His scent wafted through her nostrils. *What is that smell?* It was sweet and intoxicating. It filled her lungs like a sensual drug, infusing her blood and giving her a shock of titillating tingles throughout her body. *What the hell is that?* He smelled amaaaazing. Sinful. Mind-blowingly delicious. Every erotic nerve in her body lit up, throbbing and aching.

No way. She stepped back, pushing her ass all the way against the edge of her desk. How could she want him? *No. No. Not possible.* She looked at his giant beer belly, unkempt hair, and untoned legs and arms, feeling revolted by the lack of pride in his appearance. Yet...he still had a beautifully masculine face—strong jaw, full lips, and deep, soul-penetrating turquoise eyes that gave her goose bumps. Was he really seeing through her, right into her soul, or was that her imagination running wild due to lack of sleep?

It's definitely your imagination, and he needs to go. Clearly something was not right in her head.

PRAISE FOR MIMI JEAN'S PARANORMAL ROMANCES

"If you've never read anything by Mimi Jean Pamfiloff, then you're in for a treat here. Especially if you love laugh-out-loud tales that have tons of depth to the plot and engaging characters to latch on to."

—*Sara, Harlequin Junkie,* on *Tommaso*

"It's full of sexy gods, bat-shit crazy goddesses, wise-cracking immortals and enough snark to make me laugh out loud."

—*Leigh, Guilty Pleasures* on *Tommaso*

"Pamfiloff injects smart-ass humor into every scene…plot and characters are pure fun."

—*Publishers Weekly,* on *Sun God Seeks Surrogate*

"Smark, snarky storytelling and an inventive plot will keep readers turning the pages. Throw in a host of amusing, distinctive characters, and Pamfiloff's latest is hilarious, sexy and just plain fun."

—*RT Book Reviews,*
on *Accidentally Married to a Vampire?*

"Every time I read one of these books in the series I think it is the best one. I get proven wrong by each one. They just keep getting better and better."

—*Romancing the Book*, on *Sun God Seeks Surrogate*

"Mimi Jean Pamfiloff is a paranormal romance (PNR) author that never disappoints. She writes the type of PNR that has readers smiling and laughing one moment, and cursing and making stabby motions the next."

—*Reviews by Ruckie,*
on *Immortal Matchmakers, Inc.*

"This first book in the spin-off is everything I love about Mimi Jean Pamfiloff's paranormal. Sarcasm, snark, smartassness, and big sexy alphas in leather pants. Getting down and dirty no holds barred romance."

—*Hannah's Words*, on *Immortal Matchmakers, Inc.*

"Oh my, Mimi has done it again, woven that wonderful web of hilariously messed up paranormal matchmaking. I'm really not sure who I adore more in these books, as all the characters are so brilliantly warped!"

—**#Minxes Love Books**, on *Tommaso*

God of Wine

THE IMMORTAL MATCHMAKERS, INC., SERIES.
BOOK THREE

MIMI JEAN PAMFILOFF

A Mimi Boutique Novel

Cover Design by Earthly Charms (www.earthlycharms.com)
Development Editing by Latoya C. Smith (lcsliterary.com)
Line Editing and Proof Reading by Pauline Nolet (www.paulinenolet.com)
Formatting by bbebooksthailand.com

Like "Free" Pirated Books?
Then Ask Yourself This Question: WHO ARE THESE PEOPLE I'M HELPING?

What sort of person or organization would put up a website that uses stolen work (or encourages its users to share stolen work) in order to make money for themselves, either through website traffic or direct sales? **Haven't you ever wondered?**

Putting up thousands of pirated books onto a website or creating those anonymous ebook file sharing sites takes time and resources. Quite a lot, actually.

So who are these people? Do you think they're decent, ethical people with good intentions? Why do they set up camp anonymously in countries where they can't easily be touched? And the money they make from advertising every time you go to their website, or through selling stolen work, **what are they using it for? The answer is you don't know.** They could be terrorists, organized criminals, or just greedy bastards. But one thing we DO know is that **THEY ARE CRIMINALS** who don't care about you, your family, or me and mine. **And their intentions can't be good.**

And every time you illegally share or download a book, YOU ARE HELPING these people. Meanwhile, people like me, who work to support a family and children, are left wondering why anyone would condone this.

So please, please ask yourself who YOU are HELPING when you support ebook piracy and then ask yourself who you are HURTING.

And for those who legally purchased/borrowed/obtained my work from a reputable retailer (not sure, just ask me!) muchas thank yous! You rock.

DEDICATION

This book goes out to all of my crazy, unicorn-lovin', paranormal-obsessed, horn-doggy readers who've shown such astounding loyalty to this wacky series. From the bottom of my heart, I thank you. And, as promised, I made this book a little extra dirty for you! You guys rock with all of your #MakeItDirtyMimi! requests, to which I replied: #DontTellmyMom! LOL

WARNING

This dirty, dirty book contains a buck-naked god, sloppy drunkenness, the c-word, f-word, p-word, d-word—okay, neverthehell mind! It has a lot of fucking bad words. Okay?—invisible unicorns, outrageously sized penises, cocktail recipes, leather pants, no pants, and one healthy eating tip.

If you do not like dirty, dirty books with buck-naked gods, sloppy drunkenness, the c-word, f-word, p-word, d-word—yes, yes, all the bad words—invisible unicorns, outrageously sized penises, cocktail recipes, leather pants, no pants, and healthy eating tips, then this book might not be for you. (But feel free to gift it to your naughty, slutty friend with the gutter mouth.)

God

of

Wine

CHAPTER ONE

Acan, God of Wine and Intoxication, entered the upscale fitness club that boasted some of LA's tightest asses with one thing and one thing only on his mind: Sweet. Fucking. Revenge.

"Fucking human." His eyes scanned the ocean of disgustingly healthy people, all tanned, glowing, and annoyingly perky for five a.m. *I want to end them all.* Starting with the woman from last night. Because of her—one lowly *human*—he had been unable to partake in his usual one hundred tequila shots and fifty beers or "accidentally" burn down the posh Santa Monica hotel with one of his legendary, crowd-pleasing, exploding mojitos. All because of a random woman he'd met in the hotel elevator whilst in transit to last night's rooftop party. He'd said, "Hiya," paid her a "compliment" and then invited her to the event. She'd shockingly said, "Fuck off," more or less. So he'd said, "Fuck off back, you old bag." She'd said, "Shove it and come to my gym so we can see who's really old."

You! You are, you wilted vag. Yeah. That's right!

She was some disgusting fitness-freak mortal who spent her days denying the truth: she would grow old, her beauty would fade, and her little lady "flower" would wither and die like an old tomato.

Yet *she* had the gall to metaphorically slap his perfectly bronzed cheek and challenge him to a fitness duel? Simply because he'd complimented her by saying she had nice tits or something like that? (Honestly, he couldn't remember.) But *nooo...* She'd turned her nose up at him in the elevator. So what if he hadn't been wearing any pants! Or underwear. *Honest mistake.*

What a fuzzy cunt! With his horribly clear vision, due to the lack of alcohol, Acan zeroed right in on the blonde woman in her forties as she did squats and hip thrusts inside the fishbowl aerobics room.

"There you are..." His growl faded into the background as she raised her toned arms above her head, clapping her hands, laughing and "wooing" with the other fitness hags in the room. Acan suddenly felt his heart beating so hard that his knees began to knock. His breath stuck in his lungs, and his eyes didn't seem to want to move away. *She is so...radiant. So lively.* Her lovely creamy skin, pert nose, and beaming smile reminded him of an angel. *With really nice jugs.* And something about the woman's tight, tight ass and long legs made him feel a little tingly.

What? No. I can't stand her. Must be the lack of tequila in my system, making me all crazy. Being sober was awful.

"Hey, dude. No offense, but that's pretty fucked up," said a male voice.

Acan looked down—way, waaay down since he was over seven feet tall—at the stumpy little weight-lifter dude with bleach blond hair, wearing a black spaghetti strap tank top.

"What?" Acan pushed his snarled brown hair from his eyes, but it wouldn't move. *Why is my hair so sticky?* Was it always like this?

Stumpy dude's eyes flashed to Acan's groin. "Pants, man. Pants. I mean, yeah, that's a huge shlong, but there's a time and a place to impress the ladies. Yunnooo?"

Acan looked at his lower extremities. "Hell." He'd forgotten his pants. Again. And his fucking underwear. Again.

That's the fifteenth time this week! I think. Either way, going to kill Jill, he thought. Jill, his full-time assistant slash deity-nanny, was supposed to make sure he didn't go out the door showing off the man-gear anymore. Of course, it was now five in the morning, and she was never on duty this early because he was never awake before noon unless on his way to bed after partying all night, which was almost every night. Jill didn't usually get in until— well, he didn't really know. He was passed out most of the time.

It's a tough job being the party god, but someone's got to do it.

Acan jerked his head, playing it cool. "Thanks, dude." He turned to leave, wondering how he'd arrived to the gym naked. Uber? Chauffeur? Battery-powered kiddie tank?

Gods, I hope I didn't ride my bike. That seat was the worst on his bare balls.

"Hey!" an angry female voice called out.

Acan turned. *Dammit all to hell.* It was her. The giant CrossFit fuzzy cunt. Okay, she was hot and all vivacious and whatnot. But so? She was rude! And she didn't know her place in this world. He was a god, a force to be feared and…well, to have fun with. After all, he was the embodiment of festive excess.

"You showed up. I didn't expect…" Her voice faded as she realized he was down a pair of pants (and underpants) and up one man—involuntarily, of course. "I didn't expect to see your penis." She swallowed and made a disgusted face. "Erect."

He crossed his arms over his chest. "What? Never seen a god before?"

"If you're referring to a beer-bellied slob reeking of stale beer, who's standing nude and aroused in the middle of my gym, then no. I've never seen a god."

"Boom!" He threw up his arms, making eagle talons with his fingers. "Well, now you have." He turned and strutted from the gym with his head held high. *Godsdammit. I gotta get a drink.*

᷾᷾ ᷾᷾

"You did *what?*" The Goddess of Forgetfulness winced as she slid the uncapped Corona across the narrow width of the bar into Acan's awaiting hand.

He licked his lips, greedily grabbing the ice-cold beer, and chugged it down, not spilling a precious drop. He slammed the empty bottle on the counter and pushed it to the side with the other ten he'd just guzzled. "I think you—" *Hiccup!* "—heard me."

Forgetty, as he liked to call her, was a tall blonde who usually wore nightclub party clothes—white go-go boots, miniskirts, or little tank dresses like she had on today—because, like him, her life was all about the party. After all, nothing complimented a night of getting hammered better than blacking out and forgetting all about the crazy shit one did the previous night.

We are like peas and carrots.

In any case, his "sister"—the gods were not related by blood since they had no parents—DJ'd at their global chain of successful nightclubs and bars they owned together. She also worked the private parties for their immortal brethren while he bartended, which was his gift. As God of Wine and Intoxication, he merely looked at a person and knew what sort of drink to serve and the quantity they required to reach the ideal state of jubilation. Between him and his sister, they served a vital function that allowed humans—and the occasional immortal—to blow off steam.

Forgetty blinked her turquoise eyes at him. "I did hear you, brother. I merely cannot believe you went into a gym. At five in the morning. Are you absolutely certain you're feeling all right?"

He tapped his index finger demandingly on the bar.

Forgetty reached into the trough of ice behind the counter, uncapped another cold one, and plunked it down in front of him.

"Feeling great!" He grabbed his frosty treat, saluted her with the bottle, and then threw it back.

"Belch, Belch, Belch." She shook her head with worry, using his nickname. "I mean this in the kindest way possible, but you just called the elevator woman a cunt."

He set down his empty bottle and shrugged. "Correction. Fuzzy cunt. And so?"

She tipped her head to one side. "So you called her a cunt."

Where was Forgetty going with this? He stared at her, hoping she'd open another beer.

His sister sighed and then rolled her eyes. "Belch, don't you find that just a tad bit abrasive? Even for you?"

"Fuck no! She was being a bitchy shrew. I should rip out her throat and make a Bloody Mary out of it."

Forgetty stepped back, cringing.

"What?" he snapped defensively.

"Belch," she said softly, "you are many things—a drunk, a flasher, a very loud snorer, and occasional arsonist. But you are not an asshole."

"I *am* an asshole!"

She slammed her fist down on the counter. "No, Acan." She used his real name. She never did that. "You're nice, and you're fun, but you're never cruel or so outrageously rude. Especially not to women."

He wasn't? "Well, fuck that! Let the bitches die. Burn them all." Belch slapped his hands over his mouth. "What was that?" he mumbled.

Forgetty's face turned ghost white. "I think—and please don't panic and break out the absinth when I say this—bad, bad things happen when you break out the absinth—but I think you're flipping."

Fuck. "Fuck." Maybe he was.

She nodded. "Yes, brother. It is the only reason I can think of for your recent change from happy drunk to mean drunk. Which means—well, you know what it means."

Fuck, I do. Acan sat there on the barstool, staring into the empty bottle, his quickly sobering mind feeling far too lucid for his taste because he actually understood the implications. He didn't like it one little bit. Cimil—world-renowned garage-sale huntress and Goddess of the Underworld—announced almost a month ago that something had upset the order of the Universe. No one was sure why, but the evidence was there: good immortals were beginning to change into bad immortals and vice versa, the only remedy or vaccination being a mate. Yep, a significant other. Having a special someone seemed to act as a counterbalance of sorts to prevent the immortal from "flipping," as they now called it.

"Blahhhh!" Belch swiped his hand through the air. "I don't need a woman, I need *women*. Lots of them and a new one every night. And I need my mojito tank." Yes, it took a lot of upkeep, but the mojito tank was the highlight of his day. An indoor two-person glass tank filled with mojito goodness was ideal for total submersion, drinking games, or a very long straw.

"You're acting too dense, even for you," she said.

"I am the party god. Density is my immensity."

"Acan, stop! If you're turning evil, think about what this will mean for humanity." Her turquoise eyes—same color as his and all of the fourteen gods—filled with intense emotion. "Everyone else might underestimate your powers, but—" she tapped the side of her head "—I know. We've been partying for ten millennia. You have the power to influence an entire hemisphere. You do it every New Year's."

True. New Year's Eve was all him, with New York City being the epicenter. He influenced billions around the planet to drink in excess and party hard. It was the equivalent of his Super Bowl.

"Brother," said Forgetty worriedly, "New Year's is less than four weeks away."

He looked up at his sister, who stood on the other side of the counter, *not* reaching for the tequila bottle behind her on the mirrored shelf like she should.

"What are you waiting for?" he scolded.

"I'm cutting you off, Belch." She crossed her arms over her chest.

"What?"

"You heard me. No more cocktails. No more beer. No more flaming assholes or Jell-O shots or even cough syrup."

Belch gasped. *No more flaming assholes?* But those were the highlight of his mornings:

- ½ ounce grenadine
- ½ ounce crème de menthe
- ½ ounce crème de banana
- ½ ounce 151 rum

Light on fire.

The breakfast of champions. "What is this blasphemy I hear from your lips, sister?"

She poked his forehead from across the bar. "You! Have to. Get. Sober."

Why the hell would he do that? People needed to party. *He* needed to party. It was the Universe's will and purely instinctual for him. Asking him not to party was like asking the sun not to shine or for glue to stop being sticky.

"Because you have less than four weeks to find your mate—wait, make that two weeks."

"Why two?" he asked.

"You know we all like to take the last two weeks of the year for vacation. So should you fail to find a mate, we really should lock you up beforehand. Wouldn't want to ruin everyone's fun, would you?"

"No. Fun is an essential part of a balanced and complete existence. Which is why I refuse to give up mine." He stared defiantly, feeling disgustingly sober already. After all, he'd only had a few—ten or eleven beers. Or was it twelve?

"Brother, you can't find your woman if you're passed out or drunk. You need to be coherent and focused, and above all your senses cannot be dulled, or how will you know when you find her?"

He grumbled incoherently and stared into the mirror behind his sister, watching the old janitor sweep between the empty tables to his back. The bar wouldn't open until four p.m., but he always loved to come early and prepare to greet the sad, the forlorn, the overworked masses in need of a little fun. To stressed-out humans, he was like an instant happy pill, and frankly, he enjoyed seeing their faces light up when he prepared the beer bong.

"Sorry. Nocando. I've been partying for over ten thousand years." Merely a teenager in deity terms, but he'd been a late bloomer in finding his special powers.

"And?" Forgetty grabbed a rack of clean glasses

and a dish towel and began checking for spots before storing them under the counter.

"And…and…if I stop, I will get a hangover. An epic, immortal-sized hangover."

Forgetty blinked at him. "Don't be such a child. You can handle a little headache."

"Headache? Dear gods! I thought a hangover was feeling tired. Now I have to deal with a headache, too?"

She rolled her eyes.

"What? I've never had a headache, and in case you haven't heard, headaches hurt. I am not a fan of pain."

"You either get it over with now, or you'll be doing it when we lock you up in Sedona, where there'll be no booze, no fun, and no partying until the Universe has sorted things out and this flipping issue is flipping resolved, which might be a very, very long flipping time."

Gah. Sedona. That was where his brother Kinich had his massive estate. Nearby was one of their largest immortal prisons and Uchben bases. Uchben served primarily as the gods' mortal army; however, Uchben of every profession—doctors, teachers, accountants, scientists—were dispersed throughout the globe. After all, fourteen gods could hardly keep an eye on so many humans. Thankfully, however, the gods' role was not to babysit every being on the planet. It was merely to ensure humans weren't wiped out as a species, as was the case seventy thousand years ago when the super-volcano Toba erupted. The entire human population dwindled down to a few hundred as ash blocked out the sun for a decade. That was when the gods simply appeared. No one knew why or how exactly, but over time, they evolved along with humans and slowly began to specialize. Lately, the gods had begun taking mates and having children. A very new event in their history. Some had even transferred their powers to their significant others and shared their divine duties.

Well, fuck that. I'm not sharing my powers! And I'm not going to that horrible prison. Arizona is hot, and they have big bugs. Ick.

"I won't do it. I'd rather die. Now, pass me that tequila." He pointed to the expensive stuff on the top shelf.

"Nope." Forgetty shook her head.

"How dare you defy me when I'm thirsty and in need of a tasty Mexican spirit…" His words faded as she dialed on her cell phone. "Who are you calling?"

She gave him her back. "Hi, all. This is you-don't-know-who. I'm leaving a message in the emergency voice mailbox to inform you that Acan's evil switch is flipping."

Oh no! Forgetty was sending out an alert to his brethren.

He jumped and reached across the counter, swiping the phone from her hands. "You quisling! You cannot do that."

She cocked a blonde brow. "I can. I will. And you'll end up locked away."

"Fine. Okay. Name your price. I have some thirty-year-old Margeaux tucked away. Or how about a nice Chateau OohLaLa." He couldn't remember the name of the winery, but OohLaLa sounded fancy, right?

"You will stop partying. You will get into shape. You will make yourself appealing to more than just drunk women looking for a good time they'll forget they had, and you will find your mate in two weeks."

Now standing and trying not to get annoyed by the room not swaying, he planted his hands on the bar. "Just how do you propose I do that?"

She smiled, her turquoise eyes twinkling. "We're calling the Immortal Matchmakers."

He scoffed. "Zac and Cimil? They couldn't find their way out of an empty beer can." Zac, God of Temptation, and Cimil, Goddess of the Underworld, had been banished to the human world for breaking several divine laws—illegal use of powers, lying to fellow deities, acting without regard for another god's mate, the list went on and on. Zac and Cimil had also been stripped of their powers until they matched up one hundred immortal couples. The punishment was supposed to teach the two about the importance of love, family, and helping others rather than themselves.

Stupid. Zac would never learn, and Cimil was

evil to the core. Always would be. *Gods, I love her. So much fun.*

"They do not have powers. What is the point?" he asked.

Forgetty sighed. 'They don't need powers to throw a party and invite every eligible single immortal woman they know. All you need to do is show up sober. And wear pants. Pants would be a nice start. Feel free to practice that one starting today." Forgetty lifted a brow.

He looked down, past his beer belly, finding his big salami dangling against his thigh. "Damn. I could've sworn I stopped by my taco truck and grabbed my pants."

"Taco truck? What happened to your house? Wait." She stuck out her hand. "Don't tell me. You threw another wild party and burned it down."

How did she know? The woman was psychic. "Not on purpose. It is simply that I enjoy creating those flaming drinks the crowds so love."

"You could make them outside."

"What fun would that be?" The thrill of a flaming cocktail was just as much about the flavor and presentation as it was about the subconscious fear of something exploding in a blaze of glory.

Forgetty picked up her cell and began dialing.

"Who are you calling now?" he asked.

"Jill, how the heck are you?" Forgetty said with a bland tone, speaking to his assistant. "We've got a situation." Forgetty listened for a moment. "Nope,

Belch did not superglue himself to the Empire State Building again." She listened and then laughed. "Ouch. Yeah. I forgot about that rope burn accident. But his junk appears to be intact and enjoying its usual fresh air."

Belch grumbled at Forgetty, knowing that she and Jill were discussing the time Cimil dared him to walk a tightrope over the Grand Canyon. Blindfolded. A very bad choice because when he slipped, he hadn't been wearing any clothes and…well, his balls took the first hit. He then fell to his death. Luckily, however, when a deity's body was destroyed, they were sent back into the cosmos, where they could return to the realm of the gods—if they weren't currently banned—or return to the human realm with a new body. The whole process *usually* took a few days since the gods depended on sacred portals (aka cenotes, aka underground springs) in the Mexican jungle to rebuild them one molecule at a time—very low-tech, but tried and true. Still, ruining one's human shell hurt like a sonofabitch.

Forgetty continued her conversation with Jill over the phone. "Sadly, this is a serious matter. Belch has got to find his forever someone or he'll turn evil and be locked up. I'm putting you in charge of keeping him sober." A moment passed. "Hello? Hello?" Forgetty pulled her cell from her ear. "I think she hung up on me." Forgetty dialed again. "Voicemail! Can you believe her?"

"Was going to fire her anyway. I think I've gone

weeks without pants." *Oh well.* Belch shrugged, feeling his throat dry out and hearing that frosty cold beer calling his name. "How about a beer to celebrate going on the wagon?"

"No!" His sister shook her finger. "And so help me, Belch, if you touch one drop of alcohol, I'm going to—"

Forgetty's cell beeped, and she took a peek. "Cimil is calling an emergency midnight meeting at her office."

"Wow. We've never had one of those before. Must be important."

His sister gave him a look.

"What?" he asked defensively.

"You turning into a threat to humanity *is* important. And we just had an emergency meeting last week."

We did? "You must've made me forget."

"I've never used my powers on you, brother."

Really? Because he could barely remember the last ten thousand years.

She added, "It's also against our laws to do so without permission."

"Then why's it all a void?"

"Uhhh…because you've been wasted for more millennia than I can count. But not like you've missed much. A few near misses with the apocalypse. Cimil got married to Roberto, the king of vampires, and had evil half-vampire, half-divine quadruplets, and…a bunch of the other gods got married. Even Votan has a son."

The God of Death and War is a father? I definitely need to drink a keg. ASAP. "When did this happen?"

"Over the last couple of years."

Gods. He'd only been sober for two minutes and already realized how much he'd missed.

He looked at his sister and blinked hard. *Whoa. That's what she looks like?*

Mistaking his expression for despair, Forgetty reached across the bar and squeezed his hand. "Do not worry, brother, we'll figure this out."

"No. It's not that."

"Then what?" she asked.

"I always thought you had four eyes and two heads."

"Ha. Funny."

"Who said I was joking?" He really wasn't.

"All right. I need to finish getting everything ready for tonight's party."

"Oh, is it ladies' night? I love ladies' night." Just last week, he'd gone home with five women, who pleasured him all night long. That was the nice thing about being a deity—women found them irresistible. Their scent, their hypnotically sexy turquoise eyes, the divine energy wafting from their bodies. In his case, his very large cock was also a nice chick magnet. There was never a shortage of admirers. The only downside was that a god's energy could kill a person—fry their brain—if the god didn't make them wear a very special black jade to help absorb their potent powers. He personally had a lovely collection of black jade bracelets back home.

You mean the taco truck?

Oh yeah. Burned down my house. He'd have to go shopping tomorrow for a new house. *Maybe I'll go big this time and buy a bouncy castle.*

"Well, I'm ready to help welcome the women." He rubbed his hands together.

"You're getting locked in the closet until I leave for the meeting," said Forgetty.

It was only eleven in the morning. "No. I'm not." He defiantly took a seat on the stool again.

She reached out and grabbed his arm. "Acan, listen to me. The party is over. And you need to grow up. Your reckless teen years are over."

Grow up. Grow up? I'm the party god and this party ain't ever gonna end!

"Are you going to serve me or not?" he growled.

"Not."

"Fine." He rose from the barstool, his bare ass making a *qwiiip!* sound as it peeled off the vinyl cushion. "I'll see you at Cimil's office."

"Hey! Where are you going?" his sister yelled as he headed for the door.

"To do what I do best!"

"Belch! Dammit! No more partying!"

Screw that. If he had to find a mate, he wanted one who knew how to throw down and worshiped at the altar of wine like he did, not some teetotaler. *Going to find myself a real woman. Fit for a god.*

CHAPTER TWO

Downtown LA

With a long stick in hand, Zac, God of Temptation, sat at his desk on the fourteenth-floor office of the Immortal Matchmakers, Inc., dating agency, feeling bored and miserable. His heart ached, and it was driving him mad.

He sighed. *Maybe my mortal shell is broken, and I should go get another.*

"Please, man, please…" sobbed the hogtied man lying on the gray carpeted floor. "Just let me go, man. I promise I'll never sell again."

Zac lowered the deadly wiggling scorpion dangling from the end of the stick, only inches from the man's face. "Careful there, Joe. I am not the God of Square Knots." That honor probably belonged to his crazy sister, Cimil, the Goddess of the Underworld. She was also known as the Goddess of repurposed material items—aka garage sales—the Goddess of Clown Hell, the Goddess of Lies and Truthful Misnomers, Microwave Ovens, Reruns,

Unicorns, Ping Pong, S'mores, and General Mayhem. "Do not mistake me. I have many names and talents, but tying knots is *not* one of them. Get it? Not?" Zac chuckled and lowered the scorpion, letting its little legs tickle the man's nose.

The guy screamed and rolled to his other side, wincing and weeping like the giant meth-pimping pussy that he was. "Please, man. I'm begging you. Show mercy."

Zac suddenly had the urge to lift his desk and let it fall on the guy's head.

No. No. You will fight your evil urges. You can't let anyone know. The truth was that like many unmated immortals, he too felt his polarity shifting as if gravity herself had decided to do a handstand. He wanted to do wrong. He wanted to hurt rather than protect. He wanted to binge-watch Netflix rather than participate in life. Yes, he was in a downward death spiral, the only remedy being a mate.

Not gonna happen. He threw back his head and gazed up at the textured ceiling. *Dammit, Tula. Why couldn't you have been born less hotter?* Tula had been their human assistant. She was smart, sexy as hell, and purer than freshly fallen snow on a mountaintop. She also had the brightest aura he'd ever seen.

And I miss her so much it hurts. Yes, him. The baddass God of Temptation, sex symbol to the female masses, had allowed a mortal woman to get under his skin. It had all started when he'd tried to tempt her and her petite little body into bed, but she'd turned him down. Cold.

Of course, the rejection only made her all the more fascinating, so he tried again and again to seduce her without any luck. But then it finally happened: Last night, at the engagement party for their immortal friend Tommaso, Tula kissed him.

Mind. Blown.

Her lips had tasted of sweet innocence, and it had been the sort of sinfully delicious kiss that could make a god go crazy and believe he was in love. It could make him forget the pain of having to live for eternity.

And it almost made you forget your role.

Bottom line. He was the God of Temptation. She was an innocent, pure-souled human. He would only break her spirit and ultimately her heart. Which was why he'd done what he had last night: showed her his true man-whoring colors. Now she was gone.

Dammit, I miss her. Her big blue eyes, her bright smile.

He leaned forward and slammed his fist on his desk. "Fucking hell!" He slid his cell from his leather pants and stared at Tula's number, his thumb cocked to dial.

No. You pushed her away last night for her own good. It had been the hardest thing he'd ever done because all he'd wanted was to carry her off to a room in that hotel and deflower her. Hard, hot, passionately. A thorough fucking that would leave no leaf unturned, no thigh unlicked, no nipple unsucked. However, after they'd kissed, he did the honorable thing, the right thing, and hooked up with another woman. Yes, right in front of Tula. She disappeared from the party, and he had gone home with some woman with whom he was unable to perform. Limp as a soggy noodle.

But still hung like a horse, so at least there's that.

Nevertheless, now he felt even worse, like he'd been unfaithful merely for kissing another woman.

Gah. What's wrong with me? Zac slowly placed his phone on his desk and looked at the motherfucker lying on the floor. *Good thing I know how to let out my frustration*

"Consider your suffering the price one pays for selling drugs to children." Hell, even *he* stayed away from tempting minors. *Like they need help. Especially teenagers.*

"Please, dude. Let me go. I won't ever sell again."

Zac stared at the human, feeling the evil urges take hold. "Sorry. But you showed no mercy to those young ones you just got hooked on meth." Zac lowered the scorpion onto the man's face and watched as it stung him repeatedly. The man screamed for a few minutes and passed out.

Zac felt nothing. Nothing but sadness and a longing to end his misery. No. Not suicide. Not possible for a deity. Ending his misery meant claiming Tula.

"Zac! What in the name of the gods' green Earth are you doing?"

He looked up to find Tula in a pink turtle-necked sweaterdress with her golden hair in a ponytail. "Tula?"

"Zac." She parked her fist on her hip. "I sure don't know what you're doing to that man, but I know you don't want him to die."

"Wha-wha-what are you doing here?" Gods, she looked so fucking hot, all riled up and sweet as pie, dressed like a furry pink teddy bear. *So fucking sexy.*

Tula lifted her chin. "Cimil texted me, saying it was an emergency. Why wouldn't I be here?"

"I merely thought I'd never see you again."

Tula shook her finger at him. "You think some narcissistic deity who worships sinful acts of sexual temptation can keep me away from my friend in her time of need?"

Oh gods. Oh gods. She actually considers Cimil a friend. His heart melted right through his leather pants onto the floor, where it twitched in a gooey warm puddle. Tula was so loyal and kind and saw only the good in others. She had nothing but love in her heart. *Except for me. She hates me now.*

Yes. Exactly as it should be.

Zac cleared his throat and leaned back in his leather exec chair, crossing his big manly arms over his big manly chest, propping his black biker boots atop his desk. *Must show her who's boss and the perfect man for her.*

Wait. No. Must show her who's the dick.

"Well, technically," he said, "I embody all acts of temptation equally—chocolate, orgies, shoe shopping, eating the delicious fat on the edge of a steak, anal sex, and sleeping in and—"

She held up her petite hand to stop him. "Whatever, Mr. Zac. I don't care. I don't care about you or your tempting ways or man slutting or insane-fitting leather pants that show the outline of your ample hacky sacks and baseball bat. Because I'm marrying Gilbert. That's right. Gilbert. With nice, normal golf balls and probably packing a solid five-incher—okay, three—he comes across as a grower, not a shower. In any case, he's got equipment that a nice girl can find comfort in, and once I say my vows to him you will become dust."

She's going through with marrying that douche? Zac felt his insides blacken with rage.

Tula leaned forward, planting her delicate hands on his desk. "You. Will. Be. Dead to me."

"You can't mean that," he muttered under his breath.

"Not only do I mean it, I vow to make it happen." Evilness gleamed in her eyes.

Evil? In Tula's eyes? Holy fuck. He'd already ruined her!

"No!" He bolted from his chair, finding no Tula. The meth dealer and scorpion remained, however. "What in the gods' names was that?"

I just hallucinated about Tula. What does that mean? What does that mean?

"Nothing," he told himself. "It means nothing. You're fine."

"You don't look fine." Cimil stood in front of the elevators, wearing a giant rain poncho with a picture of the Love Boat on the front and a red Moroccan fez that almost matched the red of her long crazy hair.

"What are you doing here?" Zac asked. Cimil only showed her face at the office when...when... *Pretty much never.* "And what the hell are you wearing?"

"I think the proper question should be why is a man passed out on our floor?"

Zac didn't want to tell her that lately he'd been taking up a new, evil hobby: torturing humans. Luckily, he'd been sticking to the bad ones. He could only hope that would keep his evil urges at bay until he figured out what to do. He needed a mate to stay on Team Good, but the only woman he wanted was the one he couldn't have.

"Someone dropped him off," he lied. "Special delivery for you, I assumed." It was Cimil's job to escort evil souls off to the Underworld. Only, it wasn't really an Underworld. More like waiting areas where the souls of the dead, who existed in a place without time, congregated until they decided if they wanted to come back for another round in the game of life or be reunited with the cosmic soup of the Universe.

"Oh, look. The person who brought him included a scorpion on a stick!" She clapped. "Today is a lucky day!" She turned her head and yelled, "Kids! Get in here. There's a treat for you!"

From the stairwell, four very short-looking beings emerged in mime outfits. They had red hair, pouty lips, tiny hands, and big eyes—sort of marbled with turquoise and black and a thirst for destruction.

"Oh, I see you brought your children. How…lovely." A ripple of fear washed through him. *Those kids are creepy as hell.*

Cimil snapped her fingers, and the four tiny ones dragged the man off to the other side of the room. The entire office space was empty save Cimil's corner office, Zac and Tula's desks smack in the middle of the room, and the little waiting area Tula had made by the elevators. There was also a makeshift break room and some filing cabinets in one of the corners.

The children started mime yelling and mime kicking the man in complete silence. *So disturbing.*

"Wait. Aren't they only three months old?" asked Zac.

Cimil shrugged. "Age is just a number. I mean, look at you. You're a gazillion years old, yet you look like a homeless college student."

Zac looked down at his black, grease-stained Batman T-shirt and black leather pants. *Nuh-uh. I look like a tough, manly dude.* Seven feet of divine masculine hotness with a perfectly muscled body—maintenance-free, of course—turquoise eyes the ladies swooned over, and shiny jet black hair with that perfectly unkempt look that screamed, *"Step back! Badass on board!"*

"The human ladies warming my bed each night would happen to disagree," he lied, knowing that his bed was as cold as an iceberg since his man-stick was on the fritz. "And I'm not a gazillion—I'm only seventy thousand years old." Same as the rest of the gods, give or take a few days.

"Yet you look like a disturbed pilgrim in search of their holy land of Fuck-I'm-Pathetic. Or maybe you look more like the Wild, Wild West depression wagon ran you over. I can't quite put my finger on it, but you're definitely vibing vintage crazy. Oh. Wait. Maybe that's your smell. When's the last time you bathed?"

Huh? "Uhhh...yesterday." Perhaps Cimil was sensing the evil inside him. He had to divert her attention.

He glanced over at her kids, who now stood over the man, pretending to stab him and remove his heart. *Dear sweet deities.* "What are they doing?"

"They're playing Maaskab—their favorite game. What else?"

The Maaskab were an evil sect of ancient blood-thirsty Mayan priests who excelled in the dark arts and cold-blooded murder, which was why the gods had them nearly exterminated. All but a few, including the one who'd recently flipped to Team Good and now served as Cimil's nanny.

And wow. He's such a positive influence, too. Just look at that knife-twisting technique.

Cimil shook her gaunt finger at him. "Hey. Don't change subjects on me. Why do you look so awful?"

Zac wiggled his lips from side to side. He really didn't want to tell her the truth, so he went with, "Tula's gone. Why wouldn't I be in a bad mood? Not like I know how to organize singles mixers and get Belch out of jail every time he burns down a building."

Cimil eyed him warily. "Uh-uhh…Nope. You're lying, and you better not be thinking what I think you're thinking."

"Which is?"

"Crashing Tula's wedding."

What the godsfuck? She's already set a date? So she had run back to her fuckstain of a fiancé, Gilbert, a human male who'd broken off their engagement when she refused to have premarital sex. *Asshole.* Tula's innocence and virtue were reasons to love her more, not toss her aside. Sure, Zac personally didn't see the point of abstaining from one of life's greatest treasures and pleasures—ejaculation; however, Tula had her beliefs and stayed true to them. This Gilbert was in no way good enough for her. He had made her feel unloved simply because she wouldn't do the nasty.

Asshole. I'm the only one who's allowed to pressure her into doing carnal, indecent things. I'm the God of Temptation. It's my job.

Zac felt the rage twist his insides. "When and where is the wedding?"

"Nooo." Cimil wagged her finger in front of his face. "I'm not telling. You'll only show up and ruin it."

"Damn straight I will." *And I'll ruin her, too, while I'm at it. Ruin her for all other men.*

Cimil stomped forward. "No! You must let Tula go, Zac. It is as I told you. You are a flame. She is a moth. Only she wears long flowery dresses and granny panties."

Ooohh…those granny panties. So not sexy. Which made them hotter than hell because nothing screamed "I need temptation in my life" like giant underwear.

"Your point?" he asked.

"I've seen what happens, Zac. If you don't stop intervening in her destiny to be with Gilbert, she will die. A horrible, tormented death. She is pure and kind and loyal. You are the god of entice-ments—late night snacking, infidelity, the easy listening sounds of the '80s—all very bad things. At least on Wednesdays." She shrugged. "It's cool on Fridays."

He crossed his arms over his well-defined chest—*My awesome, well-defined chest.* "Temptation also means desire, which can be a positive thing when someone is suppressing their true path in life—living their dreams of becoming an ice skater, climbing Everest, learning to play polka music—you know, really important things."

Cimil gave him a look. "And they call me bat-shit crazy?" She leaned forward and poked his chest with her razor-sharp fingernail. "You are a bad, bad boy who likes making people do bad, bad things. And the moment you get what you want from Tula, you will no longer feel anything for her. You'll toss her aside and move on to the next temptation challenge."

No. Impossible. Wasn't it? "Tell me exactly what you saw in these visions of yours. I want every detail."

"Do I look like a fortune-teller?" Cimil rolled her eyes.

He felt his blood pressure shoot through the roof. *Damn her.* Always playing her ridiculous games. He still wasn't one hundred percent certain that her doom and gloom prophesy crap about Tula wasn't simply an attempt to torment him. Cimil liked tormenting people. It gave her deep joy.

"No. I'm not trying to torment you," Cimil said. "That only happens on leap year."

"Hey! I thought you didn't have any powers." He had not said that last bit aloud.

"I don't. I am the Goddess of the Underworld. The dead told me what you were going to say and I listen with my ears. Nothing supernatural about that."

"Sure. There's nothing supernatural about knowing what I'm thinking via conversing with the dead from the future."

"Don't forget the dead from the past and alternate universe timelines. Boy—" she slapped her knee over the plastic poncho and chuckled "—those guys can tell a joke. Did you ever hear the one about the clown and a black hole?"

Zac winced. "Please, please, I beg you *not* to tell me." Cimil hated clowns, which was why he suspected the answer might give him nightmares the next time he chose to sleep. No, gods were not required to sleep or eat; however, they did many things merely for pleasure. Listening to Cimil's clown jokes was not one of those things.

"Oh no. You have to hear this." Cimil giggled like a psycho who'd just found a box filled with knives and hockey masks. "What's red and white and black and screams, 'Help me…'?"

Dear gods. Why do I allow her in my life? "A clown in a black hole," he said blandly.

"A clown being crushed by the insane gravity of a black hole and exploding into tiny bits. The white parts are his teeth!" Cimil cackled loudly, but then, like a switch had been thrown, her laughter melted away and she went catatonic.

Good gods. Not again. Cimil zoning out generally meant one of two things: A) she was thinking of a way to make your life a living hell or B) she was in the process of hearing something new from the plane of the dead souls.

"Cimil?" Zac clapped his hands, but it did nothing. "Hey! Do not do this, you psychotic tart. No more bad news or new schemes to derail my life." After all, it was her fault he'd been banished to the human world, left powerless, and sentenced to help one hundred immortals find true love. All because he'd had a thing for the mate of one of his brothers. Cimil had promised that if Zac did everything she'd said, it would all work out. It had for everyone but him. He got into deep shit with his brethren, his brother still won the girl, and he got banished. At least Cimil got punished, too. On the other hand, he was stuck with her, running this stupid agency.

Cimil suddenly pointed at the ceiling. "We're not finished," she growled at no one and then smiled at Zac as if nothing had happened.

"Oh hell. What is it?"

"What's what?" She shrugged coyly.

"That. You just saw something."

Mischief flickered in her eyes. "Yes. I did."

"And?"

She started to snicker. "Don't worry. You'll soon find out."

No. No, no, no. "Is Tula all right?"

"Yep. As long as you stay away. But that wasn't what I saw."

"Then what?" He hoped it didn't have to do

with his switch flipping. His worst nightmare would be turning evil and doing something horrible to Tula.

Wait. If I turn evil, I might actually hurt her. But the only way not to flip is to take a mate. And a god couldn't take just anyone. It had to be *the one.* Someone they could love for eternity with a connection that ran soul deep.

Is that Tula? He didn't know. Yes, he wanted her. Yes, he felt insanely possessive of her. Yes, he cared about what happened to her and had even put her well-being ahead of his own desires last night. *Crap. I think I do love her. I'm fucked.*

Cimil's turquoise eyes flickered to black for a moment. Did she know what he'd been thinking?

"Cimil, tell me what you saw!" he demanded.

"I saw you helping me get the inflatable chairs blown up and fold-out table assembled. We have an emergency summit meeting to prepare for, and our brother Belch requires our assistance. It's a matchmaker emergency!" Zac watched Cimil skip away towards her kids, who were still using the drug dealer as their sort of playground apparatus. "Babies! Now what did Mommy say about *pretending* to hurt people? We must make them pay the right way and drag their souls to the dark place like I taught you."

Psycho nut. Why did he believe anything she said?

Zac pulled his cell from his pocket and dialed Tula. It went straight to voicemail. "Tula, it is I,

Zac. You cannot…you cannot marry…" *Fucking hell!* He could not do this to her. But he could not let her go either. *I must try. What if Cimil is correct?* "You cannot marry without receiving your severance check. I have added a special bonus to help with the expenses. I will leave it in your desk." Zac ended the call and headed straight for the elevators.

"Hey! Where are you going?" Cimil yelled. "We need to help Belch!"

"To find a distraction." Preferably one with soft curves, a mild case of reluctance to satisfy his urge to tempt, and who didn't remind him in any way of Tula.

CHAPTER THREE

"You sure this is the place, baby?" The young brunette with big brown eyes and heavy eyeliner licked her lips as she shoved her hands down Acan's jeans, insisting on letting her suck him.

"Stop that." He jerked her hand away.

"Oh, come on, big man. You promised to let me do anything I wanted."

Normally, elevator blow jobs were his favorite, but tonight he wasn't in the mood. He couldn't get that horrible elevator woman out of his mind, and being in an elevator definitely wasn't helping.

"I'll make it fast, baby." The woman kneeled in front of him, clawing at his cock through his jeans.

"Stop that." He helped his date to her feet—or more accurately stated, onto her four-inch heels. He'd already forgotten her name or why he'd lied to her and told her they were going to a party. In his defense, however, she had picked him up—begged for some fun and promised to do anything he liked just as long as he spent the night with her. He had not wanted to—so many heavy thoughts on his tequila-saturated mind—but one look at her needy eyes and dull gray aura, well, he did what he was meant to do.

Yep.

Tequila shots.

Yep.

Dirty dancing.

Yep.

A promise to take her home and play naked Twister.

But then the text came in from Forgetty, reminding him not to forget the emergency meeting at the Immortal Matchmakers' office. He'd somehow ended up inviting... *Oh hell, I forget her name.*

His date shimmied down her black dress and checked her lipstick in her mirror as the elevator slowed to the fourteenth floor. "Looking good!" she said to herself.

Acan frowned. She had red smeared clear across her cheek. "Eh, I think you missed a spot." *Gods, drunk people can be so annoying.*

Wait. What? Acan shook his head from side to side. *Who the hell am I?* He closed his eyes. *I am the party god. I do not judge. I seek to bring fun and lack of inhibition to the masses so that they may tap into their wild sides. I am the party god. I do not judge. I seek to bring fun—*

The elevator doors dinged, interrupting his serenity prayer.

"Oh, wow!" said the woman in a high-pitched

voice, stepping out into the large office with very little furniture.

Acan stepped out behind her, seeing ten of his brethren standing in a semicircle, waiting for him.

"What the bloody hell is this?" he said, feeling the buzz of his five bottles of tequila quickly wearing off.

Cimil stepped forward with a wicked gleam in her eyes. "This, my dear brother, is your intervention."

"Baby, we should go." The brunette tugged on his arm. That was when he noticed he'd forgotten to wear a shirt.

Hey, at least it's not my pants.

"Intervention?" he asked. "Like for those alcoholic humans who refuse treatment?"

Cimil laughed. "You're a god, immortal and immune to such things as alcoholism."

"Exactly."

"But you are addicted to something far more potent," Cimil said.

"I am?"

"You're addicted to the party life of a bachelor, and if you do not set aside your philandering, cock-plundering ways and settle down with one female—only one—millions will die."

Acan felt his anger bubbling up. This entire thing was ridiculous. *And no one—I mean no one—is going to stop the party!*

"Prove it," he said.

Cimil blinked at him in question.

Acan crossed his arms over his chest. "That's right, you fib factory. I'm calling your bluff. There isn't a god in this room who hasn't been misled by your lies, your exaggerations and manipulations. So prove it. Prove to me that you are telling the truth and that death and destruction will ensue if I do not settle down."

Cimil's red lips flapped for a moment. Apparently no one had ever challenged her in this manner before. Or perhaps he'd never put so many words together to form a…a…a sentence! Yes, that was the word.

"Well…well…" She shook her head from side to side, her long red curls flopping about. "Are you sure, brother?"

"Sure about what?"

"Hey, baby. This party bites. Let's go!" His human date yanked vigorously at his arm.

Acan whipped his arm away and urged her to be silent with his eyes.

Suddenly, it all went black.

∂∾ ∾ઉ

Zac had spent the evening with two smokin'-hot women—black, delicious, and French—who'd come to LA, looking for a taste of fantasy, sex, and drama. So he had tempted them all the way to his penthouse for some serious exploration of their limits. Waste of time. As a god he had very few inhibitions, but these two ladies seemed more adventurous than even himself. Toes, toys, and teeth. Anyway, he'd barely been able to get the old man-*pho* working, so the women ended up getting each other off. He'd then fled his own apartment, wishing for something less sinful. *Or a certain someone less sinful.*

Zac glanced at his watch, realizing the emergency summit meeting had started ten minutes ago. *Fuck, they're going to kick my ass.*

The elevator doors slid open. "Hey. Sorry I'm late, but…" His voice faded as he looked across the room. Blood everywhere. Ten of his brethren lie decapitated on the floor. Belch stood in the middle, panting, dripping with red, fists clenched.

"What the fuck?" Zac gasped.

Belch's head whipped up, his normally turquoise eyes solid black.

"Belch, wha-what have you done?" Zac stammered.

Belch frowned and seemed to be awaking from a diabolical trance. "I-I-I don't know."

A strange woman, who cowered in the corner of the office space with Cimil's weeping children, jumped up. "He killed them all! He snapped his fingers and their heads fell off!" The woman ran for the stairwell.

What in the gods' names? In all his years, Zac had never heard of such a power.

"No. That's not possible. I would never do that." Acan's eyes scanned the carnage before him. "Forgetty!" He fell to his knees.

"He did it. He did it," yelled Cimil's kids.

Zac stepped back, staring at the lifeless heads on the floor. "Dude, they are so going to be pissed."

CHAPTER FOUR

Acan felt certain he'd wandered into a nightmare from the deepest reaches of Cimil's basement—or walk-in closet—whichever—but after a few sobering moments, he had little doubt that the carnage before him was real. And his doing. Ten of his brothers and sisters—Cimil, Votan, Ixtab, Akna, K'ak, Ah-Ciliz, Colel, Chaam, Máax, and Forgetty—lay dead on the floor. Their heads, with various shades of hair ranging from golden blonde to jet black, were scattered about like marbles spilled from a jar. To be clear, they were immortal and would return, but there was no bigger dishonor than killing your brethren.

What have I done? And how had he done it?

Acan knelt beside his beloved sister, the Goddess of Forgetfulness, her turquoise eyes vacant of life. He gently rolled her head back to her neck and covered the horrific separation with her long blonde hair. "I know you can hear me, sister. I know at this moment you are en route to the realm of the gods, cursing every profanity ever created." He took her lifeless pale hand and held it to his cheek. "Please forgive me. Please. I would never do anything to hurt you. Except for this removing-your-head thing, which I clearly just did. But other than that, never."

Acan felt a sharp stabbing sensation in his gut and a flame scorching through his heart. He dropped his sister's hand and pressed his palm over his chest, feeling like he might pass out from the pain.

"Aaah…" he cried out. Was this their doing? His brethren reaching through their divine connection to teach him a lesson? "I promise I will find a mate. This will never happen again."

The pain stopped and Acan fell back onto the blood-soaked carpet, his arms sprawled to his sides.

"Belch?" Zac stood over him, his eyes ten different shades of pissed off.

"What?" Acan groaned, feeling his soul sink into the abyss. How could he do that to someone he loved so much?

"You'd better get the hell out of here because Cimil's husband just texted. The kids probably called him, and he's on his way."

Fuck. Roberto. Also known as Narmer, king of the vampires, ex-Egyptian pharaoh, and one of the Ancient Ones. He was the original badass vampire, as potent and lethal as he was fast and strong. While he was not truly immortal—vampires could be killed—he was not the sort of man one wanted to mess with. Nor did he appreciate anyone fucking with his mate, Cimil.

Zac reached out his hand and helped Acan to his feet. "Take the stairs down to the garage," Zac said. "My Mustang is parked next to the elevator." He reached into his pocket and produced a set of car keys. "Here. Take 'em."

Acan looked at the keys, then at his brother, and then at Forgetty. "I don't want to run. I don't want to hide." The only thing he wanted was his sister back and to know with absolute certainty he would never harm her again. Through thick and thin, she'd been by his side when they were merely infant deities trying to find their purpose. He'd been a late bloomer compared to the others, and when he had finally discovered his gift of cocktail slinging and celebrating, the other gods looked down on him. They were gods with respectable powers—God of Death and War, God of the Sun, Goddess of the Underworld. But him? God of Wine and Intoxication. No one had ever taken him seriously except for his sister, the sister no one ever remembered or missed. She was the only true family he had in this world.

"Sister, I will make this right. Just please, when you return, do not castrate me."

"Belch!" a deep, deep voice raged from the direction of the stairwell.

"Daddy! Daddy!" Cimil's children rushed toward the towering man with long black hair, mocha skin, and dark eyes.

Zac stepped in front of Acan, something Acan found strange. Why was his brother moving to protect him? Zac didn't care about him. None of them did except for Fergetty.

Zac stretched out his meaty arm. "Back the fuck off, vampire."

Roberto's dark eyes drilled into Acan as his children hugged his legs. Legs encased in black leather pants.

"Nice pants," said Zac, "but you know I cannot allow you to harm Belch."

With fists clenched, Roberto's nostrils flared, and his eyes speared Acan with hate. "You fucking killed my wife."

"Technically, she cannot die," Zac pointed out. "So this is more of a three-day body-pause. A long rejuvenation weekend."

Roberto stared down at Cimil's lifeless head and pointed. "Vacation? Vacation! I will dismember you with a teaspoon and then strap your bits to firecrackers. I will watch every particle of your human shell disintegrate into nothing, and then I will do it again!"

Zac was about to speak, but something inside Acan snapped. *What is happening to me? I feel…brave.*

Weird.

Acan cleared his throat. "Roberto, there is nothing I can say for what I've done. I don't even know how I did it." He blew out a breath and tried to run his hands through his hair, but it was matted into long ropes. "Simply know that it was unintentional, the result of flipping, a situation I will rectify by finding a mate as Cimil has instructed."

Roberto blinked at him. "Why are you not slurring or scratching your gonads?"

"I am not intoxicated and my balls do not itch."

"Fair enough," said Roberto. "However, what guarantees can you provide that this situation will not repeat? You are nothing but an untrustworthy, infantile, belligerent slob."

Acan felt a rage deep in his chest. He did not appreciate anyone challenging him, not even the most deadly, powerful vampire on the planet. *I am a fucking god. And it is time people take me seriously.*

"Roberto, I would back the hell off if I were you," said Zac. "Because apparently Belch is not merely the God of Wine and Intoxication, but the God of Decapitation, too."

I am?

Yes. I fucking am.

"What he said," added Acan.

Roberto eyed him warily as if trying to puzzle out a Picasso. The one with the crazy guitar. "Very well. Find your mate. But if you so much as look at Cimil the wrong way, I will call a thousand of my finest warriors. We will draw and quarter you and await you at the cenote so we can rinse and repeat for a few thousand years."

"Bring it, vampire. I am not afraid of you." And

he wasn't. Acan finally understood. He wasn't simply the party god. He was the god of sweet and sour, exactly like the others. Each had dark and light sides with powers that dabbled in the playful and deadly. Cimil had her garage sales and unicorns, but ruled the world of dark souls. Votan—God of Death and War—was also the God of Drums and Algebra. Ixtab, once the Goddess of Suicide, was also the Goddess of Happiness. Yin and yang. Night and day. The Universe always demanded balance.

Fuck yeah. I'm the God of Decapitation. He could snap his fingers and heads rolled. Of course, this also complicated matters exponentially. If he became evil, it was no longer a question of turning a significant percentage of the population into violent, raving lunatics on New Year's. Now he might kill millions with the snap of his fingers. This definitely placed him at the top of the list of the Universe's most deadly beings, even deadlier that his brother Votan, God of Death and War.

Gods almighty. If I lose control, that will be a lot of heads to clean up. And unlike his brethren, those humans would not be returning to their families through a cenote.

"If you'll excuse me, gentlemen, I have a mate to find." Acan took one last look at his sister and committed the horrific image to memory. He could never allow this to happen again.

≈ ≪

Feeling more determined than he had in his entire existence, Acan drove to his realtor's home, woke his ass from bed, and called his lawyer, demanding that they have a new dwelling purchased immediately—something grand and worthy of a woman's approval. Yes, it had been two in the morning. No, he did not give a shit about waking them up. That was what he paid them for. All right, it was usually to deal with matters of arson—arrests and being burned out of home and hearth—but whatever. Today was a day for firsts. So he'd spent most of the early morning hours reviewing listings with Gomez, his realtor, and then headed to the tailor.

This was not just any tailor. Mr. Damien Greystone had been dressing the gods and other large males in the immortal community for a decade. He'd inherited the business from his father and his father before that. They never asked questions. They never complained about the odd hours or rush jobs. They simply went to work, knowing exactly what to do and how to make clothes for men of large proportions, specifically pants—leather, denim, or cloth—to accommodate extraordinarily large dicks.

"I'll require some T-shirts, athletic shoes, and whatever else men of this era wear on the bottom to keep their cocks in place while they exercise."

Damien—on the tall side for a human at six three—dipped his head of thick light brown hair. "And will you be wearing these shorts multiple times, sir, or merely losing them like the others?

Because I have a very nice shipment of ten-dollar shorts—"

"My drunken, pantsless days are over." Acan waved his hand through the air while examining a variety of holiday sweaters with reindeer and snowmen hanging on the wall. He wondered if he should buy them. They kind of called to his party side.

No. No. I'm a serious grown god now. No more partying.

"You mean…you're actually going to exercise in them?" Damien blinked with confusion.

Acan gave the man a hard look.

"Very good, sir. Then I will bring you something a bit sturdier." Damien proceeded to the stock room and returned with several outfits—expensive-looking jeans, T-shirts, a few nice dress shirts, and gear to work out. "Your suits will be ready next week."

"I need everything by tomorrow." He had two weeks to find his woman. No time to lose.

Damien blinked and then smiled. "I will make arrangements, sir. And might I say, sir, it's quite refreshing to see you so passionate about dressing yourself."

Acan growled a few choice expletives under his breath. *Yeah, yeah. So I walked around pantsless for a few thousand years.*

"My party days are over. At least until I find a mate." Acan slipped a piece of paper from his pocket with his new address—a house he'd chosen only an hour ago. It was vacant and the owners were more than happy to let him stay in it while the paperwork got pushed through. He'd paid two times the asking price. "Have the suits sent to this address along with the bill." Acan grabbed his six bags of new clothes and headed out to his taco truck parked in front of the store.

"Hey, man. Can I get two steak quesadillas?" said a young guy as Acan stepped into his grease trap on wheels.

Acan looked at the man, then at his taco truck, and then back at the man. "Where's the nearest luxury auto dealer?"

"There's a Tesla dealer a few blocks that way." The guy pointed down the street.

"Thank you." Acan started up the rumbling diesel engine.

"Hey! What about my food, man?"

"I am on a mission to wow the perfect woman. There is no time for snacking. However, show up to the dealer in half an hour and the truck is yours." He sped off, spewing smoke into the air. *Watch out, ladies, because here comes the God of Wine.*

CHAPTER FIVE

Forty-five-year-old Margarita Seville toweled off her face and neck at the end of the Zumba class she'd just given, filling in for one of the instructors who'd called in sick today. She waved goodbye to the ladies filing from the room, a room with a glass wall on one side and a view into the world-class gym.

Her gym.

She sighed with a sense of accomplishment. She'd started Club CrossFit Santa Monica ten years ago, putting everything she had—money, blood, sweat, and tears—into this place to make it a success. To her, it was more than a business that provided an income for herself and her now sixteen-year-old daughter, Jessica; it was a statement about her values and will to survive. Her past, for lack of better words, had been one giant shame-fest, riddled with many mistakes, the biggest being Mike—her ex-husband and the saddest chapter of her life. The only thing good to come out of all that was Jessica.

She looked around at the packed gym, people doing the circuit with their trainers—weights, pull-ups, squat thrusts, rowing, and running. It really gave her a rush to see her establishment helping people achieve healthier bodies and lives.

Well, she thought, *all that pain led to this.* Her dream. Freedom. Being healthy and helping others achieve the same. Today marked the gym's ten-year anniversary.

Margarita glanced at her watch. Seven a.m. Time to text Jessica and make sure she was up and ready for school. Jess already had five tardies this school year. *Teenagers—the laziest, fittest people on the planet. So unfair.*

Margarita exited the aerobics room and headed for her office on the other side of the gym to grab her cell. She punched the code on the number pad to the side of the door and entered.

There you are. She reached for her phone atop a stack of papers on her desk and heard the door close behind her.

"You," said a deep male voice filled with accusation.

She turned and saw a towering male figure standing there staring at her. Beer belly. Turquoise eyes. Messy, long hair.

"Oh, hell," she muttered. "Not you again." *At least he's wearing pants.* In fact, he almost—*almost!*—looked handsome in his worn jeans and "If you're happy and you know it, clap your hands!" T-shirt.

He stepped toward her, and instead of showing an expression resembling someone lost or daydreaming—*or shitfaced*—like the last two time she'd seen him, he looked serious. *Possibly sober?* That was a relief because she hated being anywhere near a drunk. Mike had taught her how cruel they could be.

She crossed her arms over her chest, thankful she wore a loose-fitting T-shirt with her gym's red logo and black Spandex shorts. The first time she'd seen this guy—drunk, staggering, reeking of beer—she'd been on her way to a private training session with an A-list client staying at the Shangri La Hotel. She'd been wearing one of her smaller outfits—small sports tank and short shorts, better for a stretching and yoga routine—when she bumped into this disgusting clown in the elevator. He'd taken it upon himself to tell her she had a tight ass and nice tits. *Pig.* Didn't he know how threatened it made a woman feel to be trapped in an elevator with a huge, seven-foot drunk guy wearing nothing but a pair of tightie whities?

She shivered at the memory. "What do you want?"

The man—Belch he'd called himself—pointed his finger in her face. "You! Blondie," he barked with a deep menacing voice, "you will make my body into a divine temple to attract many females."

She pulled her head back. *What in the world?*

Belch stepped closer, leaving a foot of space between them, and glowered down with intense turquoise eyes, freezing her in place. "What are you waiting for, woman?"

She tried to make her mouth move, but there was something about him. Something so very different from the last time she'd seen him. Dopiness converted into a powerful authority. Magnetism instead of pure repulsiveness.

And he doesn't smell like booze.

"I am in need of fitness." He placed his large hand on her shoulder and gave her a little push. "There is no time to lose. Chop-chop."

Did he just push me? "Did you just push me?" Because no man laid his hands on her. *Never again.* She'd played the role of victim for one tragic chapter of her life. She'd survived and would never allow anyone to put her in that place again.

"Yes, and I will do so again if you do not get moving," he said.

"Get. Out. Of my. Gym," she snarled.

"Are you refusing to assist me?"

Why did he seem so shocked? Didn't he remember their last interaction? Or the one prior to that?

"I don't allow disgusting, womanizing drunken slobs in my gym," she growled.

"Ah, I see. You are nothing but one of those judgmental trolls who enjoys criticizing others less physically perfect. I should've known." He lowered his head, placing the tips of their noses together.

His scent wafted through her nostrils. *What is that smell?* It was sweet and intoxicating. It filled her lungs like a sensual drug, infusing her blood and giving her a shock of titillating tingles throughout her body. *What the hell is that?* He smelled amaaaazing. Sinful. Mind-blowingly delicious. Every erotic nerve in her body lit up, throbbing and aching.

No way. She stepped back, pushing her ass all the way against the edge of her desk. How could she want him? *No. No. Not possible.* She looked at his giant beer belly, unkempt hair, and untoned legs and arms, feeling revolted by the lack of pride in his appearance. Yet…he still had a beautifully masculine face—strong jaw, full lips, and deep, soul-penetrating turquoise eyes that gave her goose bumps. Was he really seeing through her, right into her soul, or was that her imagination running wild due to lack of sleep?

It's definitely your imagination, and he needs to go. Clearly something was not right in her head.

"Leave," she snapped.

Eyeing her with those stunning blue-green eyes, he crossed his large arms over his flabby chest. "I will leave when you, you foulmouthed little female, give me what I came for: a hot sexy body."

She laughed. "Not possible. Now go before I call the police." This man was a mess, both inside and out. No manners and vile. *But dammit, he smells so good. Why?* She felt the warm tingles between her legs turn into a hot dampness.

"I do not fear the police or anyone for that matter—except the clowns. They make my skin crawl.

Nevertheless, I will go, but know this: you are a member of this world, same as anyone, and you have failed it."

"Whatever, Arrow. Just know you are the biggest loser to ever walk the…" Her words faded as she watched him turn to leave. Something inside her—a very, very strange something—did not want him to go. No. She wanted him to stay. She wanted to ravish him.

"Wait. Tell me what you're willing to give in exchange?" *What the hell am I saying?*

He glanced over his wide shoulder in her direction. "What do you want?"

She couldn't bring herself to say the unbelievable words: She wanted…she wanted him! *Oh God. Did I smack my head on a barbell? He's so unhealthy.*

His eyes flickered with suspicion as if puzzling something out. "All right." He sighed his words. "If I must." He returned to her, placing his hands on her hips and lifting her onto her desk.

"What are you doing?" she whispered.

"What do you think?"

I think you're going to have sex with me on top of my desk. And more shocking than anything, she wanted him to.

What's happening to me?

CHAPTER SIX

Fine. If this stuck-up, horrible woman required a thorough fucking in order to be persuaded to help him, then that was what he'd give her. What did he care? He actually might enjoy shutting up her rude, condescending mouth with something big in his pants. Because the nasty tone in her voice had instantly set him off. And turned him the hell on.

He ripped off his shirt and pulled down the top of his pants, exposing his large, thick cock. He was already hard, ready to show her how the natural order of species worked—him on top. Her on the bottom.

"What are we doing?" she asked without any fear in her voice.

She so wants me. He saw her dilated pupils and hard nipples poking through her thin T-shirt as proof.

"Remove your shorts," he commanded.

"You're disgusting. And insane."

"And you're a mean, nasty old woman."

Her mouth dropped. "I am *not* old."

Actually, she wasn't. She looked to be approximately in her early thirties; however, her aura and vibe told him she was a bit older. *She takes very good care of herself. Serious MILF.*

"Prove it. Shut up and take off your shorts," he egged her on.

She was about to say something, but there it was. A flushness in her face and chest. Rapid breathing. She was about to lose her mind if he didn't fuck her. It was a simple fact that humans found gods irresistible. Perhaps it was nature's way of making them more complacent so the gods might effectively do their jobs. Who knew? But he could not recall any woman ever getting this excited nor did he recall wanting to fuck someone as badly as this. He wanted to pound her into submission.

"Well, I do not have all fucking day, woman." He gripped his enormous throbbing cock in his hand, waiting for somewhere warm and wet to put it. *I am a true romantic.*

"Fine." She reached for her waistband and began shimmying down her shorts. "But you're still a disgusting slob. This changes nothing."

Dear gods. He glanced at the perfectly smooth creamy skin between her thighs and the barely there landing strip of dark hair between her legs. Now *he* was the one who might lose his fucking mind if he didn't get in there.

"No more talking," he commanded.

With her tennis shoes still on and her shorts

around her ankles, he lifted her legs and slid between her thighs. He pushed her back onto her desk and leaned over her, staring into her wide, hate-filled eyes.

Gods, she's so mean. And he so wanted her.

With his cock firmly in one hand, determined to make her eat her words, he slapped her c-spot a few times, teasing her with the head.

She gasped with pleasure.

"Yeah, you like that, don't you?" he whispered in a deep voice.

"No. Shut up. You make me sick."

He laughed. "Liar." He slapped her clit again with his heavy shaft. "Tell me you want it. Tell me to end your torment and fuck you."

"Never."

He spanked her c-spot once more with his stiff dick, unsure of how much more he could take of this.

She bucked with pleasure but stared defiantly. "I have no idea why that feels so damned good. You're awful. I can't stand you." She smiled wickedly, taunting him.

Oh. So this was her game. "Fine. You win." He quickly positioned the head of his shaft into her slick entrance and grabbed her petite hands, raising her arms above her head while staring into her mesmerizing green eyes. She looked absolutely lovely, like a wild creature, her long blonde hair loose, her body pumping with adrenaline.

He stilled, refusing to give her what she wanted. Eleven inches of thick, hard flesh.

"What are you waiting for?" she complained, wiggling her hips, trying to get him deeper.

He pulled back, maintaining enough pressure to torment her and keep the tip of his shaft inside. "Say it. Tell me to fuck you."

"I hate you," she growled.

Oh, that did it. "I think I hate you, too." He thrust hard, driving into her until he could go no further. Not nearly far enough.

She gasped and threw her head to the side. "Fuck. Fuck, you're too big."

He pulled out and drove into her again, the desk creaking. *Damn!* He could barely get halfway in. He never remembered a woman being so damned tight. But then again, every inch of her body was solid, lean muscle.

"Relax," he commanded, "or it won't work."

She nodded, panting, "Okay. Okay. I'm relaxing."

"That's right." Slowly, he eased into her, feeling her walls clenching, resisting the sensual invasion. He increased the pressure, watching the intense pleasure build on her face as he drove inside one inch at a time. "There you go." He brushed his hand over the top of her blonde hair, admiring her natural, timeless beauty—full lips, golden brown eyelashes that fanned out in thick curtains, and the loveliest smile lines etched into her cheeks. He slowly pulled back, enjoying the feeling of her warmth and wetness all around his dick. *Gods, she feels so perfect. So good.* Being with her was like having sex for the very first time. Was it because of her or because he had nothing in his bloodstream to dull the pleasure? And the way she reacted to him, bucking and moaning, her skin flushing. He couldn't wait to show her what would happen when he came inside her. Instantaneous, mind-blowing orgasms. And he could come as many times as he liked. All night long, if he wished. It was good to be a god. *Sometimes.*

She bowed her body forward and slid her hands around his ass, pulling him closer, deeper. "Harder. I'm ready now."

He looked down at her needy face and grinned. *Oh, yes.* She was enjoying this, and he was enjoying making her eat her words. She fucking wanted him. *In your face!*

He thrust his hips forward, this time going as deep as her body would allow, but still unable to completely bury himself. He would have to try another position to get his cock in the entire way.

"Oh, god," she panted, "I'm so close."

He pumped a little faster, allowing his balls to tighten. He would wait for her natural climax and then…he'd ejaculate deep inside her, allowing his energy to seep into her womb and give her an orgasm that would have her salivating for the rest of her life.

The good thing was that once he removed the black jade bracelet, she could not get pregnant.

Acan froze. *Wait. I didn't give her a jade bracelet. Oh shit.* He probably had three seconds not to fry her brain. Panicked, he quickly pulled out and looked at her. *Oh, gods. Oh, gods. Please tell me she is all right.*

Her hooded green eyes went wide. "Why did you stop?"

Thank gods. He sighed with relief. *She's fine.* He'd pulled out in the nick of time.

"Well?" She lay there in front of him, glowing with sweat, and the valley between her legs wide open, tempting him to return to her glistening wetness.

He could not tell her the truth—humans were on a need-to-know basis about the gods, meaning they had to be a part of their human army, the Uchben, or they were essential in some other way. Mates were also allowed to know, but this woman did not fall into any of those categories.

He lifted her legs, slid out from between her thighs, and put his cock back in his jeans, painfully adjusting himself so it would go sideways instead of sticking straight out like a giant horizontal flagpole.

"Oh, my god." Her mouth dropped. "You're going to leave me hanging to get back at me, aren't you? I should've known."

Acan glanced down at her lying there so angry and aroused. *Fuck, I want to get back in there and*

*give her the real punishment—the orgasm that will
ruin her for all other men.*

"You're a disgusting asshole," she said. "Or
maybe you're just too drunk to come."

He narrowed his eyes. "I am never too drunk to
come. And you should watch that nasty mouth of
yours." His eyes involuntarily moved down and
stuck to her entrance. *Godsdammit, I want her.* In all
his years of existence he could not recall feeling so
aroused by a woman. And the way her body felt
pressed against his was nothing shy of amazing. Had
this been what he'd been missing out on all of these
years? Sure, black jade—which enabled gods to have
sex with humans—was a fairly recent discovery, but
since then, he'd had sex all the time. Of course,
never like this. Like she'd lit up his body from the
inside out.

Must be the lack of party juice. Nonetheless, it
had been intense.

He sighed longingly at her unsatisfied and swollen c-spot.

She snapped her legs closed. "Loser."

He glanced back up at her angry face. "Dried-
out cougar."

"Dysfunctional dickhead."

"All right. That does it." He would slide inside
her, come hard, and pull out. He'd have to be
quick, but then she'd know who she was messing
with.

He reached for his cock but stopped. Despite

everything, he cared what happened to this woman. He could not risk harming her.

"Oh, big man can't finish the job?" she said bitterly.

Gods, she looked so hot. And beautiful. He would give anything to reach out and touch her again. *Godsdammit. Look how full she is of sexual energy and life and whatnot.* He could look at her all day long.

He sighed and stepped away. "I have to go. I'm late for a meeting."

She snapped up her head. "Yes. You should go." She pulled up her shorts and began pushing him toward the door. "Like now. Right now. Now, now, now, and don't ever come back. Got it."

"You are not going to assist me with my fitness needs simply because of this?" he asked. "That is called sexual bullying. I feel violated."

"Yep. Absolutely. That's me. Exploiter of men." She pushed him again, trying to move him toward the door. She was behaving like a lunatic.

"Ah. You must be worried about a boyfriend or significant other who will no longer be appealing to you after you've come so close to male perfection."

She looked up at him. "What the hell's that supposed to mean?"

"It means that you are a sore loser and can only attract insecure men."

Hate shot from her beautiful green eyes. "You. Are. Such. A disgusting pig."

"Yes. I know that. Thus the reason to change my ways to impress more women, starting with my body, which you've now refused to help me with."

She blinked at him and stuttered, "Wha-what? Oh God. You're insane, and you really need to leave."

She was serious. She really truly refused to help him. How was that even possible? Humans were supposed to want to do anything a god said. *Dammit. I feel the need to party and release the negative energy building in my chest.*

No. I cannot. I made a vow. But the urge to give in to his instincts, his divine place in this world, felt like gravity pulling him down. He could hear the masses chanting his name and begging him for fun. *So much suffering, such need for libations and drink!*

"You truly want me to go?" he asked.

"Yes. There are plenty of other gyms in the city you can go to for your 'fitness needs.'"

Of course. However, now he sort of liked her sour attitude and smart mouth. And clearly this woman, who was in incredible shape, knew what she was doing.

Again, the pull to party was tremendous. He could hardly stand it.

"All right," he said. "I will leave, but you must do one thing for me."

"What?" She looked up at him, thoroughly agitated.

He leaned down and kissed her hard. Her

mouth, resistant at first, melted into him and her lips became soft and welcoming. He moved his tongue inside her, softly stroking and sliding. Her breath, sweet and fresh like a spring meadow, filled his lungs. Everything about her was so damned rejuvenating and uplifting.

But I bet she's never had real fun. I bet she could stand a night of getting wild and letting loose with— the perfect drink popped in his head. *Oh, oh, oh…what a naughty girl, this one.* She was in need of a banana daiquiri, or as he liked to call them, banana cockeries…

In a float glass:
- two shots of vanilla vodka
- one shot of banana liqueur
- a scoop of vanilla ice cream
- a dollop of whipped cream
- drizzle of caramel

Slide an entire peeled banana down the side and place a thin straw carefully through the top of the banana, pushing it all the way down.

The *drinker* had to suck the banana bits from the straw in a very salacious manner before getting to the creamy good stuff inside the glass.

Very provocative. Yes, he must prepare it for her immediately and kiss her all night and—

He pushed back, breaking their kiss. He'd almost forgotten again. Prolonged contact was dangerous without the black jade.

She opened her eyes and blinked at him as if waking from a long sleep. "Okay. I kissed you. Now you have to go."

"That wasn't good enough." He walked her backwards until her ass hit the desk. He cupped her between her legs, allowing a pulse of energy to hit her right where it counted.

She gasped with pleasure.

"One more kiss, and then I'm gone," he said.

She hesitated for a moment. "Promise?"

He nodded and covered her mouth with his, cupping her ass.

That ass. So fucking tight. He thought about how easy it would be to turn her around, push her forward, and fuck her hard from behind. *In and out. Five seconds.* Quickly and safely. He could slide inside her, open up the gates and flood her with cum. She would whimper, given his semen would make her orgasm instantly, and then she'd be grabbing fists of papers, moaning his name. Why coming inside a woman made them orgasm instantly, he didn't know, but it came in handy.

Dear gods. I must try.

Whoa. Whoa. I am too excited. The thrill of sexual arousal without any alcohol to stifle the pleasure had gone to his head.

Must go! Without a word, he made a swift exit through her office door.

"Wait!" she called out before he was halfway out the door of her gym. She'd obviously dressed but looked freshly fucked, her blonde hair a mess and her shirt hem caught in her gray sports bra, showing off her flat stomach.

Nice abs. He gave her a look, wondering what she might say. Maybe "come back later?" or "please don't go, I need you?"

He waited. She said nothing.

"Well?" he asked.

"You're still a disgusting slob, but good luck. And don't ever come here again."

What the hell! What was her problem?

"Horrible woman, I wouldn't come in you if you cried and begged me."

Her face turned bright red. "God, I hate you."

"Gods, I hate you back."

CHAPTER SEVEN

For the rest of the horrific morning, Acan traded texts with his realtor, his lawyer, Zac, and his assistant, Jill—she'd miraculously resurfaced after he'd reluctantly offered to double her salary. Desperate times. But there was much to do in preparation for finding (and keeping) his future Mrs. God of Wine, including Zac's task of organizing a singles mixer for later in the week.

Would his brother pull through? The guy seemed to be a complete mess over the loss of his assistant, Tula.

Yes.

No.

Trust, but verify?

Halt the chatter. He will make it happen. If anyone knew how to gather women, it was Zac.

*Hmmm…*Acan wondered what his mate might look like. Tall? Red hair?—*Wait. No red hair. Reminds me of Cirail.* He shivered with disgust. *All right, brunette or blonde. Young.* Energetic and extraverted so she wouldn't mind accompanying him to parties. *Or beheadings?*

He shook his head. *Gods*, there was nothing on this earth he'd rather do less. Why had the Universe bestowed such a gruesome power upon him? *And where the hell does popping heads off come in handy?* As for killing, there were hundreds of cooler, less gory ways to do it. Take his brother K'ak (pronounced "cock"), for example. K'ak still had not found his flagship gift—a power he truly connected with—but nevertheless he had many skills, one of them being the ability to summon lightning. Very badass. He'd once taken out an army of Maaskab priests—those bloodthirsty Mayan witch doctors. Just when all had seemed lost...boom! Sizzle, sizzle. Evil priest charcoal. Not a drop of blood. K'ak was not only the hero that day, but he'd looked like a manly deity while doing it. Over seven feet tall with ankle-length black hair and a two-foot-high serpent headdress, K'ak put the "awe" in awesome, the "zing" in amazing, the "tudi" in pulchritudinous.

Not so badass, however? Belch. God of drunken pantlessness.

In any case, it was time to turn over a new image-leaf. *Perhaps I will go exclusively by my given Mayan name, Acan.* It would help him to forget his party days—i.e., yesterday. And Acan was the very first name given to him by the humans. He and all of his brethren honored this tradition. They first came to the human realm via the River Tlaloc, a current of energy flowing between the two worlds, one end of the current emerging at the very spot where Mayans once thrived. They were the first to see the gods and to whom the gods spoke. The Mayans were the first to produce written records specifically about them and, more importantly, they knew how to party!

Speaking of partying…dammit all to hell! I miss having my afternoon box-o-wine. Why had the Universe decided to create this mess and torture him? Who the hell knew.

Well, I really only have to last until I find my mate. He could resist the urge to "bring down the house" for two weeks. Right? Zac was hard at work, doing his best to organize a mate mixer in a few days, which was not an easy task given that his assistant had quit. She was off planning her own wedding, at which Acan was supposed to tend bar. He didn't know if he could handle the pressure of being around so much temptation at such a critical juncture. And then, he'd have to attend the party being planned by Zac. *I will need to remain very focused.*

Acan stood in the circular driveway of his new, superluxurious, beachside palace and watched the movers unload five large vans—red and black sofas, plush area rugs, big-screen TVs, refrigerators for every room, ten king-sized beds, lamps (with naked lady bases), pool table, portable dance floor for the backyard, trampoline, bouncy house, giant bar set with fun saddle-shaped bar stools, a mechanical bull, hay, mojito tank, an assortment of crazy hats, massage table for quiet evenings at home with four or five women (he hoped his mate would be a swinger), case of frosting for orgy night (gods, he really, really hoped), a bubble machine, ten-person video game center, disco ball, jukebox, loudspeakers for Forgetty's DJ magic, fifty cases of alcohol (for after he found his mate), a supersized ice machine for parties, five blow-up sex dolls (party decorations for one of his favorite holidays: Valentine's Day), a hot-pink Ping-Pong table (for Cimil and her unicorn) and…a pony (just for shits and g's).

"Ah, I love LA." He sighed contentedly. There was nothing money couldn't buy in this town and, as a god, money was the one thing he had plenty of. It almost felt like cheating to be so rich, but he looked at it as a simple necessity (and perk) of the job. One could not roam about, going from party to party, worrying about money. Not when his flock needed him! Bottom line, his lifestyle required capital. No, now that he was on the wagon—no more partying until he found Mrs. Get Down and Get Funky—he would behave, but after he found her, he'd be prepared to give the party to end all parties. *I cannot wait to honor her with such fun.*

His mind drifted to the woman at the gym. The way her green eyes viewed him with such intensity. Lust mixed with hate. Need met with disgust. The dichotomy made him wonder—not only about her duality but his, too. She genuinely made him ill with her piety and judgmental ways. Yet, he felt drawn to her vigorous thirst for life, and the way she'd needed and craved his body made him feel like a god.

Wait. I am a god. I do not require measly mortals to feel like my awesome self. What he really needed now was to keep his eye on the woman prize. Yes, he lusted after this horribly fit woman like no other, but so what? Lust was replaceable. *Focus, Acan. Focus on the vacant gaze of your beloved sister after you took her head.*

I am searching for the one. A woman to challenge him, balance him, love him, and please him.

But what if he did not find his special someone? He would end up imprisoned for the safety of others, and he wasn't so certain that would contain the situation. After all, on New Year's Eve, his powers spiked off the charts and reached humans on the other side of the planet. If he were not in control at the time, then what would a few steel prison bars and cement walls do? Nothing. He would still be a menace to society.

I will find her. I will find my mate. And when he did, she would not be able to resist him and everything he had to offer. *Including the pony.*

And after the movers left, the decorator would get to work to create an impressive party palace. Jill had also made him an appointment at the gym down the road—no snooty mean ladies he wanted to sleep with there—and in the morning he would go to the salon for something called a "man-over," which was apparently a makeover for men.

Acan's phone rang, and he slipped it from his jeans pocket. *Hey! Look. I'm still wearing pants. Nice.*

He answered the call. "Hello?"

"Belch, it's me, Tula."

"I am now going by my formal name, Acan. How may I be of service?"

"I haven't heard back from—dangit. Why can't I remember her name? Anyway, I haven't heard back from your sister."

Crap on a cracker. He did not want to tell Tula what he'd done.

"She's been busy."

"Okay. But Cimil hasn't been sending her usual hourly text messages with photos of guinea pigs dressed as evil gnomes. They're so creepy, but I know she looks forward to tormenting me. Something must be wrong."

"Eh…no. Everything's fine. My brethren are all out of town at the moment. They'll be back in a day or two."

Tula sighed. "Phew. That's good to hear, Mr. Acan, because my wedding is next week. You are still bartending, right?"

"About that, I am afraid you will need to find someone else—"

Tula began to sob on the other end of the phone. "But how am I going to find someone on such short notice? And you know I don't have much money." Sniffle, sniffle.

Dear gods, he did not need this right now. "I will give you the money to hire someone—consider it an engagement gift.'

"I don't take charity. You know that. Besides, you're the only one I trust to serve drinks. This wedding party must go right, and Gilbert's father is the pickiest man on the planet. He likes everything a certain way. Including his drinks."

My kind of guy. After all, partying with the perfect beverage, prepared perfectly, was a sign of respect for the time-honored tradition of celebrating. Any moron could crack open a cheap beer or those premixed cocktails in a can, but a sign of general awesomeness was pairing the occasion to the drink. For example, one did not perform wedding toasts with "turds in a punch bowl" punch, even if it was a classic and one of his all-time favorites:

In a large punch bowl, mix:
- one liter of white chocolate liqueur
- one pint of peppermint Schnapps
- five cups of ice
- cover surface of punch with chocolate-covered marshmallows. Can substitute with dollops of chocolate Cool Whip

Serve in a glass mug to allow a clear view of the floating turds.

Hmmm…delicious.

"Tula, I am truly sorry, but I am afraid I must

insist on finding you a replacement." They had plenty of fine bartenders who worked in their nightclubs and bars.

"You're just like Zac. You don't care about anyone or that you made a commitment to me after I helped you."

She'd helped him? "What do you mean, Tula?"

"Who got you out of human jail the last four times? And who kept you from going to jail when you lit that Beverly Hills hotel on fire at the last singles mixer, huh?"

Oh dammit. He'd forgotten about that. "You did."

"That's right. Me. I stuck my neck out and convinced the police to let you go. I posted bail and called your lawyer. And I did it all without blowing your cover."

Acan now recalled several small pieces of these wild events—*god times, god times*—when Tula had been there to help him. Which was why he promised to be there for her if she ever needed him.

"Very well," he sighed with a grumble. "I will bartend for your wedding." This would not make things easy for him, but he was a deity. Strong. Determined. Insanely handsome. He could handle going to a party and not partaking in the fun. Couldn't he?

"Thank you, Mr. Acan. Thank you for keeping your promise."

"Of course, but might I ask you a question?"

"Okay," she replied.

"Why must you worry so much about impressing your fiancé's family especially at your own wedding? You're a very nice human. Do they not approve of you?"

"I-I-I can't risk upsetting Gilbert, so everything for the wedding has to be perfect. And we have to marry soon."

How very odd. "This doesn't have anything to do with Zac, does it?" After all, she had just mentioned something about him: *"You're just like him. You don't care about anyone..."* she'd said.

"No. What would make you think that?" she snapped in an uncharacteristic manner. Everyone knew Tula was kind and pure hearted. They could all see her perfectly pristine white aura.

"Tula, there are few secrets among the gods, and everyone knows Zac has been pursuing you."

"Well, he blew it! He showed me who he really is—the God of Temptation. Only I wasn't tempted, and it made him try harder. And then he just...he just..." Tula began to cry again. "This is why I have to marry Gilbert like Cimil said. Then I'll be happy."

Whoa. "You cannot, and I repeat, you cannot believe anything Cimil says. She prays to a shrine made entirely of Twinkies—only on Wednesdays, of course, but still. She's out of her freaking red head. If you marry this Gilbert man, it must be your decision."

"Cimil is my friend. She wouldn't lie to me."

Acan stifled a laugh. "Tula, I have known Cimil for over seventy thousand years. She is not capable of friendship—not by your human definition, anyway."

"You only say that because you don't know her like I do. She gave me a job so I could finish college when no one else would. She believed in me when no one else did, and she trusted me with your secrets. Where I come from, that's a good friend."

Acan groaned. Should he tell Tula about the time Cimil lured everyone into a giant freezer, had them frozen into a block of ice, and then dropped them into the middle of the ocean so they would have to swim to shore once they defrosted? Or how about the time she tried to end the world simply for fun? A few hundred times? Of course, he thoroughly enjoyed Cimil's chaotic side. She knew how to party like no other. Twister, for example? No one could beat her. Not even those shifty vampires. And her *Love Boat* marathon sleepovers complete with fish sticks, marimba music, and those little stick-on anchor tattoos? The best.

"Tula, all I am saying is that you must never do anything simply because another tells you to. Always think for yourself."

"Point taken. I think I should marry Gilbert. See you next week at the wedding." She ended the call, and Acan simply stood there in his driveway, wondering why he felt so displeased by her choice or why he cared so much about what happened to her, as if she were a little sister of sorts?

Strange. He scratched his scraggly short beard, watching the last of the furnishings being loaded into his new mansion overlooking the Pacific Ocean. He suddenly felt a sharp pinch in his gut.

Hell, his brethren were coming through the portal. They were going to kick the shit out of him when they returned.

Must hurry and find my mate. He closed his eyes for a moment, trying to sense her presence out there in the Universe, but all he could hear was the call of the masses in need of libation. Belch, Belch, Belch!

I am sorry, my flock of fun-doers, but the God of Wine is on a leave of absence until he finds his woman. It was for their own good. But after that, the party would go on.

CHAPTER EIGHT

After a long *hard* day at work, Margarita entered the front door of her modest two-bedroom condo in the even more modest Sawtelle neighborhood just east of Santa Monica, hoping to God her daughter, Jessica, would not notice the residual guilt plastered on her face.

For as long as Margarita could recall (and it was age appropriate), Margarita had told her daughter to always use care. Not only with her body, but with her heart. "Men are not in charge of protecting you—you are." Margarita's ex, Mike, had taught her the lesson. When they'd met seventeen years ago, she'd been working as a manager at a twenty-four-hour fitness chain. He'd been one of those guys who'd turned every woman's head in the gym. Ripped from head to toe, gorgeous, completely cocky.

At first, she didn't give him much attention—she was far more into competing with herself than with another woman for a guy—but after a few months, he began asking her out. She'd said no.

Then he asked her out again. And again. No turned into maybe. Maybe turned into yes. Fast-forward a few months, and she'd allowed one night of superficial lust to overcome her sense of responsibility. Nine months later came Jessica and big changes in Mike. Looking back, however, the changes started happening the day she told him she was pregnant.

By day, he'd worked as a car salesman, but on weekends, he competed in bodybuilding competitions. Perhaps it was the pressure of knowing he would have to support them while she took time off with the baby, or maybe he simply felt trapped, but he'd started taking performance enhancers, pushing himself to the limit. Then he snapped. Literally. His hamstring tore, and Margarita found herself taking care of a new baby and her damaged new husband while trying to make ends meet with not two, but three part-time jobs and a lactation schedule. Somewhere in that sleepless nightmare, he began drinking and hitting.

She never knew where she'd found the will to leave him, but she had, and it was the toughest time of her life. Worse than being hit. Worse than being eighteen and telling her Amish parents and two sisters that she—officially known as Margaret Miller at the time—wanted to live a different life with "the English." Worse than trying to adapt to a world she didn't understand, but desperately wanted to be a part of for the simple reason that she felt her calling was elsewhere.

Alone with a new baby, living in her car because Mike refused to leave the apartment she was paying for, Margarita was terrified. Absolutely terrified. So she'd prayed like she'd never prayed before. She begged for the strength not to go back where there was a warm bed and roof for her and her child. She prayed for the strength to face the unknown.

Then something unexpected happened: She hit emotional rock bottom. And the funny thing about rock bottom was that there was absolutely nowhere else to go but up. Suddenly, the mountain she'd been destined to climb became crystal clear, and that rocky bastard was one she became determined to conquer. That night she went to a shelter and began figuring out what it would take to climb high. From there, she didn't stop. Years later, it had cost her everything she had to do it—tears, pain, sweat, food stamps, donated clothes from churches or anywhere she could get them, and secret handouts from her estranged older sister—but she'd scraped together a living for her and Jessica. They'd shared a one-bedroom apartment in a run-down building in Sawtelle, but she eventually saved enough to move them to a slightly better place and open her own gym.

Why a gym? It hadn't really started out that way. Her idea had been to offer single working moms a place to come and exercise while their kids were supervised. It sounded strange, but at her lowest points, those days when she barely had anything to eat because there was only enough money to buy food for Jessica, or those days where she only slept two hours because she needed to work, she remembered being grateful that she had her health. It had saved her and Jessica. Because as long as she could work, there was hope for a better life. Her wish became wanting to give that same hope and health to as many struggling mothers as possible.

But soon, word started to spread. People liked the laid-back vibe and the classes she gave. From there, the gym kept on growing and she eventually qualified for a loan to expand her business. It took Margarita sixteen years to pull her life back together a piece at a time after Mike, but Jessica had been her motivation every painstaking step of the way. Now, she finally made enough money to pay off her debt, save for Jessica's college, and put a little bit away for retirement. In LA money didn't go far, but Margarita's life was tied to her business. She could never leave unless she sold the gym, and it wasn't worth enough. *Not yet.*

Please let me get that second loan. Please… With it, she would open two more locations and be impressive enough to franchise.

Yet you risked it all for sex with some horrible strange man in your office? What if word got out? Everyone would see her as a fraud. Her gym had been built on her reputation for living a clean, healthy life where fitness was at the center. If her customers knew she'd cavorted with a drunken slob who clearly did not believe in caring for one's body, they'd all think she was a giant hypocrite.

God, I hope he doesn't have any diseases. Really. What had come over her? It was so unlike her to become overwhelmed with so much…well, hard hot lust.

She shook her head. *Stress. It's got to be stress.* Or perhaps her hormones were messing with her?

Margarita threw her keys and purse down on the small glass entryway table of their very modest condo overlooking a sushi restaurant. "Jessica! I'm home!"

No reply.

"Jess?" The lights in her daughter's room were out and her school backpack wasn't on the bed—its usual place.

Margarita went for her purse, dug out her phone, and dialed Jessica's cell. *Voicemail? Dammit, Jess. Don't do this to me again. I can't support us and be home to babysit you, too.*

She looked up at the ceiling, tears of frustration welling in her eyes. This was the third time this month that Jessica had decided to do as she pleased, ignoring the rule to come home after school and to always tell her where she was. LA was a big, big city and no place for a young woman to be running around. If anyone knew that, it was Margarita.

Why? Why would she do this to me?

Margarita sat on her brown, secondhand couch

and pushed her palms to her eyes, trying her best not to cry. Jessica meant everything to her, but it felt like everything she sacrificed meant nothing to her daughter. Every day they grew further and further apart.

Margarita clasped her hands together and closed her eyes. "Dear God, please help us get through this."

"Gods, not God. Either way…you rang and I'm answering," said a snappy female voice.

Margarita shot up from her couch. "What the…" She found the room empty. *Holy shit. What was that?* Her blood chilled.

"I think I need a vacation." She picked up her phone and started calling Jessica's friends. It was going to be another dramatic night. *And yippy. I'm going crazy.*

෨ ෯

The next morning, Margarita got up early, opened the gym and rushed home through the insane traffic to make sure Jessica was up in time for school. They'd spent two hours last night, after Margarita picked up Jessica from the mall, going around and around about the fact that Jessica was grounded for breaking the rules again, to which Jessica responded, "You're never here, so what are you going to do if I go out with my friends? Huh?" Margarita had pointed out that every day she wasn't working her butt off put them further away from finally having enough money to buy a house or to have more money available for Jess's college. But Jessica just didn't care, and she was right. Margarita couldn't do much to physically force her daughter to obey.

Dammit. Teenagers were so tough, and even tougher on single working mothers. She had to keep Jessica on track, away from any paths of recklessness that would lead Jess down a path as hard as hers. So from now on, she'd be picking Jessica up from school—forty-five minutes each way in traffic—and bringing her back to the gym to do homework and study. Hell, maybe Jess would see how hard she worked to support them.

For the time being, though, Margarita had to rush to the salon to get her hair touched up—always had to look her best. And in LA "best" meant looking young and hot.

CHAPTER NINE

What is this place? Acan had stayed at the gym all night—all right, two hours—okay, okay, an hour and forty-five minutes—but he felt exhausted. Last evening he did more exercise than he had in seventy thousand years, and he was in no mood for stupid games. Okay, also not entirely accurate. He was very much in the mood to put on his tequila shot-glass belt and do the rounds at a retirement home, as was his custom on weekends. If anyone needed to have fun and live a little it was the elderly, who understood their days were numbered. He also found the older humans to be…well, comforting. He liked that when they smiled, they meant it. When they lectured, it came from heartfelt experience, and when they told you to make every minute count, they said it out of love.

Old people rock. This place does not. Acan looked around the stuffy salon filled with snobby-looking women and wondered why the hell he'd allowed Jill to send him here. Couldn't he get a trim at the zoo with the llamas like he normally did? Yes, like old people, llamas were cool to hang around. They didn't judge and found pleasure in the simple things in life. Hay. Chewing. Making fun of zebras. Simple.

"Sir, may I, like, help you?" said a young female with spiked blue hair, standing behind the reception counter, her brown eyes wide with lust.

Instinctively, Acan looked down to ensure that he indeed wore pants. *Check! No need for help there.* "Yes, I have an appointment to trim my hair."

The young woman looked over his entire body like a squirrel eyeing a tree it wanted to climb in search of nuts. "We can totally help you with that. What's your name?"

"Acan."

She scanned her appointment book and made a pouty frown. "Oh no. I'm not seeing ya."

Dammit. Jill likely put him under his nickname. "Try Belch."

"Belch?" She giggled and then looked at her magic book. "Here you are. Under 'Mr. Belch, God of Wine.'" She looked up at him. "OMG. You a celebrity? 'Cause that's some name, mister." She winked at him. "It screams fun. So do you."

Sure. He was a celebrity in a way, but not in the manner she meant. He was more like toilet paper—people needed it but only noticed its importance when lacking. When fun went missing in their world, the journey of being alive felt more like a burden. Which was why he needed to get back to work as soon as possible. *Duty calls.*

"Haircut. Now," he ordered. "And you must cease the flirtation. I'm on vacation."

She gave him a confused look. "Uh…right this way."

He followed her into the depths of the chemical-scented girly jungle and took a seat in the chair, facing the mirror. The women—customers and stylists alike—gawked and drooled behind him.

"Linda will be right with you," said the blue-haired girl. "Can I get you water or coffee? Or meee?"

He tried to hide his impatience. This hair-grooming business was seriously annoying. "No. Thank you," he said dryly. "I am looking for the perfect woman to dedicate my existence to, and though it pains me to say it, you are not her."

"Okay. If you change your mind." She sighed and slinked away.

"Good morning, I'm Linda. Jill said you needed a…" The Asian woman, with lovely hazel eyes and short ringlet hair, stopped in her tracks and stared at his face in the mirror. "Oh, dear god of hotness."

"No. I am not the God of Hotness." How ridiculous. No such god existed. Of course, he could not disclose he truly was a god or what his call signs were: Mr. Decap and Mr. Goodtime.

The woman shook her head from side to side, trying to get a hold of herself. "Uh-uh. All right. You're here for a trim and deep-conditioning treatment, right?"

"Yes. You must make my hair soft and silky so that it beckons a woman's attention and fills her with the irresistible urge to run her fingers through it as I make passionate love to her body with my enormous cock."

The woman's mouth fell open, and she wobbled to the side.

"Are you all right, Linda?" he asked. "Because you do not look all right."

She swallowed hard. "Um. Yeah. I'm, uh...uh...really—phew! Is it hot in here?"

He understood that humans became a little wild in his presence, but he never recalled them swooning.

"Gods, this was a dumb idea. I should have gone to the llama man at the zoo." Acan stood to leave, not wanting to waste another moment.

"No. Please, I'm sorry," Linda said. "I'm not sure what came over me. I'll have you done in twenty minutes, thirty tops." She held out a black poncho-looking thing. "Let's get this on you." She glanced at the chair, urging him to retake his seat.

"What is the poncho for?" He hoped it did not have a picture of unicorns, clowns, Buck Rogers, or Hannibal on the front, as Cimil's often did. Her poncho collection was getting out of control.

"It's to keep the hair off your clothes." Reluctantly, he sat back in the chair, and the woman quickly fastened the annoying cloth around his neck. She went to work, dousing his hair with spritzes of bottled water and then applying some other stuff. With a giant comb, hand a trembling mess, she raked through his hair. The tangles came out quickly with her magic solution, and she then moved to the trim.

"Not too much," he warned. "The hair is a symbol of my sexual prowess." He'd worn his hair short many times in his existence after accidentally lighting it on fire; however, he liked it long the best. As the official party god, his look needed to scream "reckless abandon."

"No-no-no, sir. Ju-just the ends," the poor woman said with an unsteady voice. "And might I add how incredible you sme-smell."

Hell. She looked like she might pass out at any second. Honestly, he did not comprehend why women were suddenly behaving so strange around him.

After about ten minutes, Linda beamed at him from behind, staring at his face in the mirror. "All done. Now let's ge-get that power conditioner rinsed out."

Eager to get the hell on with his day, he stood from the chair and accidentally snagged the poncho on something. It fell to the ground and wet sticky hair dropped on his white shirt.

"Oh no! I'm so sorry!" She began trying to swipe the bits from his shoulders.

"Do not concern yourself." He whipped off his

shirt and then quickly witnessed Linda fainting backwards.

"What in the gods' names?" He crouched to help her while the rest of the women in the salon simply stood there staring at him. "What's the matter with you women? She needs assistance. Call those ambulance people."

Nobody moved.

"Now!" he barked with his deep, authoritative voice, jolting them back to life. He looked down at Linda and inspected her head. He saw no blood.

"Linda, can you hear me?" He tapped her cheek, and she began moaning—a good sign because it meant she had not expired.

"So fucking hot," she mumbled.

Acan sighed with a deep grumble. What was getting into these female humans?

Margarita was in the back room of the salon, getting the hair dye rinsed out, when one of the stylists rushed in. "Kay! Linda passed out."

Margarita's stylist, Kay—a woman in her sixties with hot pink hair—stopped rinsing.

"What happened?" Kay asked.

"This guy just came in and—" the woman shook her head from side to side "—I don't know. But you should see him. He's so damned hot. I mean hot, hot."

What in the world? A woman had passed out in the front of the salon and this gal was fawning over a man?

Outraged, Margarita sat up, took the towel from her shoulders, and wrapped it around her dripping wet hair. "Did you call 9-1-1?" she asked.

"I don't know, actually."

"Well, go make sure!" Margarita grumbled a few choice words and got up, heading toward the front of the salon. She knew basic CPR and first aid—a necessity when one owned a gym and people got hurt or overexerted themselves from time to time.

Margarita turned the corner and spotted a very large, shirtless man hunched over a woman lying on the floor. His back was pure muscle.

The women in the room sort of just stood there staring at him as if he were the last man on Earth.

Seriously, people?

"Linda," the man said in a hypnotically deep, sexy voice to the woman on the floor, "can you hear me?"

That voice sounds familiar. Where do I know it? As she approached, the man came into view. First, she noticed those eyes. Deep, penetrating, and turquoise like the Caribbean. Then she noticed those lips, the bottom one just the right amount of fullness to give a woman the urge to suck on it.

Wait. That face. It's that Belch guy. But as that thought reached her mind, "Belch" stood, her gaze following his face as he rose up, up, up. Then her eyes went down, down, down.

Crap. Look at those abs. The grooves were so deep and perfectly formed that they almost looked fake. And the pecs were two smooth mounds of chiseled muscle. His arms were just right. Not overly meaty, but naturally strong and swelling with power.

Perfect. He's too perfect. There wasn't a fake, overly done thing about him. One hundred percent man. One hundred percent ripped. One hundred percent naturally gorgeous. She blinked several times, wondering if she'd been the one to fall and hit her head. In all her years of running a gym that boasted some of the most sculpted bodies in the world, she'd never seen a guy like this.

But he looks like...no! It can't be! The Belch she knew had a beer belly, flabby arms, and perma-bedhead. This guy was not that. This guy was a god. A sex god.

"Ohmygod!" She covered her mouth with a gasp. "You're Belch's brother, aren't you?"

He frowned down at her as if insulted.

Why would that make him angry? Unless he wasn't that guy's brother. *No. No way. Their faces are identical.*

Maybe they didn't get along. Wouldn't surprise her. That Belch guy was a piece of work.

"I'm so sorry," she said. "I didn't mean to upset you. It must be difficult having a brother like that and always having to apologize for him."

The man continued frowning.

"What? Did I say something wrong?" she asked. "I'm sorry. It's just that I've bumped into him a couple of times—totally random and—"

"What is your name, woman?"

Woman? How very antediluvian. "Margarita."

"Well, Margarita," his turquoise eyes twitched with irritation, "this woman is injured and in need of assistance. Are you going to help or simply stand there?"

He was right. She'd been blubbering over this man like all of the other women in the salon.

Without another word, Margarita lowered herself to the woman's side. She was conscious, but clearly in pain and in need of attention. "Can you hear me…?"

"Linda. Her name is Linda," he said.

"Linda, the paramedics are on the way. Can you talk? Can you tell me where it hurts?"

Slowly, the woman raised her arm and pointed at Belch's brother. 'So hot," Linda gasped.

CHAPTER TEN

After the paramedics arrived and hauled Linda away to the hospital—merely a precaution, as she seemed to only be suffering from extreme horniness and a bump on the head—one of the other women in the salon took Acan back to the sinks to rinse out his hair.

He was absolutely going to kill Jill for this disaster, he thought while having his scalp massaged. For starters, she'd sent him to a salon where fitness woman, Margarita, just happened to show up—*very funny, Universe, harhar*—forcing him to pretend to be his own damned brother. *All right, perhaps Jill is not to blame; however, I do not have time for such ridiculous charades.* Nor did he have time to deal with human women fainting and requiring medical attention when he entered a room simply because he'd done a few hours of toning.

Prior to his God of Wine days, he did not recall such bizarre behavior, although ten thousand years ago, the human population was significantly less and he rarely spent time in it. Nevertheless, he was a deity. He supposed he should've known that his form would bounce back so quickly and that the ladies would become excited by it.

Still, that was a bit extreme.

As the stylist finished his soothing scalp pampering, he reached to touch his stomach. *Although, I must admit, the ripples are quite magnificent.* And strangely, while he'd been working out last night, he hadn't thought about partying one little bit.

Nor had he thought about fucking her, the CrossFit fuzzy cu—

No. That is your evil side speaking. Her name is Margarita.

He glanced over at *Margarita* from the corner of his eye. She was at the sink next to him, having her hair rinsed out, too. His eyes washed down the length of her stretched-out body in tight workout clothes. Plump breasts, lean arms, and long, long legs.

Very fucking sexy. Ironic. Her name is Margarita, one of my all-time favorite drinks.

"So," she said with her eyes closed, "do you come here often?"

"Are you speaking to me?" he asked.

"Yes."

"No. Never. I rarely have time for such things." *I'm quite busy partying. And if I'm not partying, I'm thinking about partying.*

"Of course. You must spend a lot of time working out."

He tried not to laugh. "More like working."

"Really?" The woman rinsing Margarita's hair turned off the water and began towel drying her hair. "What do you do?" Margarita asked.

Besides showing the entire world a good time, turning evil, and accidentally decapitating my brethren? "I own a global chain of nightclubs and bars. My sister is the co-owner." *But headless. And soon to be very, very cranky with me.* He wondered if he could get Forgetty to use her powers on herself.

Margarita sat up. "Wow. Very impressive. So when do you find the time to work out?"

He stared blankly at her.

"Oh. Sorry. I'm not trying to be nosy. It's just that I own a gym and many of my clients are successful business owners or working mothers. They find it difficult to juggle family, work, and exercise."

"I have no wife or children, and my work allows me plenty of leisure time." In fact, his work was leisure time.

"Right. You probably have a lot of downtime during the day."

"Yes," he replied. *And downtime at night, weekends, and holidays, too.*

The young blonde stylist, who was currently drooling over him while rinsing out his hair, finished and wrapped a giant towel around his head before sitting his chair up.

Margarita snickered at him.

He must look like a fool with a towel on his head. *No. Never. I am a god. I look awesome.*

All right, but just to be certain, perhaps I should remove my shirt again. He thought about that for a moment and decided that would not be prudent. Accidents and all.

"Well, if you're free tomorrow," she said, "you should join me—I'm one of the sponsors for the Run Wild Marathon and we don't have a man on our team."

Run Wild? That sounded like something he should stay away from until he was cured and settled down. "I'm afraid I will be occupied tomorrow."

She nodded politely and then looked down at her lap. "Sure. Of course you are."

Her words and body language told him that she had just regretted her decision to ask him for a playdate.

Loud banter in the front of the salon, followed by women hollering and woop-wooping, echoed through the room.

"Sounds like they're having fun." Margarita stood.

"Indeed. Listen, about tomorr—"

"I should get going. Nice to meet you…"

"Acan." He pulled off his towel. "It has been a pleasure meeting you, too." He felt a twinge of guilt for lying to her, but what other choice was there? He couldn't very well tell her he was a deity who had transformed his body with merely a few hours of exercise or that he couldn't waste time on any females who were not potential mates. Millions could die if he became distracted.

She beamed down at him with those wide green eyes. "How is it possible that two brothers could be so different?"

"In what way?"

She laughed. "Oh, come on."

"Come on to what?"

She made a little huff and cocked a golden brown brow. "You really don't see the difference?"

"Aside from our physical appearances, not much." In fact, there could not be two brothers more alike. *Simply because we're not brothers.*

"Oh no. Trust me. You're like night and day."

"Elaborate." He crossed his arms over his chest.

"He's a misogynistic a-hole." She rubbed her forehead and added with a mumble, "And yet, still surprisingly attractive at the same time."

Interesting. So his little CrossFit queen saw something sexy in the sloppy, beer-belly version of him?

"So you feel like he might have a few pleasing qualities?" he asked.

Margarita gave him a strange look, one he could not interpret. "Only one, and he's got a lot to learn about women." She glanced at the clock on the wall above the sinks. "Dammit. I'm late. Gotta run." She smiled at him again, and he thoroughly enjoyed it. Perhaps because her smile was genuine.

Just like the old people. Maybe that was the reason he'd hit on her when they'd first met. He liked her authenticity.

"Bye, Acan. Nice meeting you."

He watched her sexy little behind exit the room while a few thoughts clicked around in his mind. He genuinely found her tempting and attractive, which was odd given her squeaky-clean persona and lack of immaturity. *Can you say uptight and in need of some fun?* That said, he could not afford distractions because his priority was finding Mrs. Party Like It's 1999.

Hold on. All is not lost. Margarita seemed to have an informed opinion about what he might need to change in order to increase his chances of catching his special someone. With mates, it wasn't always love at first sight. Sometimes it took a while for things to settle into place and for the two to realize they couldn't live without each other. Take his brother Votan, God of Death and War, for example. He'd met his mate when she was born and obviously had no clue she was the one. As she grew older, he felt more protective and possessive. She hated his guts. When she finally grew into a woman, those two fought every time they got into the same room, like two snakes determined to devour one and other. Then it happened: They realized who they were to each other. But it was a painful process for them or anyone near them, including the gods. *I'd rather rip out my ears than listen to those two fighting.* And he could not afford to wait years.

That reminds me, I must check in with Zac. He had heard nothing about this mixer to assist him with quickly finding a mate. The party was supposed to happen in a few days. By then they'd be done with the house setup, his brethren would be back—looking for a little sweet revenge—and he would have to show them that he was in control of the situation.

Sadly, I am not. He felt miserable, haunted by how he'd hurt Forgetty. He also had no clue if his efforts to find Mrs. Right All Night would pan out.

Alone in the back room of the salon, he slid his phone from his pocket and called Zac. It went to voicemail. "Zac. It is I, Acan, God of Wine—I mean to say…Decapitation, so you should fear me when I tell you that we are running out of time and this party better happen. Call me back."

Acan shoved his phone into his jeans pocket and made his way out front to pay. Before he could utter a word to the receptionist, the women in the salon rushed toward him, screaming like a mob of sex-starved groupies. "There he is! Ohmygod! So sexy!"

"Back off, ladies!" He held out his hands, but they continued to scream like wild kittens, grabbing at his arms, torso, and hair.

"What in the world?" He reached into his pocket, threw a wadded-up hundred at the receptionist, and ran for the door, not stopping until he reached his eco-friendly, chick magnet of a car—a black

Tesla. The saleswoman had told him that being green was the new black, so he went with it.

Once safely inside his vehicle, Acan took a deep breath, but an effort to find calmness only resulted in millions of voices chanting his name across the planet: "Belch, Belch, Belch…"

"Dammit." It killed him to turn his back on the people he was hardwired to help. "And I need a Big Gulp-sized mojito." It was Friday, after all.

No. No partying. He started the engine and headed straight for the gym. He would do crunches until his urge to throw down passed. *Yes, I will focus on perfecting my body for my future mate.* Of course, his body was already perfect—a forgotten perk of being a deity. But keeping away from the fun and focusing on his abs was the only thing standing between him and world destruction.

CHAPTER ELEVEN

Zac lay on his king-size bed atop his red satin comforter, shirtless, leather pants unbuttoned, and staring at the cell in his hand. He'd had two women over earlier tonight but lost his motivation the second he thought of Tula marrying that buffoon. He'd sent the women home—or more accurately put: they left in a huff, pissed off that he had not pleasured them. But it seemed his own temptation demon now ruled his life. Simply stated, he couldn't have Tula, yet he couldn't allow her to marry this man Gilbert. Yes, yes, it was the classic case of "if I can't have her, then no one can." Yet he truly did care for her and wished her to be happy.

I need to be happy, as well.

Zac set his phone down to his side and slid his hand into his pants, closing his eyes and thinking of Tula's sweet little legs and round ass. He'd only seen her body once when he'd convinced her to wear her enormous granny panties and granny bra—and nothing else—on casual Friday at the office. He'd claimed that if she started acting and dressing a little more provocatively, it would subdue his urge to tempt her. Little had he known that her prudish, nun-like undergarments would only give him a perma-erection.

Saucy little vixen.

With his hand tightly fisted around his cock, he began stroking hard, imagining taking her over his desk at work, hiking up her giant flowery muumuu she often wore—*so sexy*—while kissing her neck and mouth, and then plowing his hand into her giant panties. He would find her wet and ready. *Yes. Ready for her first time.* Ready to experience a god who knew exactly how to take her virginity and leave her begging for more. He would be rough and gentle. He would show her how good it felt to be ravished and fucked and touched softly with his breath. He imagined her sweet vanilla perfume filling his nostrils as he ground himself against her thigh while he massaged her bud and prepared her for the mind-blowing event to come. She would moan softly in his ear, *"Yes...yes—"*

Zac's cell phone chirped the "Hotline Bling" song in his ear. "No! No!" He picked it up with his free hand and glanced at the screen. *Tula?*

"Hello?" he answered, eager to hear her voice.

"Zac?" Tula's voice trembled.

What was the matter? "Yes. How are you, Tula?"

"I'm fine. Great, really." The sadness in her tone told him otherwise. "Am I bothering you? I know it's late—but oh god. Do you have guests? I know you like to have guests."

"No. I have no guests. I was just—" Zac glanced down at his hand, which was still wrapped around his hard cock. He jerked it away. "I was just reading."

"Anything good?" Her tone perked up.

If you enjoy stories of me wacking off, then yes. "Not really. Just some articles about global warming—the usual god stuff."

"Oh."

"So what can I do for you?" *Gods, I miss you. Please come back. Please.*

"I, uh…" There was a small crack in her voice followed by a muffled sniffle.

"Tula, are you all right?"

Silence.

"Tula?" he said with a deep voice.

"I'm fine. It's just that…"

"Say it. What is on your mind?"

She sighed. "I can't help feeling like this is a mistake. That I'm marrying Gilbert because…" She paused for several long moments.

"Because why?" he asked.

"Just tell me that this is what you want me to do. Tell me that you will never be faithful or love one woman. Tell me that you are a womanizing man-whore and that it truly makes you happy."

Her words instantly made him feel as though he stood on the edge of a great cliff overlooking a bubbling volcano. Tula was giving him another chance. Why? Why would she do that? He'd treated her like garbage. Yes, yes, on purpose to push her way, but why would she want to forgive him?

She went on, "Tell me the truth, Zac. I need to know."

I just can't fucking win. If he told her the truth—that he didn't know if he could ever be a one-woman god because he'd never tried, but that he wanted to try with her—it would be enough to tempt her away from Gilbert, the man Cimil claimed Tula was destined for. But what if Cimil was right? What if the moment Zac had her, he didn't want her anymore?

Just another notch in the ol' temptation belt.

However, if he lied to Tula to push her away, he knew that his torment would only continue, and for an immortal, that torment might endure a very, very, very, very, very long time.

"Fuck," he muttered, feeling his soul and body pulling in opposite directions.

"Okay."

"Sorry?" He sat up.

"Okay. We'll do...*that.*"

"You mean fuck?" he asked.

"Yes. That. Maybe I need to know what it's like to be with another man before I'm married."

What the hell? Having premarital sex was the one thing Tula had sworn never to do, and he genuinely respected that about her. *Yeah, but if the woman wants to fuck, let her fuck.* Who was he to get in her way?

"You know where I live." He ended the call. This was the perfect solution. He'd have sex with her and give her a night to remember. He would sate his desire and then be able to let her go.

But what if I'm wrong? What if I fuck her and want more and she still marries that loser?

Frantic, Zac quickly dialed Tula back, but his call went to voicemail. "Tula, if you get this, don't come. I didn't mean it. You can't come here. If you do, I won't answer the door." He snarled out a breath, knowing it was a lie. He was so going to open that door. "Fucking call me."

Zac let out an agonized moan. *Why am I such a greedy, sadistic asshole?* He could not sleep with her no matter what. He could not get in the way of her life.

Oh, but you can. And you will.

He looked up at the ceiling. "Universe, I'm sorry. All right? I'm sorry for being such a self-centered ass. But please, I'm begging you, don't make Tula suffer for it. Make her change her mind before she gets here." Because if she came here tonight and offered herself, he wouldn't be able to resist this time around. He just wouldn't. She was his Achilles' heel.

CHAPTER TWELVE

At five in the morning, Acan finally felt like he might be able to breathe again. It was now Saturday, and last night, he had felt the excruciating pull to get out there and party. Somehow, pumping iron had kept him focused. Anyway, he'd gone home, discovering that Jill had been hard at work organizing his new kitchen and decorating his bathroom—a marble palace with fluffy his-and-hers towels next to the glass-encased walk-in sauna and shower, a bath salt bar next to the jet tub, and a variety of candles on marble pillars positioned strategically throughout the enormous room.

"Very nice." He glanced at his cell and noted the time. The marathon would be starting in an hour. He'd decided he would go, ask Margarita some questions about his "brother," and then stop by Zac's place. Zac had not returned his calls and Acan could already feel his mood beginning to darken. It was difficult to describe, but the sensation felt like a cancer spreading slowly through his body, devouring the positive charge in his molecules one by one.

It's all right. You can push it back. You can do this. He hopped in the shower, using a nice-smelling citrus soap. *Hmmm…Jill will have to get another raise.* Now that he wasn't hammered all the time, he could see how hard she worked to take care of him.

Margarita met her team near the sign-in table, just before six o'clock. Most were members of her gym, but a few girlfriends of hers—Kris and Lauran—joined them, too. Kris was an accountant with three girls ages six to fifteen and Lauran was a divorced PE teacher at a high school in Malibu. They'd met when Margarita first opened her gym years ago and used to run on the beach Sunday mornings. But then life got busier with their kids and work and life. They still got together every now and then, but the Run Wild Marathon was their thing. This year, the team decided to wear purple. Purple underwear, purple bras, and purple sun hats. And yes, purple tennis shoes. It sounded a little risqué until you knew that everyone dressed up (or down), wearing everything from superhero costumes to unicorn heads to almost nothing at all.

Margarita clapped her hands as the team of eleven women helped each other fasten their team number and name to the backs of their bras. They were "Victorious Secret."

"Okay, team!" Margarita bellowed. "We came in fifth last year. That can't happen again." She pointed to Lauran, her good friend, who was a blonde in her late forties, same as Kris. The rest of the ladies ranged in age from mid-thirties to early fifties. "And you! You leave out the bar crawl this time, okay?"

"But the crawl is the best part," Lauran whined.

Several other women, including Kris, agreed and booed jokingly at Margarita.

Margarita rolled her eyes. "Come on, guys. Isn't it enough fun just to be running together, showing everyone how hot us middle-aged women are?"

Everyone continued lobbing the boos and then began chanting for "boos" the kind spelled with the letter Z. "We want booze! We want booze!"

Several men, dressed like giant beer bottles, wandered by in the enormous crowd and hooted, "We'll be waiting at stop number one!"

Margarita's team cheered. It seemed she was the only one who took the competition seriously. Of course, she didn't drink—she hated alcohol—but it seemed her team needed to have a good time.

"Okay, fine." She shook her head at her running shoes. "We'll make one stop. Just one. But then you'd better run your butts off."

Luckily, this was only a 5K for charity and many of the contestants never crossed the finish line because there were roughly twenty cocktail stops along the route down Highway 1, but her gym could still use the publicity if they won.

"Margarita?" said a deep, deep masculine voice from behind her, sending goose bumps up her spine.

The women on her team froze, staring like they'd just spotted a delicious pile of chocolate behind her.

Margarita turned to find the hottest man ever to walk the Earth. His long brown hair, streaked with ribbons of caramel brown and gold, shimmered in the early morning sunlight. His eyes, a stunning turquoise green, sparkled with the promise of supreme lovemaking. His tall, tall form—*Jesus, he must be over seven feet*—was perfectly muscled in all the right places, including those rock-solid arms and legs. He was too sexy for words. *God, I feel really sleazy for wanting him so much.* She'd just slept with his horrible brother, an incident that still boggled her mind.

Margarita's mouth went dry. "Acan, you came."

"Not yet. But given your outfit, that might change." His eyes washed over her body.

She felt her face flush red. Wanting him so much had to be wrong. "Oh, uhh…yeah. I guess I forgot to mention my team's costume. Last year we were the B-52 Boobers." They'd worn hats in the shape of airplanes and stuck little cutouts of boobs all over their bodies. "We always run for breast cancer awareness."

And…it appears to be working well this year.

Acan would not stop staring at her boobs. Why the hell had she invited him, again? Yesterday at the salon felt like a giant blur, the only thing she recalled clearly being the mind-crippling lust she'd felt in Acan's presence. He had all of the strange masculine magnetism of his crude brother, with the unfathomable good looks of a sex god. But Acan was so out of her league, not to mention probably about twenty years younger.

Wait. Out of your league? You're a hot older woman with the bod of a twenty-year-old. And he is here because I invited him, isn't he?

Just to be sure, she had to ask, "You're not running on another team, are you?"

He didn't reply. His brain was too occupied.

"You can stop staring at my breasts now," she said.

"Oh. My apologies. It's simply that I never got to see them."

Huh?

His eyes snapped up. "Sorry. I meant to say I wouldn't dream of running on another team." He glanced around at the nearly catatonic group of women in purple underwear and purple sun hats. "Hello, ladies. Love the outfits."

From the surprise—and delight—on his face, it dawned on Margarita that he might not have heard of this event. "Acan, I should've asked if you've run this marathon before or even know what it is." She'd simply assumed everyone in LA knew it.

"I'm not exactly from around here, but I come

prepared." He started lifting up his black T-shirt and the ladies gasped in unison.

"Oh, God. No, no, no." Margarita grabbed his hand to stop him from going any further. "You should keep that on."

He flashed a devilish grin. "Afraid that I might be a distraction?"

Absolutely. What was I thinking telling him to come? She would be tripping all over the place while her boobs jiggled like crazy. Kinda funny in front of a mob of crazy drunk runners dressed as zoo animals, burlesque dancers, or peanut butter and jelly sandwiches, but not so much in front of a man as perfect as this.

Oh God, I can't believe he actually showed up. And he was so freaking hot. And young. But how could she possibly ever tell him that she'd sort of slept with his disgusting brother for no other reason than he smelled really nice and she'd suffered from a moment of temporary insanity.

He'll think I'm pathetic. And a little loose.

Wait, Margarita. What the hell is the matter with you, pining for this guy? Did you learn nothing from Mike? He had been a pretty face, skilled at charming women. He'd taught her that a man who worked so hard on his exterior only did so to hide some serious flaws on the inside. *Still, look at this guy.* It was hard not to drool.

"So it looks like everyone is queuing up. Shall we?" Acan gestured toward the massive crowd closing in on the starting line.

She smiled stiffly. 'Sure. Come on, ladies! Time to win."

Her team sort of just followed Acan like hypnotized sheep in purple panties. She noticed a bunch of women from other teams following him, too.

How odd. It was like they were all in a trance.

As she stood there next to him, unable to do her usual stretching for obvious scantily clad panty-related reasons, she noticed his shoes were untied. Then she noticed they were brand new, the edges of the rubber soles a pristine white. His black running shorts and T-shirt looked new, as well. No spots, stains, pills, or wrinkles.

Had he gone shopping for workout clothes simply to look nice for her? *Nah. That would be silly. Just look at the guy. With a body like that, he must be at the gym three or four hours a day.*

"Margarita, would you mind if I ask you a question?" Acan said.

"That was a question." She smiled. "And your shoe is untied."

"Ah." He chuckled and bent over to tie it.

"Ohmygod," a woman gasped behind him along with twenty others. They all just stared at his ass or the bulge between his legs or whatever they were getting a view of.

Oblivious or indifferent, Acan stood and then looked down at Margarita.

"What was it you wanted to ask?" she said.

"I'd like to know why you slept with my brother."

CHAPTER THIRTEEN

Acan did not have a clue what he'd said wrong, but his question had triggered Margarita's face to turn ghost white, her lovely plump lips to flatten into a hard line, and her golden brows to crinkle together. *Oh hell. Perhaps I should take off my shirt. That will distract her.*

"I'm—I'm sorry," she stammered. "What was that?"

The starting gun went off just as he was about to explain—all right, he was about to lie, lie, lie—that he and his brother had no secrets.

Margarita and her gaggle of horny women friends all took off, and rather than get run over by a few thousand humans in the most awesome clothing ever—*oh, look, those ones are dressed like martinis! My people, your king is here!*—he began running along, trying to keep up. After a few blocks, Acan felt his lungs beginning to burn while his heart thumped out of control.

"Hey, you okay, sweetie?" said some random woman dressed as a hotdog.

"How," pant, pant, pant, "much," pant, pant, pant, "further is the," pant, pant, "finish line?"

She laughed. "Uh, we've only run about two blocks, so you've still got a ways! Oh, look, there's the first refreshment stop."

Refreshments. Thank the gods! He needed water, and he needed to catch up to Margarita, whom he'd lost in the crowd mostly because he was now surrounded by a rowdy group of screaming, groping women who seemed attracted to him like steel bolts to a powerful magnet

Dammit, I feel my powers spiking. He was setting off the crowd, driving them into a party frenzy. *So this is how you want to play it, Universe?* He wanted to stay away from the party, so now she would bring the party to him? *Such a bitch.* He was not negating his duties simply for fun. He had made a vow to his brethren to make things right and take this whole finding-a-mate thing seriously, which was why he needed to find out the reason for Margarita's expression turning into something resembling a human who'd accidentally stumbled upon a pile of dirty diapers after he'd asked her his very innocent question: He wanted to know what it was about "Belch" that had persuaded her to fuck him. Was it more than simply his godly pheromones and energy, or was there some other quality that intrigued her? After asking that, he then wanted to know what he might do differently to attract women in a genuine manner. *Leverage my strengths, improve my weakness-*

es, but still be me.

"This way!" Hotdog woman and her team of other fast-food-related menu items—a pickle, cheeseburger, fries, and a bottle of catsup—crowded around him and herded him into a tavern. People from the marathon with numbers and team names pinned on their torsos flowed in and out in a steady stream through either side of a double door.

He entered, following the pickle, and someone pinched his butt.

"Hey!" He turned but couldn't tell who had done the groping. "I am not a piece of meat, ladies! Okay, yes, I am. But not for you." Several women booed at him. Then someone shoved a paper cup in his hand.

He glanced down at the purple liquid. *Punch?* Or perhaps some sort of sports drink? He didn't care. His parched throat and burning body required moisture.

He chugged it down and the crowd from behind urged him forward past more tables of cups filled with punch. He grabbed two more, threw them back and then continued around another set of tables where everyone made a U-turn to head back out the door.

Suddenly, he felt funny. A deep warmth in his chest and a rush in his veins. *Oh, hell.*

He turned to the sandwich behind him. "Is there alcohol in those drinks?"

"Of course! It's the breakfast of champions."

She's so right, but...oh no. Oh no. Acan stepped to the side between two drinking stations and doubled over. He felt his body stalling like a car that had been given syrup instead of gasoline. His belly began pushing out, his muscle turned to flab, his perfect abs grew a spare tire.

"You okay, sweetie?" said a woman.

Slowly, he stood, his mind not feeling the usual cocktail bliss, but something else. Something dark and sinister.

"Hey! Acan! There you are!" He glanced across the crowded tavern flowing with a steady stream of runners slash breakfast partiers. *Oh no. Margarita.* He'd never been so unhappy to see one in his life. There was no way to explain his...his...well, his transformation into Belch. *Who gives a fuck about that?* The evil was spreading.

Panicked, Acan dashed through the crowd, toward the back of the tavern, away from Margarita.

"Acan! Where are you going?" she yelled.

He popped open the emergency exit and headed into a back alley. *Godsdammit.* She'd seen him. *All right. Think. Think. Think.* He could not allow her to know that he and Belch were one and the same because she was not allowed to know about the gods. He also needed her to get the hell away from him as quickly as possible. He was not safe.

Acan whipped off his shirt, slid down his shorts, kicked off his running shoes and threw them into the dumpster at his side. His beer belly sort of flopped out and hung over the waistband of his boxer briefs.

There we go. Acan quickly turned away and placed his hands over his crotch, pretending to urinate into a trash can. He didn't feel drunk—not even close—but he had to convince her he was Belch and get her to leave.

Margarita burst through the door. "Acan, why the hell did you run away from…" Her words faded. "Acan?"

He looked over his shoulder at her and swayed a bit. "Hey, baby. Come for the shoooow?" He slurred his words.

"Belch?"

He pretended to tuck himself away and then faced her, making little circles over his protruding belly. "Hey, I know…you. You're that CrossFit bitch with the tight pussy."

Gods, what a terrible thing to say to a woman. It made him feel dirty on the inside.

Her green eyes widened with rage. "You are vile. Where's your brother?"

"My brother? That fucking uptight loser? Who the hell cares?"

"What is the matter with you?" She apparently did not approve of him speaking ill about himself.

How sweet.

"What's the matter with me? What's the matter with *you!* Besides the fact that…that…" *Think of something horrible.* "Besides the fact you're ooold."

Dammit, leave, woman.

Her lovely face turned tomato red. "Old. Wow. Aren't you a gentleman? And a picture of physical perfection, I should add." She stepped forward, her hands fisted.

Why the hell wasn't she leaving? *For fuck's sake, woman, just go.* He had to do something. Something so rude and distasteful that she'd run the other way. "Yeah, baby. I am a vision of perfection. See for yourself." He yanked down the front of his underwear and let his long cock fall out.

Her gaze zeroed right in. However, instead of wincing or showing disgust, lust twinkled in her green eyes. *Uh-oh.* Had he not been vulgar enough? Offensive enough? She really needed to prude up a little.

Acan decided to go for broke, saying the most horrible thing he could come up with. "Why don't you suck it?" He reached for his dick and sort of wiggled it at her.

Her face twisted with abhorrence. "What is the *matter* with you?"

"Nothing. I just like having my dick sucked." True. However, he would never say that. At least not sober. Which instantly made him realize how he'd spent the last ten millennia acting like such an immature, vile prick. He'd told himself it was what the people wanted—wild, uninhibited, and racy behavior. But had they? Or had he just been acting like a fool, the jester. The drunken idiot who provoked a laugh?

Fucking hell. What the fuck is *the matter with me?*
He put himself away. "You should return to your
race now."

"Love to," Margarita said. "Where'd your
brother go?"

Stoked by his self-perpetuated anger, Acan felt
that darkness seeping in. "What do you want with
him anyway?"

"He's running with us."

"Why?" he growled.

She didn't reply.

"Tell me, Margarita, what it is about him you
like so much?"

She blinked her eyes up at him. "He's not a
complete barbaric imbecile like you."

Oh yes he is.

Acan stepped closer, leaving only an inch between them. "And yet you wanted *me* to fuck you.
You still do." He could see it in her eyes. The eyes
never lied. Unless you were Cimil. Her eyes were
allergic to the truth. "Tell me, Margarita. Just why is
that? Why is it that at this very moment, you're
wondering why you can't get the image of my cock
out of your mind and you still feel angry that I left
you hanging? Orgasmless?" He bent down, placing
them nose to nose. "Aching for me?"

Margarita's green eyes were barren of all emotion save one. Lust.

She inhaled deeply. "What the *hell* is that

smell?"

⤙ ⤚

Margarita felt intoxicated by this man's delicious, masculine scent—sweet and light with a hint of something exotic. Not quite a flower. Not quite woodsy. Just...natural and so, so addictive. Yet she knew that the smell wasn't producing a false desire. No, quite the opposite. This intoxication made her want to lower the barriers, the apprehension, and dispel the fear keeping her from her true desire. As she inhaled, all inhibitions flew out the window.

I feel drunk. And I feel like...like I want to do wild and crazy things. Especially with him. But why? He spoke like a man who'd been born in a barn and raised by a pile of porn magazines. But dammit, if she wasn't feeling hot and throbbing down there and little reckless.

"What the hell is going on?" she muttered to herself.

"That would be your body's hormones spiking in response to sexual desire. And right now, your body is telling you how much it wants me inside you." He pinched her chin, gazing down at her with those turquoise green eyes. They were so beautiful. So hypnotic. "I'm a generous man, Margarita, and I'll help you out." He chuckled with a hint of sadistic delight. "If you answer one question: tell me exactly what you find attractive about me."

What a strange question. Where was he going with it? *Who cares?*

"Shut up and fuck me," she blurted out involuntarily.

His eyes twitched with hatred or anger or something she couldn't quite interpret.

"Fine." He bent his head and covered her mouth with his, his warm, silky tongue sliding inside. Their tongues danced wildly as he moved her back between two large stacks of pallets and wooden crates pushed against the wall. The rough cool brick scratched at her skin as he raised her up, and she wrapped her legs around his waist.

I can't believe I'm doing this. Again! But she couldn't help herself. This man, despite being physically unfit and foulmouthed, somehow rang her bell.

He wasted no time freeing his cock and pulling the crotch of her panties aside. As he kissed her hard, his breath and intoxicating scent filling her lungs, she felt the tip of his shaft enter. He then placed his hand on her ass and thrust hard.

Fuck. She broke their kiss, wincing.

"Relax," he told her. "Just like last time."

Margarita exhaled and loosened her muscles, allowing him to slowly ease his way in. She wanted him deep; she wanted him all the way.

"That's right," he said in a low, sinful voice. "Just like that."

He slid out and drove back into her, stealing her

breath, this time with pure pleasure. He was so thick, so long, she could feel every inch of delicious friction.

"Ohmygod," she panted, "you feel so good. So…" Her words faded as he pushed into her again, hitting her c-spot and g-spot at the exact same time. "Ohgod. Please tell me you're not going to stop this time. Please."

"Why the hell would I…" Still inside her, he stopped moving. She felt his hurried breath on her neck, his arms trembling, and his entire body stiff as a board.

"What's wrong?"

He unexpectedly pulled out and dropped her to her feet, stepping away and breaking all contact. A look of terror flickered in his eyes. "I must go."

No, no, no. He's not doing this again.

He put himself away and headed down the alley. She rushed past him and placed her palm on his chest. "You are a sadistic prick, you know that?"

He glanced down at her, his expression and demeanor indicating that something had unnerved him. "And you should be grateful I care so much," he growled.

What the hell did that mean? "I think the only thing you care about is humiliating me."

"I only stopped because, because…I wasn't wearing a condom. I don't wish to impregnate you. And *you* should be more careful."

What! He was right of course, and once again,

she was left wondering why she'd been so reckless. It wasn't like her. At least, not for the last seventeen years. That said, "What right do you have to lecture me, huh?" Still pressed to his chest, her hand began to heat up. She snapped it back. "What the…?"

"You must stay away from me, Margarita. You must never come near me again." The moment he disappeared around the corner, mortification set in.

"What the heck is happening to me?" She placed her hands over her face. *I'm going crazy.* The only problem with that excuse was she'd never felt more clearheaded.

CHAPTER FOURTEEN

Wearing nothing but black boxer briefs, Acan had been chased all the way to his car by a mob of screaming women—*dear gods, I must exercise more*—before realizing his keys were in his shorts. Yes, the shorts he'd chucked into the dumpster behind the tavern. Surprisingly, however, his form had bounced back the moment those few drinks left his system, which took only minutes due to his very special metabolism. So instead of attempting a rescue of his keys, he simply kept on running, which felt like the only thing he could do to prevent himself from going back to find Margarita and finishing what he'd started.

Godsdammit! How could I do that to her? His evil side had obviously driven that mind-bending lust he'd just experienced. And because of it, he'd once again forgotten about the black jade and almost hurt Margarita. *Unforgivable.*

The first time he'd had sex with her—very, very sad and incomplete sex—it had been a move he'd made without little thought until he was all up in there. And then wow! Wow, wow, wow. Such hotness—touching her body, his cock inside her, the sound of her breath. The moment he'd realized he was putting her in physical jeopardy, he'd easily torn himself away and endured her wrath. This time, however, had been a completely different story. Somewhere in the back of his mind, he knew full well that he could hurt her, yet he'd not been able to resist. The look in her green eyes—anger mixed with lust and a yearning for a little recklessness—had acted like a powerful aphrodisiac. And once he had himself inside her, all he could think about was bringing her to orgasm so he could hear the sound of her whimpering voice while he blew her mind. It had taken everything in his power to pull out before he harmed her.

Thank gods I gained control. On the flipside, he'd left her hanging once again, and now she believed him to be the world's most sadistic prick. *Better than killing her, I suppose.* Nonetheless, the entire event scared the hell out of him. How could he crave a woman so much that he'd risk harming her? *It wasn't right. It simply wasn't.*

How many more must suffer because of him? The answer: incalculable. It could easily fall into the millions if he did not hurry and quell the darkness.

Having run as far as his insanely ripped, but very out-of-shape body could take him, Acan collapsed on the side of the road, where he apparently passed out, only to be awoken by two very friendly female police officers.

Once he'd convinced them that he wasn't insane (a lie) nor on drugs (the truth), they offered him a ride home. Little had he known that they would insist on frisking him before allowing him to enter the squad car, leaving him feeling somewhat violated. *Did they really need to check inside my underwear for a weapon? And take pictures of the contents? And then text it to their "colleagues" in order to confirm his penis was not a sex weapon of sorts?*

He'd finally put his foot down when they claimed they'd need to inspect the ridges of his abs with their tongues. It sounded like a bunch of hullabaloo to him. Ultimately, they agreed to take him to Zac's apartment, which was miles away, near downtown Los Angeles.

"Thanks, ladies." Acan gave an unfriendly wave to the two officers while they videotaped him walking away in his underwear. Grumbling with annoyance, he made his way past the security guard—another female who simply stared—and up to the penthouse of the small, but exclusive building. He hoped Zac was home. It was still early enough, about nine in the morning.

The elevator doors chimed and opened to the fifteenth floor. Acan immediately spotted a small form curled up in front of Zac's door. "Tula?"

Her big blue eyes popped open with a startle, and she sat up. "Belch?"

"What are you doing here?"

"He won't open the door, and I need to see him." She immediately covered her face and began sobbing.

How odd. Everyone knew that Zac was very much into Tula, though they all agreed that she was too nice for him. Too sweet. Too pure hearted. Too innocent. And it wasn't as if they didn't know their humans. As gods, they'd been around the people-block, so to speak, and could spot a good soul from a mile away. Tula was a good, good woman. Zac was…well, in some ways like himself. Sort of a prick. All right, and a bit of a self-centered, juvenile, arrogant, insensitive prick.

"Are you certain Zac is inside?" he asked.

Tula sniffled, wiping her pert little nose with the back of her hand. "Yes. I could hear him breaking things when I got here." She stood, revealing her outfit: a skimpy tight pink dress.

"Tula? Why are you dressed like Street Corner Barbie? Not that I do not like Street Corner Barbie—she is, in fact, a lot of fun, and I'm all about that—however, you are not her."

"Why?" Tula snapped. "Because I'm a virgin? Because I'm a prude and old-fashioned? Because you think I can't be fun or have needs like a real woman?"

Whoa. Triggered.

He reached out and gently grabbed her wrist. "No, Tula. Speaking as a man who just sprinted across Los Angeles in his underwear, escaping a mob of horny women, I can say with complete confidence that you march to your very own sweet song, just as I do. And we—the gods—wouldn't want it any other way. However, you are not a woman who requires the attention of others to feel attractive or energized. Your joy comes from helping others, caring about them."

She sniffled. "How do *you* know?"

How? I have no clue. Frankly, he'd been living in a party bubble for so long he rarely reflected on what he knew or how he'd learned it. Which was why this fatherly impulse felt so foreign. For him, of all people, to have paternal instincts was just about as shocking as a gorilla doing calculus.

Still, he had to take a stab at an answer. "I suppose, Tula, I know because I've spent my life helping others after life has kicked them so hard they weren't sure they'd ever get up again."

She cocked a blonde brow. "You serve cocktails and drink like a fish—wait, scratch that. Not even fish drink like you do. They're lightweights in comparison."

He smiled proudly. "I certainly can hold my liquor, but compliments will not deter me from telling you the truth, my dear sweet human. Do not dress in a manner that does not reflect who you are. Do not bend to the will of others simply to appease them. And, above all, do not marry, fuck, kiss, or otherwise with a man who makes you feel less than the magnificent, unique creation that you are." He pinched her chin. "You got that?"

Tula's eyes filled with chubby tears. "Thank you, Belch." She threw her arms around his midriff and squeezed.

"Uhhh…" He patted her back, feeling awkward. "There, there?" He was not accustomed to connecting with anyone on such a genuine level, with the exception of his sister Forgetty.

Zac's front door flew open. "Get the hell off her," snarled a fierce-looking Zac standing shirtless in leather pants, his dark shaggy hair a wild mess.

"Ah. The hermit emerges," Acan said as Tula released him. "I believe this young woman has been crying at your doorstep for many hours in hopes you will speak with her."

Zac's turquoise eyes, drastically contrasting his black stubble and dark eyelashes, glared down at Tula. "I told you not to come."

"Don't you think I deserve an explanation as to why?" she barked back.

"No. You do not!" he bellowed in an ominous voice that did little to frighten the tiny woman.

"Yes. I do!" she replied.

Zac stuck his finger in Tula's face. "I will not deflower you, woman! And you can't make me."

"Oh yes I can!" She shoved him, using the entire weight of her very tiny body to send his brother—equal in size and weight to himself—reeling back.

Before Acan could say a word, Tula slammed the door in his face. From the other side, Acan heard the two yelling at each other, Tula screaming that Zac would sleep with her or risk a painful death with her knitting needles, and Zac yelling that she should remove her "wholesome paws from his cock" and that he would not be used in such a sleazy manner simply to "fulfill your sexual fantasies before you marry the world's worst lover!"

Acan almost wanted to laugh, except that it became abundantly clear he was on his own. Given the tension with Tula, Zac would not get squat done for the mixer. Without Zac, Tula was apparently a mess. Yet they could not see a path forward together, which meant they would continue to fight for a very, very long time.

And no singles mixer for me. He would be on his own to find "the one" and he had no time to lose. New Year's Eve was but a few short weeks away, and his brethren were due back at any moment. If he could not convince them that finding his mate (and keeping her) was imminent, then they would lock him away.

Dammit, I need to throw my own party.

Wait. I can do that. I can throw the biggest singles mixer ever to be seen on the planet. And with the way women followed him, going completely mad in his presence, it wouldn't be difficult to ensure they showed up and brought friends. One or two immortal women were bound to come, too.

Acan knocked on Zac's door. "Hey, I know you two are busy in there, but could you call me a cab?

Or Jill? I don't have a phone or wallet."

Zac and Tula continued going round and round. "Yes, you will deflower me." "No, I will not!"

Dammit. I'm going to have to hitchhike. I hope they don't try to take pictures of my penis again.

CHAPTER FIFTEEN

That afternoon, Acan began instructing Jill on the details of the party—when, where, and who. They would hold the event at their biggest LA nightclub, the Randy Unicorn, and post invitations that included a picture of himself all over social media. To enter, the women had to be between the ages of twenty-one and thirty, love the night life, look sexy, and be able to hold her liquor. He hoped his photo, which showed off his eyes—a telltale sign of his immortality—would attract the attention of a few immortal women, too: sex faeries, vampires, and demigoddesses. Hel., he'd even be okay with a succubus, although there weren't many of those around these days. The gods had killed most of them off, but their offspring were beginning to pop up and the females were quite attractive.

Speaking of attractive, *Margarita...Mmmm...Margarita*. So soft in all the right places.

"Belch!" a familiar voice screamed as he sat outside next to the pool of his new estate, making the list of what to buy for the party.

Acan looked up to find a face he'd been missing with all his heart yet dreading to see again.

"Forgetty." He sighed.

Wearing a short pink skirt, white tank top and white go-go boots, Forgetty stomped toward him with clenched fists. "I am going to break every bone in your body!"

He popped up from the lounge chair and held out his hands. "Now, sister, I know you're upset, but let me explain—"

"Explain?" She poked his chest. "Explain! You removed my head! And what the hell happened to your body?"

He glanced down at his muscular form, which he was in the process of suntanning in the buff. He'd read somewhere that women liked a man who looked like he spent excessive amounts of time in the outdoors, doing things such as bicycle riding or sailing. He wasn't much for water or mounting things with wheels—he much preferred things with boobs—big boobs—so he took Jill's advice and lay out.

Acan smiled. "My body is in nonparty mode at the moment, just as you asked. And I have been preparing to win my mate, including having purchased this fine home with a built-in sprinkler system."

"Too little, too late! Votan and the others are on their way, and you, my dear brother, are going to jail."

Why was she speaking to him as if he were a child getting a time-out for naughty behavior?

Acan crossed his arms. "No."

Her turquoise eyes shifted a bit from side to side. "No what?"

"No, I won't go to jail, and you can't make me." *There. How's that for not sounding childish.* He patted himself on the back.

"Wanna bet?" She reached for his wrist, but he held it away.

"I do wanna bet, Forgetty, because there are two things you are not thinking of."

"That you're an ass and you're an ass?"

"Yes and yes. However, I'm referring to the fact that the immortal prison in Sedona is only capable of incarcerating my physical form. It will not prevent my spike in powers on New Year's Eve. So given that my condition is deteriorating rapidly, everyone's best and only option is to assist me in finding my Mrs. Party All Night."

Her eyes twitched with irritation. "We could just kill you and then wait for you to reemerge at the cenote with a new body and kill you again."

Balls. That didn't sound pleasant. "You could. Yes. But then I'll have to point out the fact that I am the God of Decapitation, and therefore, if I'm permitted to completely flip, my brethren would be no match for me. So it is you who would be executed over and over again, leaving the lot of you suspended between worlds and the human population at risk to all of the immortals out there who are turning evil, yours truly included."

Forgetty growled. "Godsdammit. Since when did you become so logical and articulate? It's incredibly annoying."

"Agreed. Which is why I intend to find my woman as quickly as possible, prevent myself from flipping, and then return to my old self—completely oblivious to everything and nauseatingly juvenile. Just as I was meant to be. So are you going to assist me? Because I am throwing a party tomorrow evening."

"You just said you were not partying."

"It's a casting call of sorts—for my mate."

"Why isn't Zac organizing your mixer?"

"He has been distracted by Tula."

Forgetty crossed her arms. "Fine. I'll talk to the others so they don't kill you."

"And will you help me throw the party? Because I cannot risk having anything happen to you ever again. Hurting you was a nightmare I do not wish to repeat. Not for as long as I live." He genuinely felt sick to his stomach.

She sighed and reached for his arm. "It's okay. I know you were not yourself."

"It is not *okay*. Even though we are not related by blood, I am your brother. It is my job to protect you, sister, and I did not."

She made a noncommittal groan. "Fine. I will

help Jill with the party. And you know, brother, you might want to try apologizing more often. You have done a lot of reckless, insensitive things over your lifetime and this is the first time you've ever said sorry. I think I like this new side of you."

"Noted."

"But you really need to start wearing pants."

He glanced down at his groin. "I did not want tan lines."

Forgetty rolled her eyes. "Whatever. I gotta intercept our brethren before they find you."

"Thank you, sister."

"Yeah, yeah. Go find some clothes and stay out of trouble." Forgetty sauntered off.

That was easy. Who knew that a simple apology would go so far? Perhaps he should apologize to Jill so that she'd do an even better job on his mixer.

His cell chirped. Jill had retrieved it from the dumpster along with his keys, shoes, and shorts before picking up his car.

He glanced down at the small table where his phone lay next to the lounge chair. *Unknown number.* It was likely Cimil calling to tell him what an epic immortal douche he was.

He hit the green button. "God of Wine, Intoxication, Loose Morals, and Lost Heads."

"Acan?" said a female voice.

Oh shit. "Margarita?"

"Yes."

"How did you obtain this number?" he asked.

"I called the salon, who gave me your assistant's number. She said it would be okay if I called you. By the way, she's wonderful. So polite and friendly. Where did you find her?"

I wish I could remember. In his mind, Jill sort of showed up one day and never left his employ.

"She came recommended through a friend. So to what do I owe this pleasure?" *I wasn't expecting to hear from you. Ever again.* But it pleased him to hear her voice after this morning's horrific episode of "alley fuck with a god gone wrong."

"You disappeared during the marathon, and I wanted to be sure you were all right."

She wanted to check up on him? How very thoughtful; however, he was the one who should be inquiring about her. She'd tangled with the Decapitator this morning—a brush with evil that had left her feeling rejected and angry once again, when really he'd only been saving her.

I'm a godsdamned hero. Did it matter that it was his fault that she'd been in danger? *Nah. Me. Hero. All the way.*

"Yes, I'm fine," he said. "But I'm afraid I'm not much of a runner. You left me in the dust after the first block."

"That's strange, because I could see *you*—I mean you are pretty tall. About seven feet, right?"

*Hmmm...*Margarita seemed suspicious. He decided to play innocent.

With a chuckle he said, "Then you must've witnessed my very masculine display of panting."

"Not exactly."

"Oh? Do tell."

"Cut the crap, Acan. I watched you being corralled into a tavern by a horde of sandwich fixings, and I followed you inside. You scrambled out the back door when I called your name."

Uh-oh. It seemed that she'd figured him out.

Not good.

He could not afford any more problems, and problems he would have if she'd caught on to who he truly was. He would have to report it, and the gods would demand that her memory be wiped—a disaster for her because they usually left it to A.C., the God of Eclipses, or K'ak, the God of…well, he didn't have an official title yet, but Acan supposed he'd be the God of Enormous Serpent Headdresses, Togas, or Lightning All very respectable skills, of course. In any case, when they wiped a memory, it was the equivalent of using a sledgehammer. The human sometimes lost years of memories.

I must nip this in the bud. And he'd use Forgetty, who could easily reach into the mind of a human and extract particular memories. *She's like a neurosurgeon without the scalpel.* But before he did that, he would need to determine if the rules had truly been broken.

"I assure you, Margarita, I was in no such tavern. You must've mistaken me for someone else. My brother perhaps?"

"Yeah. That's the thing. I could've sworn I saw you leaving out the back door, but I found your brother in the alley. Just why is that, Acan?"

All right, she was either catching on to him or she believed him to be a very sly and sleazy man who worked with his belligerent brother to trap women in alleys in order to have their way with them. Which was it?

Ha. I know what to do.

"Margarita, would you like to have dinner with me tonight?" If she believed him to be one of those scoundrels who preyed on women, then she would not want anything to do with him.

"What I want are answers. Be at my place. Nine o'clock. But no bullshit. I want to know what the hell is going on."

Jesus Hey-sus Cristo. Please tell me she has no clue. Because if she knew too much, it would mean that he'd have to ask Forgetty to handle this. *And then she will forget all about me. Forever.*

His heart fell to his bare feet. *Wait. Waaait...* He froze and witnessed with absolute clarity how his body seemed heavy, drooping with sadness. He then thought of seeing her again, those large green eyes, her tight little butt, the other unmentionables he would gladly mention if it were not for his current state of undress. *Dear gods, could fuzzy cunt be the one?*

No. No! You cannot refer to your mate like that.

What? Dear gods! No. Why did I think that? She

could not be his mate. She hated him. He thought she was uptight.

Yet she still finds you hot enough to shag you in your state of awesome beer belliness. Acan rubbed his brow. He had to be mistaken. *Fucking horrible Universe, you would do this to me, wouldn't you?* If the Universe had mated him with his polar opposite, someone who didn't like to have a good time and party, he'd rather die. Only he couldn't die.

Yes. But you can reject her and choose another. It used to be unheard of—this not marrying the one your mother (aka the Universe) picked out for you—but there were instances popping up of immortals rejecting their intended mates in lieu of a soul mate. That demigod Andrus had just done it, and then Andrus's rejected mate, Charlotte, mated with another demigod, Tommaso. They'd been shuffling the deck of love cards, so to speak.

Then I shall do the same. He would meet with Margarita, confirm what she knew, and then have him wiped from her memory. He'd have his mixer, find a more suitable woman, and party happily ever after.

"Text me the address. See you at nine." He ended the call, feeling completely annoyed. The thought of seeing Margarita again made him all squishy inside. Likewise, the thought of never seeing her again rubbed him the wrong way.

No. I must end this. She's just not right for me.

CHAPTER SIXTEEN

From the moment Margarita hung up with Acan, she felt completely ridiculous. What exactly was she accusing him of, anyway? Doing magic tricks and switching places with his brother to try to fool her? *Yeah. Because they look so identical.* She shook her head at herself, loading the dishwasher. *I'm ridiculous.*

What reason would Acan have to play games with her? Yet she couldn't deny that something big and horrible kept nagging away in the back of her mind. She was not a needy, reckless, or an overtly horny woman. She did not and would not simply throw herself at a man—twice—simply because he smelled nice. *Nope. Nuh-uh.* She knew herself. She was a strong, mature woman who knew exactly what she wanted. *And that Belch guy isn't it.* He was the most socially inept, offensive man she'd ever met. No filter whatsoever. No class. And he was a flasher! Or a nudist with no sense of propriety. Yet she'd wanted him.

Why?

Perhaps the guy had roofied her somehow. Yes, an airborne roofy that he sprayed on his body or something like that.

That's even more ridiculous.

Ugh, she growled, putting the last mixing bowl into the dishwasher. She'd prepared one of her famous healthy meatloaves, a recipe she'd made up when Jessica was little and refused to eat veggies. Since then, she made it a daily habit to sneak finely chopped or shredded veggies into their food—burgers, spaghetti sauce, quesadillas—and switched out beef for turkey in order to cut down the calories. This recipe was her favorite, though.

In a large mixing bowl, combine:
- 1 lb lean ground beef
- 2 lbs ground turkey
- 2 cups of dry, quick-cooking oatmeal
- 1 cup of egg whites or egg substitute
- 2-3 cups of firmly packed shredded vegetables. Carrots, zucchini, yellow squash or cauliflower. A cheese grater can be used if a food processor isn't an option.
- 1 medium-sized, finely chopped onion of any kind
- 1 tbsp of chipotle chili peppers, powdered or from a can
- 2 tbsp of Italian herbs, depending on taste: oregano, thyme, basil. Tarragon is also a great add.
- 2-3 cloves of chopped garlic or 1 tbsp of

    garlic powder
-   2 tsps salt

Mix the ingredients well.

Test: Take one spoonful and either microwave for thirty seconds (or until done) or fry the sample in a pan with a dab of oil. If the mixture tastes great, go to the next step. If it needs more salt or isn't sticking together enough, add a little extra egg or salt. Test again before cooking.

Spread mixture in a shallow glass baking dish (approximately 2x10x16) and cover with a thin layer of organic catsup. The shallow dish will make it cook faster and more evenly.

Cook at 400 degrees for approximately forty minutes. Test middle to ensure it's cooked all the way before removing.

Viola! A complete healthy meal.

Margarita hadn't really invited Acan over for dinner, but she had to cook for herself and Jess, so if he showed up expecting to eat, she wouldn't feel unclassy. If he showed up only expecting to talk, her famous healthy meatloaf never went to waste.

Margarita removed her apron and glanced at the clock on the wall of her insanely small kitchen—white cupboards, brown tile counters, and a ten-year-old electric range—the space barely big enough for one person to move around. Someday, she'd buy a house with a gas stove, chef's island, and tons of cupboards for her juicer, food processor, and other gadgets. She so loved to cook, although there was never enough time. Still, thinking about a better life, home, and financial situation got her out of bed each morning. There was so much to look forward to, but for the moment, she would settle for a daughter who arrived on time. Jessica was an hour late from her study group.

Study group, my study ass.

The door buzzed, and Margarita's breath hitched. *He's here.* Acan was so beautiful it hurt to look at him. That silky soft caramel brown hair, that golden brown skin, those soulful turquoise eyes. He was seven feet of lean, hard, chiseled muscle, and if anything like his brother, he was hung like a stallion.

She sighed, momentarily distracted by the image of Belch's long, thick cock, which only led her to the memories of how good he felt inside her, which then led to thoughts of how he'd left her high and dry, figuratively speaking, of course. *All right, now that I'm properly humiliated…*

She quickly checked her outfit—tight jeans, a little red sweater, and black boots—for any remnants from her cooking—*all clear*—and then jerked open the door. "Acan, how nice to…" Her eyes washed over a very tall, sexy man with a deep tan, shimmering turquoise green eyes, and waves of silky hair falling over his broad shoulders. He wore a button-down white shirt and jeans that caressed his muscular legs.

"I bet you even have perfect toes." *Oh crap. Why did I say that?*

"Errr...I'm sure yours are especially lovely, too?" He held out a bottle of fresh-squeezed wheat grass with carrot and pineapple juice.

"Wow. That's my favorite. How did you know?"

"I asked this woman at the store, who was wearing a very unflattering tie-dye dress and smelled of *sopes*, what she might drink if she wished to have prolonged diarrhea."

Margarita almost swallowed her tongue. "I'm sorry...but..." Hack, hack. "Did you say—"

"Sopes are a Mexican dish often topped with chopped onions."

Ewww. And that wasn't even close to landing near her diarrhea question, but okeydokey.

"Umm...thanks?" She took the bottle of green liquid and stepped aside to let him in.

The top of Acan's head looked like it might collide with the door jamb as he entered. "Your home is so small and lacking any festive qualities. How do you have parties here?"

Wow. Nice manners. "I don't, and it suits me and my daughter just fine."

He turned with a startle in his translucent green eyes. "You have a child? How old is it?"

"*It* is sixteen, and its name is Jessica," she said with a snap.

"So...you are married and in love with a man

who is her father?"

What planet was this guy from?

"No. Not married. No. Not in love. Her father is out of the picture, and has anyone ever told you that it's rude to ask such personal questions?"

He made a little shrug, his eyes scanning her modest living room slash eating area. "I'm not one for pomp and circumstance. Gets old after a few millennia."

"Millennia?"

"I meant years. It's been a long day at work."

"I thought you worked nights at your clubs," she questioned.

He gave her a stern look. "Are you always so inquisitive?"

"No. I'm generally too busy trying to run my business and support my daughter, so I rarely have time."

He grinned. "Excellent."

What a strange response. "So are you hungry?" She went over to her tiny fridge and put away the juice. It would be perfect for breakfast.

"I don't eat."

She frowned and closed the refrigerator. "You must eat something. I mean, look at the size of you." Her eyes involuntarily fell to the substantial bulge in his groin.

"Eh-hem. Eyes up here, woman. It may not look it, but I too have feelings."

She swallowed down a shameful lump and

looked him in the eyes. *I bet he does.* With equipment like that, he had at least eleven inches of feelings. Just like his brother.

She cleared her throat. "Sorry. I'm not usually so…"

"Sexually degrading?"

She blinked. "You feel degraded because I looked at your pants?"

"It's impossible for you to degrade me; however, had I been a lesser man, the answer would be yes. So I feel obligated to speak out in the name of weak males—basically all of them."

Huh? How had this conversation gone so sideways on her?

"Would you like to sit?" She gestured toward her espresso brown sofa and black coffee table. She'd picked them because they easily hid dirt and stains. She couldn't afford to waste a dime, so her furniture had to last.

"I prefer to stand." He crossed his arms and stared down at her like some nasty general who felt displeased. "I suggest that we get on with it."

She blinked. "With what?"

"It."

"Uhhh…and 'it' would be?" she asked.

"The reason you summoned me."

"Has anyone ever told you that you speak like a robotic pirate who's been robbed of his soul?"

"Maybe—I wouldn't remember. But that's beside the point. Why did you ask me to come? And please make it quick. I have work to do."

"Okay. If you want to push aside any sort of civility, then I can do that. But then you have to answer my questions honestly."

"I can do that, but first you must answer my questions," he said.

"I'm the one who summoned you." This felt like a game of Crazy Battleship.

"Yes. However, I drove forty minutes in LA traffic to get here, which entitles me to ask my question first."

Ugh. "Fine. What's your question?"

"What do you think happened this morning?"

"Honestly?" she asked.

"Yes. Honestly."

"I have no clue," she replied, *honestly.*

"If you were to guess?" he asked.

"I would guess that you and your brother are playing some sort of strange game with me, and the fact you're asking me this question only validates the shadiness of it all."

He bobbed his head and scratched his short brown beard that accentuated the strong lines of his masculine jaw. "So the most likely scenario in your mind is that my brother and I are two shady men who enjoy mind-fucking women for sexual pleasure in dirty alleys?"

Gasp! "He told you about this morning?"

"Answer the question. Is this what you believe to be the likeliest scenario?"

"Yes."

"And your least likely scenario?" he prodded.

"There isn't one. Now it's my turn."

"Very well."

"Why do you and your brother smell so sweet?" For example, her apartment was now filled with the most delicious scent known to woman. It made her nipples hard, her c-spot throb, and her neck tingle.

"I know not what you mean."

"Liar," she snapped. "You smell like…sex. Like sinful, dirty, hot sex." She slapped her hands over her mouth. Her words had just sort of popped out.

He tilted his head to one side. "Are you, by chance, smelling it right now?"

"No. Maybe."

"Would you like me to take you to your bed-room and fuck you senseless?" he asked.

"No! Okay, maybe. Wait. No! Definitely no! What the hell is going on? I feel like I'm going crazy, and I don't know why." It was awful. Just awful. "I'm too young to go senile. How am I going to take care of Jessica?" She looked up at the ceiling and shook her head. *Why is this happening to me?* To make matters worse, she had this beautiful—strange but beautiful—man in her apartment, witnessing her ungraceful descent into dementia.

He stepped towards her and sighed, staring into her eyes for several long moments, but not speaking. "You are not going crazy."

"Then what the hell is going on?"

He opened his mouth to speak, but instead whooshed out a breath.

"What! Just say it! Tell me! Because I honestly feel like I'm losing my mind, which is the only explanation for why I can't shake these strange feelings I have for you."

With a sadness in his sublime eyes, he reached out and ran his thumb along her lower lip while gently pinching her chin. "I suppose it won't hurt to tell you. Not now."

"Tell me what?"

"We are mates, and I am a god."

CHAPTER SEVENTEEN

To Acan's surprise, Margarita laughed in his face the moment he uttered the painful truth: She was his mate. He supposed it was a surprise to him as well; however, there could be no other explanation for her wanton feelings. Or his.

I should've known. From the first moment he'd seen her in the elevator, he'd been mesmerized. When he saw her the next morning at her gym, he should've known, too, but he hadn't been ready to accept the truth. Now, after seeing her the last few times, things became clearer. She was the one the Universe had chosen for him, only he didn't want her. Her life was fitness and eating the sort of foul-smelling healthy crap that now sat cooling in her kitchen and likely contained almost no fat, sugar, or preservatives. *Ewww...* Her life was the opposite of late night parties, delicious deep-fried snacks, and fun. He merely had to look at her to know. It was his gift, after all, looking into people's eyes and seeing their essence. Margarita was boring. Super-duper stick in the mud. Boring.

Still, he liked her. The way she smiled. The way she moaned. He especially liked the way his heart skipped when he thought about seeing her. But it wasn't enough, was it? She would never accept the real him, and that meant he'd have to give up who he was merely to please her. *And if I can't be the party god, I'd have to be the decap god.* Not so fun. Not when he faced an eternity with his choices, which was something most humans couldn't comprehend.

"You need to leave," she spouted in response to his confession.

"Margarita." He took her hand between his. "I fully realize that what I've said sounds insane, which is why I'm prepared to prove every word to you. However, before I do that, I simply need to know if you could ever love a man who stays up all night—seven days a week—drinks approximately fifteen gallons of alcohol each day, and pretty much forgets to wear clothing on his bottom half."

"Are you fucking with me?"

"Afraid not."

"No. My answer is *no*," she said with a twisted frown.

He shook his head. "As I thought."

"Acan? Please tell me this is a joke. Please tell me you're not serious."

It was time to ease her mind. At least for tonight, she'd be at peace and then Forgetty would take care of her in the morning. "I am serious, and as I said, here is my proof." He took her hand and placed it over his heart. "Close your eyes, Margarita. Listen to the Universe beating through me. Hear her whisper of life and the voices of every being on this planet calling for me. Feel your skin heating as my cells cause yours to vibrate rapidly."

He knew Margarita didn't want to do as he asked, but his scent, voice, and energy persuaded her.

With hesitant flutters, she closed her eyes and took a sobering breath. After a soul-grilling moment—him hoping she'd see the truth—her eyes flew open. "Ohmygod!"

❧ ❦

Margarita could not believe her ears. Thousands of voices silently chanted his name, and she heard each and every one: "Belch, Belch, Belch."

"This can't be." She stepped back, taking her hand with her. "You're him, aren't you? *You* are Belch."

He nodded. "I had to pretend because humans are not permitted to know about us unless it's a necessity."

She covered her mouth. She felt like a fool, but she wasn't sure if it was due to his lying or due to her actually believing he was a god.

"But how? How can you and he be…?"

"The same person?"

She nodded.

"I am not human. I do not grow old. I do not get ill. My body is predisposed for perfection. But given my role, to help humans forget their woes for an evening, the excess calories do take a toll on my figure. Although I've now learned it's only temporary."

"So-so-so," she stammered, "if you were to drink, you'd become him—that other guy."

He nodded yes.

"Jesus." She walked over to her sofa and plunked down, covering her face. *This can't be true.* Yet her heart told her it was. "Why did you decide to tell me if humans aren't allowed to know?"

He walked over and sat but looked ahead at the wall where a collage—all pictures of her and Jessica—hung on the wall.

"Something is happening to us," he said. "A plague. But only those who are single, without a mate, are susceptible."

"So you're sick?" Didn't he just say he couldn't get sick?

"In a way, yes. This plague takes a good immortal and turns them into a violent, dangerous being."

"Like rabies."

"Yes." He nodded. "However, for an immortal like myself, the damage I can inflict will be in the millions. Perhaps tens of millions. Specifically on New Year's Eve, when my powers naturally spike."

Her eyes went wide. "Who, Acan? Who will be

the millions?" Her heart raced out of control.

"I do not know." He clasped his large hands together in his lap and stared down at them.

She stood up. "So wait. You're telling me that in a few weeks, you're going to turn into a rabid god, strike down tens of millions of people, and that there's nothing you can do."

"I assure you, I will do everything in my power to find my mate and stop the change from occurring."

Her mind reeled with fear. Fear for her child. Fear for herself. Fear for all of those people who would lose family members. *This can't happen. I have to do something. Wait…*

"I'm not following." She ran her hands through her hair, trying to keep her cool. "You said that I'm your mate."

He nodded calmly.

"So if I'm your mate, why are you looking for someone else?" This made no sense.

He stood and gazed down into her eyes. It suddenly felt like the blanket had lifted from her mind. Now that he'd told her the truth, whatever tricks her brain had been playing to deny the strangeness right in front of her were gone. He wasn't human. His skin had a slight iridescent glow, his turquoise eye shimmered like afternoon sun bouncing off a calm ocean, and simply standing next to him made her body feel warm and at peace.

"Jesus, you're magnificent," she whispered.

"Thank you." He frowned. "But my name is Acan, not Jesus. Are you feeling all right?"

"You just told me that you're a god and millions of people will die on New Year's Eve, so no. I'm not all right. Now, answer my question."

"You mean...why I cannot accept you as my mate?"

"Yes."

"You said it yourself, you would not be happy living a life of nonstop nocturnal celebrations with me. And I could not live a life being someone I am not. Just these few days of behaving have been torture for me given the role I was born to play. It would be like removing a bird's wings or telling a teenager to speak respectfully to their parents—it is unnatural."

"So basically, you're saying that we're not a match?" she asked.

"No."

"But we're mates?" she asked.

"Yes."

"And you don't mean 'mate' in the Australian sense of the word," she stated.

"No."

She nodded but didn't truly understand. How had they been matched up? And by who? And why would they be matched up if they weren't right for each other?

"So your plan is to find someone you click with and then stop this plague from making you sick."

"Yes," he confirmed.

"What if you fail?"

He crossed his large arms over his chest. "I will not. I am a god."

"No. You're an idiot. Think about what you're saying: you want to find a woman who will love you and accept you for who you are—i.e., bombed out of your stupid skull—when you're this horrible, egregious version of yourself who treats women like pieces of ass, goes around flashing his dick everywhere, and looks like he has a liver the size of a watermelon."

"Your point?"

"No woman wants that, and if she does, there's something seriously wrong with her."

"I meet plenty of women who enjoy me when I'm in party mode."

"Are they drunk? Because they'd have to be." He was absolutely offensive and belligerent.

"Well, yes. But that is to be expected. I do serve the best cocktails on the planet. Humans find it difficult to stay sober in my presence."

"I have no problem."

"Because apparently your drink of choice is getting fucked by a hot god."

What? Ohmygod. How can he say that? On the other hand, could it explain why she felt the irresistible urge to get down, dirty, and naughty in his presence? Still, he was a pig for saying it like he had.

She shook her head. "I'm not clear on how you got to be a god, but your plan is a joke."

"And what then do you propose I do? Mate with a woman who doesn't know how to have fun? Who hates drinking, the one thing I'm truly gifted at? I am the God of Wine and Intoxication. My role is to help humans—"

"You're a man-child, and it's time you grew up. People's lives are on the line, including my child's and possibly my own." She poked him in his chest, his firm, firm chest. *Dammit, am I turned on right now! He smells so good.*

Wait. No. Stop! She needed to think clearly.

The truth was that she found him extremely attractive. Excruciatingly attractive. Seven feet of perfectly sculpted male muscled in such a way that her eyes couldn't help wanting to savor every inch of his exposed skin. For example, his neck. He had an Adam's apple that stuck out just a little bit farther than a regular guy. Overtly manly. His stunning face was accentuated by a short beard that didn't grow in full. Instead, it skirted the contour of his jaw, leaving his smooth, high cheekbones fully exposed. His brows and intense eyes made him look sexy and tough all at the same time. As for his chest and abs, they weren't on display, but she would never forget such perfection. Hard round pecs, rippled abs, and belly button covered in a light dusting of dark hair. His soft wavy hair that fell to his nipples was enough to...*to make a woman want to strip naked just so she could feel the silky strands brush over her nipples.*

Oh God. Don't think about it. Just don't.

Her conclusion was that in the sexual-attraction department, there was a lot to work with. But what she couldn't live with was his chauvinistic, crude behavior. If it weren't for that, she might be able to take him seriously. *As it stands, I just want to lock him in a stockade and throw things at him.*

She drew a breath. "Have you ever tried to learn how to be the party without partying? You facilitate the fun, but you don't engage in the fun."

He scratched his thick, brown scruff. "No. However, I had planned on bartending sober at my mate mixer."

"Mate mixer?"

"Yes, I am throwing myself a party and inviting only single women. It is the best hope I have of finding my soul mate on such short notice."

She shook her head. "And they'll all be drunk?"

"I hope so. Otherwise, I wouldn't be doing my job, now would I?"

He's crazy. He's a god, and he's downright crazy. "Have your stupid mixer, but I promise you that your plan sucks."

"It's a wonderful plan."

"And if you fail? What's plan B? Oh. That's right. You don't have one," she snarled.

"I told you I'm a god. I never fail."

Could he possibly be more arrogant? "What if

you do?"

"I am not sure."

"That settles it. You are going to spend a platonic night with me."

"Why?"

"While I find you morally repugnant and sleazy, I'm your best hope. We are going to test us out and make absolutely sure there's no way for us to be a match." They had to try.

"I've seen your style of fun, and while racing in your skivvies was very…well, racy, I sense that is about as wild as you get."

"Basically, yes. It took me a decade to work up the nerve to do it, but we have to try. We have to." Her daughter meant everything to her.

"You're saying you want me to show you a good time," he said.

"Sure. Or maybe we'll do my version of fun for a few hours and then I'll do yours."

"I have sworn an oath to stay sober until I've found my mate, but I suppose I can take you out."

"But you were…the other you this morning."

"An accidental cocktail. It wore off minutes after I left."

"Why exactly did you leave?" she asked.

"Ah. Yes. That. I did not want to kill you."

Huh? "Huh?"

"It is fatal for a human to have intercourse with a god. They must wear a special stone—a particular black jade—that absorbs our energy."

"You almost killed me?" She didn't even know how to process that.

"No. I mean—well...I found you very irresistible and forgot and then..." He let out a sigh. "I'm a complete asshole, aren't I?"

"Yes. I can't believe you! I'm a mother. People depend on me."

"I stopped before you burst into flames. Does that not count for something?"

She winced. "Dear God, you are so obtuse."

"Thank you. Now, shall we get on with our evening?"

The front door swung open and in walked Jessica.

Still standing in the middle of her living room, Margarita froze for a moment as if she'd been caught doing something very bad.

"Jessica, you're late." She put on a face of calmness.

"Mom, I'm sixteen. If I want to stay out until nine with my friends, I'm going to stay out." She entered their small living room and spotted Acan. Her eyes went wide and then wider.

"Who's he?" Jessica said with a flirty smile.

Nope. Nuh-uh. She would not have her daughter lusting after the party god.

Acan dipped his head. "I am—"

"He is my friend from work," Margarita interrupted. "And we are leaving. You are going to do your homework. Dinner is in the oven." She grabbed Acan's arm—so, so muscled and bulgy— and urged him toward the door.

"A pleasure meeting you, Jessica."

"Uh…" Jessica stood there drooling.

Margarita grabbed her keys and little satchel-style purse from the glass table next to the door. "I mean it, young lady. Homework."

Acan's eyes stuck on Jessica for a moment, a long moment as if he was taking her in.

Oh, no. Like hell, you bastard. She pushed him outside and slammed the front door shut. "Don't ever look at my daughter like that again."

Acan jerked his head back. "She is far too young for me."

"Then why were you looking at her like that?"

He blinked. "I do not know. But I assure you, it was not sexual. Although, she is quite lovely. She takes after her mother."

Margarita huffed. "Let's go. We have work to do."

"Work? I understood we were to embark on an evening of fun."

Yes, but his version of fun was not hers. "Same thing."

CHAPTER EIGHTEEN

Acan's head spun after his interaction with Margarita. He could see the logic in what she had said about her being his best chance of thwarting the worst disaster to hit the human race since the inception of Pokémon Go; however, he simply did not see a way for them to work out as a couple. A couple who would be together forever. For. Ever. As in eternity.

Nevertheless, he could not argue that it made sense to sacrifice one night to make absolutely certain they could not work.

"Where would you like to go first?" he asked, opening the door to his black Tesla sedan parked out front of her apartment building, a four-story brick monstrosity built in the sixties and sandwiched between a sushi joint and a pawnshop.

She deserves better.

"Are you hungry?" she asked.

"Never. But I can always eat. Where would you like to go?"

"I know just the place down the street. It's my idea of fun."

Fifteen minutes later, they were seated at a strange table with a large iron griddle in the middle. The cuisine was called "Korean BBQ," but he did not see any barbeques.

"So let me get this straight," he said. "You pay money to sit at a table and cook your own food?"

"Well, yeah. It's supposed to be fun, and it's healthy." She pointed to all of the small dishes filled with fatless meats, steamed vegetables, pickled cabbage, and various sauces. "So you see, healthy cooking isn't boring."

"But *I* have to cook."

She sighed. "Yes. But they prepare everything and wash the dishes."

He smiled. "Oh, that certainly is better. I never do dishes."

"Then who does them?" Margarita grabbed her chopsticks and began scraping them together.

"I have Jill. She does everything for me," he replied.

"And does Jill know about…" Margarita fanned her chopsticks over his upper torso.

"About my hotness? Why of course. What woman wouldn't notice?" He grinned.

"Ha. Funny. I meant about your," she leaned in, "about your nonhuman state."

"Ah. That. Yes, she's aware. But she's a necessity because she was appointed to keep me out of human jail."

"Jail? For what?"

"My specialty is flaming drinks. I often burn things down."

Margarita slid the plates of marinated meat away from him. "In that case, I will be doing the cooking." The table next to them cheered loudly and began clanking their beer bottles together. "Well, nice to see someone knows how to have fun."

"You mean to say that I don't?" he asked.

"Yes."

How could *she* say that about *him*? *This date is already a bust.*

Just then, the table of six behind them screamed, "Bottoms up!" and slammed down shots. Wild laughter broke out at the bar. The quiet, family-style restaurant suddenly turned into a rowdy, Korean saloon. The waiters started bringing out beers and shots to all of the tables. Margarita looked increasingly uncomfortable.

"Perhaps we should leave and sample your next bit of fun," he said.

Her mouth dropped. "This is you, isn't it?"

"Not on purpose. I simply have this effect on people, especially at night."

She made a strange face.

"It's part of my charm?" he offered.

"Let's go." She raised her hand for the check, but the waiter was too busy drinking with the patrons at the bar.

"Allow me." Acan raised his index finger in the air. Without saying a word, without looking away from her, the entire establishment turned their attention toward him in silence.

"Check." He shrugged.

Margarita frowned. "This is just too freaking weird."

Still spinning from the bizarre reaction of the patrons in the restaurant, Margarita decided that comfort food was in order: frozen yogurt. She knew it wasn't exciting or filled with people screaming and drinking, but there was nothing better than a sweet treat at the end of the day. One that didn't undo all of her workouts. Not that she was conceited, but she was the face and body of her business. Her livelihood depended on looking fit.

Margarita prepared a cup for Acan, filling it with carob chips, three gummy bears, and a dollop of strawberry, and handed it to him.

"What am I supposed to do with this?" he asked.

"You're supposed to eat it while we walk along the beach." Santa Monica Beach was only three blocks away. They could look at the lights of the Ferris wheel on the pier, listen to the sound of the waves, and walk off the calories of the delicious dessert they were about to enjoy.

He gave her a look of extreme skepticism.

"Just keep an open mind, all right?" she pushed.

"Very well."

She paid for their dessert—she'd insisted since he'd paid for the dinner they didn't get to eat—and they headed down the long flight of steps that would take them to the beach.

"So tell me, Margarita, why are you so opposed to fun?"

"I'm not. But I don't care for alcohol."

"Same difference."

"Okay, well, I guess it has to do with the fact that I associate many bad memories with inebriation."

"Such as?"

"I really don't want to talk about it," she said.

"You're the one who wished to test our compatibility. I think being honest is paramount."

She took a spoonful of her frozen yogurt, thinking it over. Perhaps he was right. "Okay. My ex-husband, Jessica's father, was a drunk, and he beat me. How's that for painful honesty?"

"Very traumatizing. Yes, I'm feeling traumatized." They crossed the narrow street and hit the sand, making their way toward the water.

"Well, so did I. It didn't last long, but it started right after I gave birth to her. I was still healing from the delivery when he slapped me the first time and told me how I'd ruined his life with my 'shitty little baby.' After that, he apologized but did it again and again and again until I left him. I had nothing—no job, no savings, no family to lean on. So you might say that alcohol reminds me of a time when I was at my lowest, trying to be my strongest."

Margarita couldn't see Acan's face clearly, but the distant lights of the pier allowed her to make out a frown.

"Where does he live?" he asked.

"Sorry?"

"Where does he live?" he repeated.

"I'm not sure, but why do you want to know?"

"Because I have recently learned that I am also the God of Decapitation, and I wish to remove his head."

Margarita laughed, but Acan didn't laugh with her. "You're joking, right?"

"Yes, I am joking," he said in the most non-joking tone ever. "Where did you say he lives again? And what is his name?"

Margarita wasn't sure if he was kidding, so she changed the subject. "Try your yogurt."

He stared at the cup. "Are you certain it's safe? It looks very menacing, like a frozen terrorist."

"Stop being such a baby."

Almost to the shoreline, she stopped and waited.

He took his spoon and raised it to his mouth. A moment passed while Margarita waited for a *yumm* or an *mmm....* He couldn't not like it. It was sweet and creamy and—

Acan clutched his throat, hacking and coughing. He dropped to the sand on his back, clawing at the front of his white dress shirt.

"Oh shit! Acan, are you okay?" *Stupid question! Of course not!* She dropped to her knees beside him, frantically reaching for the phone in her purse to shine a light on his face.

"Are you choking? Oh god. What do I do?" Her first aid training kicked in, and she remembered to check the passageway for obstruction. She shoved her fingers in his mouth and tried to pry his lips open to get a better look. Suddenly, he began sucking on her fingers.

"Mmmm…now that's better."

Her jaw dropped, and she jerked her fingers back. "Gah. What? You were joking?" She swatted his chest, and he began to chuckle. "What an asshole! I thought you were dying." She sprang to her feet and began marching away.

Acan followed after her, half-laughing his words. "Oh, come on, Margarita. I was merely joking. Your 'fun' yogurt tastes like a cardboard box took a crap and then coated it with fake sugar."

"So what? You thought you'd make it fun by faking death."

"Well, yes. I cannot die, so it is very funny."

Ugh. She rolled her eyes.

Acan grabbed her hand and whipped her back toward him, encasing her in his large arms. "Now it is time for my version of fun." He leaned down and pressed his lips to hers. For a moment, she thought about pulling back, but his warm hard body pressed to hers, his addictive scent, his soft mouth framed by bristly whiskers, all pulled her right in.

She dropped her frozen treat in the sand and slid her arms around his solid midriff. *He's right. This is so much better than that cardboard crap.* She loved the substantial feel of him—like nothing could ever hurt her when she was wrapped in his embrace.

As his soft tongue delved into her mouth, massaging hers with a sinful rhythm that promised all sorts of other sinful moves in the bedroom, her mind drifted to thoughts about him. A god. He was a god. She still couldn't believe they were real, but the evidence stood right in front of her, including his insanely large erection pressing into her belly.

He really was magnificent, in this state, of course. The party version of him, not so much. Why couldn't he see that? Why couldn't he see that being a drunken fool didn't help anyone? She wondered if he really wasn't able to resist playing this role he claimed he'd been born to do. Come to think of it, she had a lot of questions now that reality had sunk in. How many other gods were there? Why weren't they helping him?

Slowly, her mind moved back to his hot lips and his even hotter body towering over her. His hands slid down to her hips and pulled her into him, allowing her to feel the full length of his stiffness. She sighed into his kiss, her body melting, her insides fluttering, and the space between her legs perking up.

He abruptly broke away, leaving her breathless.

"We better stop before I hurt you." The distant light of the pier caught a concerned look in his eyes.

"Whoa!" She jumped back a foot, holding up her hands in the "all clear" position. "I almost forgot."

"As did I. And now you see how easy it is for me to become distracted by you. Perhaps we should swing by my place before the next stop of our evening. I have several black jade accessories you can wear."

Margarita suddenly felt like they were two horny teenagers in need of a condom. Only this guy was…well, she didn't know how old, but she assumed very old—and his prophylactic was a stone meant to absorb his otherworldly energy.

Don't think about how weird that sounds. Don't think about it. And stepping away from my head exploding from the surrealness of it all…and there, I'm back.

"I think if that little stone is the only thing preventing us from going to bed together—" she swallowed "—again. Then we'd better skip your house and get on to the next event."

"Ahh…" he said, his voice deep and filled with seduction. "But we can make my home the next event, one that will last—" he reached for her hand and placed a kiss on top "—for days, if you like."

Her mouth went all dry. "You can make lo-love for-for days?"

"Longer. But I don't want to break you." He chuckled and leaned down to whisper in her ear, "My cum will make you instantly orgasm, and I can ejaculate as much or as little as you like." His lips brushed across her cheek. "It's a god thing."

Dear Lord. She felt her core combusting.

"What do you say?" he asked.

"Uh-uh-uh…" She imagined them lying between silky sheets, him covering her body, pumping his thick cock into her while kissing her with those delicious lips that were framed by a thick growth of bristly whiskers. *Sigh. So manly.* And if he didn't tire, he would take his time with her, and she would let him. She would let him touch and lick and kiss every inch of her body, allow him to explore her most sensitive areas while she did the same. She would stroke him gently, take him in her mouth, and watch him come. She would lick her way up those washboard abs and then suck his nipples. She would kiss those lips for hours while riding his large shaft, enjoying the way he filled her.

Oh, boy. She fanned her face. The ocean breeze wasn't going to do the trick. And then, as if to torment her further, she caught a fresh whiff of his skin. Goose bumps exploded all over her body, and her nipples hardened into sharp points.

She gnashed her teeth. She wanted him so badly, but…

"Nope," she said in her firmest tone. "We can't. We have to stick to the program—you said yourself that millions of lives are on the line here, and we already know we're compatible in the bedroom. Even though we've only had partial sex on a desk and in an alley." *Jeez, who am I?*

He sighed. "I suppose you are right. But are you certain you do not wish to just have a quickie at my place? I can give you a sample orgasm with my powerful cu—"

"Nope. No, thank you. You can keep your powerful, uh…man-juice right there where it belongs." She pointed to his groin.

"Sharing it sounds so much better, but if you insist." He sounded disappointed, and she could relate. Right now, her c-spot was so lit up that the light pressure of her underwear under her tight jeans might make her orgasm. Worst of all, the more time she spent with him, the more intense her body's reaction.

"Why do I feel like this?" she asked, thinking aloud.

"Like what?"

"Like you're bombarding me with some strange sexual radiation."

"Ah." He nodded, his face now stone-cold serious. "That is because we are mates; it's our bond."

"Sorry. Mind elaborating?"

"The best way to describe it is in terms of energy. Everything is made from matter, tiny particles of energy bound together via an electrical charge of sorts. Energy holds us together—holds everything together. And for mates, their molecules are attracted to each other. Like a force of nature within us, only we have minds and hearts that get in the way."

How fascinating. "How does the reaction start?"

He shrugged. "The Universe. The Creator. Who truly knows?"

"So you don't know?"

"Why would I?"

"Because you're a god."

"Yes, but like you, I was not born with answers. In fact, I wasn't even born. I simply awoke one day. No body, no form, just alive, and searching for answers that eventually led us to your world, like birds who instinctually knew what direction to fly."

She'd never heard anything so incredible. "So there was no manual, no bigger god to tell you all of the secrets of the universe."

"Now, where would the fun be in that? Especially when you're destined to live for eternity."

Wow. Just wow. "You're really going to live forever?"

"Perhaps forever is not the correct word. It is likely somewhere along the lines of a really, really, really long time. Which only supports my hypothesis that just like every soul born to this Earth, the gods were meant to find answers on our own."

She would not want to live forever. She loved the idea of growing old and experiencing life as it was meant to be: every moment precious.

"So what answers have you found?" she asked.

"I like beer." He smiled. "Beer and cheese balls. Tacos are also excellent."

"Ha. Funny."

"Honestly, I have learned that gods are just as crazy as humans, and not everything has a reason because the Universe has a very twisted mind. Why else would she decide to mate two complete opposites?"

"Maybe to test us."

"Or maybe she gets bored like any living being and needs a little entertainment. Either way, we'll never know, and it does not alter the fact that at this very moment our molecules are attempting to pull you and me closer. Just like we are subconsciously driven to find our fates."

"Amazing." Because she felt the pull he spoke of. She truly did. And in some strange way, it gave her peace to learn all this. She'd grown up in a happy but very strict family whose beliefs and way of life didn't make sense to her. In her heart, she felt her calling was out there in the world among the outsiders. In her heart, she loved her parents, her two sisters, and her simple way of life, but she couldn't ignore her desire to see the world.

When she expressed her doubts, her mother and father told her to pray and work hard and in time she'd find her way. And she had. One week before her eighteenth birthday, her father began questioning why she wasn't courting with anyone or preparing to marry. The answer was simple: She couldn't see herself living that life and being happy. So on her eighteenth birthday, she did the most difficult thing ever and left. With only the four hundred dollars she'd saved over the years from small birthday gifts and handmade lace she sold to tourists, she got on a bus to Los Angeles. All she knew was that she had an aunt who'd left the community twenty years ago to live with an "English" man she'd met.

Margarita—or Margaret as she was called back then—never found her aunt, but as if an angel had been watching over her, she met a strange redheaded woman on the bus, who gave her the address of a place she could stay while she got on her feet. It was a halfway house of sorts for women from all backgrounds, and it was also a Godsend. More importantly, it opened her eyes to the ugliness of the modern world her family had warned her of. These women had come from gangs, cults, abusive relationships, and from them Margarita learned that she had to be vigilant and strong. The evils of the world were real, but that didn't mean there wasn't good or that she should be afraid. She just had to be smart.

From there, she got a job bussing tables, learned about a wonderful thing called financial aid, and began taking classes at the nearby community college. Slowly, her old life faded into the past, and she began discovering who she truly was: adventurous, brave, and compassionate. She also loved running on the beach. She'd never felt freer or more alive. She loved hiking and swimming and anything that got her blood flowing. That was when Margaret Miller of Pennsylvania legally became Margarita Seville. A lively name that fit her. From there she decided to study kinesiology, which led her to a managerial job at the gym after she obtained her bachelor's. The rest was history. However, not even to this day had she told anyone where she'd come from or what she'd endured to get here—fifteen years of finding herself, then a single mother, survivor, and business owner.

Every step of her journey had felt like a test. One after another. But now, hearing that unseen forces pulled people toward something or someone, well, it gave her a sense of peace. She wasn't crazy for leaving her world behind twenty-something years ago. She hadn't been just another teenager, rebelling, making up excuses to escape the restrictive life of her community. She was meant to be living this life; otherwise she wouldn't be here.

"Thank you," she finally said, the two of them quietly staring out at the ocean.

"For what?"

"You have no idea how long I've been living in doubt."

"About?"

"Every minute of my life."

He smiled. "I am here to serve."

CHAPTER NINETEEN

Margarita didn't say much as they drove toward Beverly Hills to the Randy Unicorn. But every chance Acan had to look at her, he did. She had a hint of a smile on her beautiful pink lips and a sparkle of joy in her almond-shaped green eyes. He could only guess what she might be feeling, but for him it was contentment. A strange, completely foreign contentment. He truly liked his sweet but ballsy, fuzzy cu—

No! You cannot call her that. It is wrong on too many levels. Perhaps it would help if I found another nickname.

He glanced over at her and took the off-ramp. "What do you think about pet names?"

She shrugged. "I don't know. I guess I've never found a use for them."

"So you've never had a pet name?"

"Nope," she replied.

"How do you like fuzzy cup?"

She frowned. "Why would you call me that?"

"Never mind."

"How about you? Any pet names?" she asked.

"Men do not have pet names—just nicknames."

"Like Belch," she offered.

"Yes."

"Doesn't that name bother you? Sounds kinda slobbish."

"Actually, the nickname evolved over time, beginning with the Mayans, who created a drink called 'balche,' a fermented beverage derived from the balche tree, also known as the drink of the gods. Obviously, they dedicated the drink to me and made many offerings. Which is why they called me the balche god. My brethren later turned it into Belch simply to tease me. I was too drunk to care, so I embraced it."

Margarita's face contorted a bit.

"This deity thing is difficult for you, isn't it?" He stepped on the brakes to wait out the red light.

"Uh, yep."

He placed his hand on her thigh. Simply touching her gave him a rush—sexual and mental. *My perfect cocktail of delights: Margarita.*

"Give it time. You'll get used to all this," he said.

"Will I?"

Ah. He'd almost forgotten. His way of life wasn't something she approved of. Not that he could blame her if her frame of reference was a man who used to get drunk and hit her.

Note to godly self: smite evil ex-spouse of Margari-

ta. There was no excuse to hit a woman.

He felt his insides coil. He'd done far worse a few days ago. He'd decapitated his sister plus nine others.

All right, man. Cut yourself some slack. It wasn't exactly the same. He'd never hurt anyone while drunk, not even when he'd accidentally burned down a few hundred hotels and nightclubs with his infamous flaming drinks. And the other night, when he'd murdered his brethren in cold blood, well, he wasn't to blame. That was all the Universe's doing.

Wasn't it?

Oh hell. Maybe it wasn't. Moving on…

Tonight was his chance to show Margarita the truth. He was a caring deity. A true giver. Of drinks. And fun. And occasional orgies. He provided a necessary service to humanity, and if his awesome manly waistline and pant-wearing abilities were sacrificed in the process, so be it! Margarita would hopefully see the importance in his work.

Still, in these few short hours with Margarita, he'd come to feel something between them almost as equally gratifying as his quest to intoxicate the masses. Friendship. It was something he never sought or needed in his life. He had his sister. He had his thirsty flock. He had drink recipes and matches. But now he had her. Someone to listen and talk with. He felt at ease in her presence. Except when he thought about fucking her tight but luscious woman grotto—okay, okay, and maybe poking her in the ass a few times with his finger to see if it might make her giggle. Dirty fantasies aside, there was a certain ease about being with her. An ease laced with unabashed lust. *And thoughts of ass tickling. Just for fun.*

"Oh, look. We're here." He pulled up to the valet, alongside a line of a few hundred people wrapping around the block. They were all dressed in a plethora of unicorn garb—hats, headbands, full-body suits, and papier-mâché unicorn heads—eagerly awaiting the world-famous Randy Unicorn experience.

The irony is if they ever met Minky, they'd never want to look at anything unicorn again. She only showed herself every few decades, but it was said that one look into her blood red eyes could eviscerate a man and liquefy his brains. Others said that her unihorn was a straw she used like a mosquito's beak to suck the blood from her victims. Personally, he'd never seen Minky—that he remembered—but he knew she did one hell of a Bee Gees impression on unicorn karaoke night every Thursday. *Free Forgetty treatment at the door on the way out!*

"Are you ready for some real fun?" He glanced at Margarita as she took in a woman strutting by in nothing but a rainbow thong and two miniature unicorn heads taped to her nipples.

"Uhh…well, this is interesting." Her voice was tinged with disdain.

He sighed with contentment. "It is, isn't it?

Shall we?" The valet opened his door, but he couldn't take his eyes off his favorite cocktail—Margarita. Not until he knew she was coming inside. The shock on her face told him otherwise.

"I realize you do not approve of drinking, but may I ask why you are so nervous?"

"Umm...I've never actually been in a night-club."

How shocking! "Why not?"

She shrugged but did not offer more.

It struck him as odd that she'd never gone to a nightclub, and whatever her reason for such an oversight, she did not seem prepared to tell him.

The loud bass from inside the building vibrated the windows of the car. He already felt the people inside subconsciously calling *Belch, Belch, Belch!*

Ah, yes! The masses were looking for their king to guide them through a night of excess, letting loose, and decompression. *Well, not tonight.* He would keep his oath not to partake in any libations, but he would serve a few rounds.

He slid his hand over Margarita's and let the beat of the awaiting party pulse through him into her. She remained frozen, staring at the windshield.

"Breathe, Margarita. It is merely a building filled with souls in need of happiness."

"Says you," she snapped.

She was behaving as if she were a nun and he the devil taking her to a demonic orgy. *Oh! Great idea for next year's Halloween party.* They threw one every year. He usually just went as the pantsless horseman.

"I just don't feel like this is the place for me. They're all so young and...drunk." Margarita frowned in her seat.

He suddenly remembered a woman who'd come into the club last year. She'd been sitting at the bar with a sour face, unenticed by his standard drinks—blue balls, a horny bandit, a chocolate T-bag. Turned out that she was an aspiring singer who'd been burned every way possible by her famous ex-husband. The man had taken her car, her home, and her three small children, all because she refused to be cheated on and he could afford a better lawyer. Acan recalled the moment clearly: The song "So What" by Pink filled the club, and that was when it hit him: The perfect drink. Acan had reached across the bar, laid his hand over hers, and said, "You're still a rock star. You got your rock moves. And you don't need him." He then handed her a fuck you hurricane, better known as the fuckuicane:

In a plastic yard glass, fill:
- ½ with ice
- ¼ with pink lemonade
- ¼ tequila
- Add a splash of grenadine for color and garnish with a slice of orange and a maraschino cherry on a toothpick.

The woman had smiled, thanked him, and hit

the floor. By the end of the night, she had a record deal and would soon have enough money to get her kids back.

God times, god times. Sometimes, people simply needed to be reminded of who they were.

He mentally patted himself on the back and then looked at Margarita. "You are Wonder Woman. Nothing frightens you, least of all a club full of people dressed as unicorns, dancing their worries away."

"Okay." She bobbed her head. "You're right. Let's go."

Ha. I really am good with people, aren't I?

They exited the car, and the moment the line of patrons spotted him, they cheered.

Acan waved at the crowd as he walked around the vehicle and took Margarita's hand. "Ready for the night of your life?"

She drew a breath. "Ready."

The bouncer unlatched the rope and high-fived Acan on their way inside.

"VIP treatment. This is nice," she said.

"Just wait. It gets better."

The moment they got inside, they were swallowed by the cheering crowd.

Daddy's home.

CHAPTER TWENTY

Wearing her favorite pink flannel nightgown, Tula lay on her flowery bedspread with a box of tissues, her mind a swirling mess of emotions: humiliation, heartbreak, frustration, and anger. This morning with Zac had been a complete disaster. Not only did he refuse to touch her, he'd tossed her out on her perky behind and threatened to call Gilbert if she didn't go home.

Can you believe that god? Just who does he think he is, treating me like a child?

She was Tula Jones. And while she was a wholesome Midwestern girl raised by two wholesome and loving parents who taught her to always be kind, compassionate, truthful, and modest, she was also a woman. A woman with a heart filled with passion. Yes, she believed with all her being that saving one's passion for the wedding night was the right thing to do, but ever since Zac had kissed her at that party, all she could think about was how right he'd felt.

And she was no fool. She knew exactly why he'd pushed her away after their kiss the other night.

Cimil had warned him half a dozen times that he would ruin Tula's life if he pursued her or distracted her from her destiny to marry Gilbert. But that was just the thing: Zac *had* pushed her away. Which could only mean he truly cared. Little did he know that to someone like herself, that was the biggest temptation of all. An irresistible aphrodisiac. Not sexy comments or flirting or promises of lust-filled nights. Nope. Nothing was hotter than a man who did right and put the well-being of the woman he loved first.

Tula fanned her flushed face. Simply thinking about it made her hotter than a Sunday morning griddlecake.

She sighed. *Oh, fiddlesticks. What am I going to do now?* She couldn't marry Gilbert. She just couldn't. Her mama taught her to always tell the truth, and that included being honest with what was in her heart. Gilbert was a good man, but his family looked down on her and her own—too simple, too poor, too uneducated, they said. Her father farmed corn, just like his daddy and his daddy before him. Gilbert's father owned the only bank in town.

Well, to heck with them! She and her family were good, honest, hardworking people. As for uneducated, well, that was a big ol' pile of last week's bologna. She was only one semester away from obtaining her degree in astrophysics with a minor in mythology—sort of a hobby she'd picked up after learning her quantum theory professor, Cimil, was an actual deity. Who owned a unicorn!

Ain't life just full o' surprises. And so what if I'm poor? She always paid her way. More importantly, she always did the right thing. *Which is why I am calling off the wedding.*

Tula's cell phone rang on her nightstand, and her heart practically leapt through her flannel nightgown. Could it be Zac?

She picked up the device. *Oh, phewy.* "Hi, Cimil."

"You can't cancel the wedding, Tula."

Tula's mouth fell open. "Wait. But I just—how'd you know?"

"I am the Great and Powerful Oz."

"Funny, Cimil."

"No. Really. You think that whole story about Dorothy and Toto is fiction? No way, baby. That shit was real, and so is this final warning. You must marry Gilbert."

"Why?"

"The Great and Powerful Oz does not give reasons. You must simply trust the Ozziness of his ways."

Tula rolled her eyes. "Unless you can give me a good reason, then I must follow my heart."

"So you're saying no to fate. No to the joyous rewards of doing what is best for humanity."

Tula gave it a moment of thought. "Uhhh…yep. That sounds about right." She wanted Zac, and if giving in to temptation had consequences, then she was ready to accept that.

"Dammit, Tula. Then you give me no choice."

Huh? Tula felt a hot breath on her face. She looked up, and hovering above her was the most frightening pair of glowing red eyes she'd ever seen.

Dripping with blood, the horrific beast smiled, bearing two giant white fangs.

Minky? "Oh, barnacles." Tula dropped the phone.

☙ ❧

Zac sat on his black leather couch, drowning his sorrows in a gallon of scotch, a pint of Cherry Garcia, and binge-watching *Supernatural*. His favorite was Lucifer, of course. Although, Dean was kinda cool, too, he supposed. *For a dude.*

Zac shoved a spoonful of ice cream into his mouth and washed it down with a swig of booze. Of course, none of this helped clear his mind of Tula.

Resisting her pleas to fuck her had been the most difficult exercise in restraint of his existence. Did she not understand the sort of torment she was provoking in his life? *For once I'm trying to do the right thing. For her sake! Oh, but nooo... Did she care? She could only see what she wanted.*

"Well, she can't have it!" He glanced down at the bulge in his leather pants. "That's right." She could tempt him all she wanted, but he was a god and had his duties to think of. Okay, and he really didn't want her to die in torment as Cimil had prophesied. He cared about Tula, and if that meant staying away, then he would do the godly thing and stay the hell away! *Door closed.*

He shoved his spoon into the container and cued up another gooey bite. Suddenly, he felt his soul icing over, covered in a dark, malevolent sticky energy.

Oh hell. His entire body drained of light, quickly consumed by something sinister evil inside him. *No. No. Fuck no. I'm flipping.* But the acknowledgment did nothing to stop every molecule of his body draining of light and goodness.

Slowly, he stood from the couch, his essence and human shell surging with a powerful thirst for destruction. *Pain. I will make the world swallow my pain. I will bathe them all in blood. I will not rest until I bring this world to its knees.*

He tossed his pint to the floor and grinned. "And I know who's going to be the first to kneel."

Tula.

His cell phone rang on the coffee table, and the name Cimil flashed on the screen. He picked it up and held the phone to his ear.

"You'll never find her, Zac," Cimil said. "So don't even try."

A blinding rage scorched through him. "What did you do with her?" he growled.

"I've hidden her somewhere safe. Away from you."

"Tell me where she is or I will disembowel you!" he roared.

Cimil laughed. "Be my guest. I don't really like my colon anyway. And before you utter another inane threat from that stupid evil head of yours, Zac, know this: I saw this coming, and I am ten steps ahead of you. You'll never win."

Fucking Cimil.

His front door burst open with a heavy thud. Five Uchben soldiers poured in, armed to the teeth.

"You think a few humans and some guns can stop me?" Zac chuckled and threw down his cell.

෴

Listening to the noise on the other end of her cell, Cimil stood in line at the Quickie Mart, dressed in full clown garb, waiting to buy cigarettes. She didn't smoke, but the evil man she was hunting tonight enjoyed dressing as a clown and hiding behind trees to grab helpless children. He would then take them to his van, tie them up, and put his smokes out on the bottoms of their feet. Tonight would be his turn. Only she planned to get a little creative with the torture before dragging his soul to the place where bad apples went.

"Oh my god, is that clown wearing a strap-on dildo?" whispered a woman to her boyfriend over by the slushy machines.

"Yay! That's right. Payback is an evil clown-fuck

of a bitch!" Cimil barked at the woman, who scurried out of the store empty-handed.

Okeydokey. Now where was I? Ah! That's right. She'd sent their best Uchben soldiers to take Zac into custody. *Oh cheesesticks.* She'd really hoped that Tula would choose to marry Gilbert. Because then, according to her sources—the dead who saw all and knew all—Zac would cling to the hope that Tula might be for him. Then...wedding day! He would see a virginal Tula marching down the aisle in her flowing white dress, looking like the purest, most ethereal creature to ever walk the planet in need of hard hot temptation. Zac would finally crack. He'd be so jealous and enthralled that it would push him over the edge and make him ready to commit to her. He would then stop her wedding, declare his love, and marry her right there on the spot. (After Minky dealt with Gilbert—that lying, cheating man-whore!) But Tula had changed course.

"Hmm...where'd it all go wrong?" Tapping her cheek, Cimil listened to the screams and grunts echoing through the phone from Zac's apartment. Well, there wasn't much to be done at this point. Zac would go into custody. Tula would remain Minky's prisoner in a safe, hidden location. Eventually, things would work out. Of course, Tula would be nearly ninety by then, but hey.

"Ma'am?" said the clerk behind the counter.

"Yeah, give me a carton of Camel's unfiltered." Suddenly, she heard a loud scream over the phone, followed by a rustle.

"Cimil," Zac's dark, sadistic voice poured over the phone, "next time, I suggest you send real men to fight me. Not these piles of hamburger waiting to happen. And tell Tula that she can run, but she cannot hide. When I find her, I will make sure there's not an ounce of goodness left in her pure sweet soul." The call ended.

Cimil blinked, frozen in fear. Zac killed all the men? And he remained free to hunt Tula? "Oh fudgeballs. I did *not* see that coming."

CHAPTER TWENTY-ONE

After saluting the rowdy masses dressed in a wide array of unicorn garb, Acan gave Margarita the grand tour. In the basement, there was a full bar, where muscular men wearing white hot pants danced around rainbow-spiraled stripper poles. The main floor, where they'd entered, had another big dance floor packed with gyrating bodies and several giant platforms—also for their unicorn-themed go-go dancers—mostly female. A huge unicorn head hung from the ceiling, its eyes flashing to the beat of the music, giving it a happy, yet possessed sort of vibe. Upstairs were offices, another bar, and a cotton candy lounge, where patrons sat around on giant beanbag chairs, nibbling on—yes, you guessed it!—cotton candy from the cotton candy bar, featuring forty different flavors, including jalapeño and bacon.

So gross. And unhealthy. Margarita shook her head. Of course, none of that was nearly as shocking as the huge amounts of alcohol everyone consumed from the five different bars throughout the establishment.

"And that bar is exclusively for me." Acan pointed to a fifty-foot-long stainless steel counter situated below a DJ booth perched above on a separate platform where a blonde woman spun records.

"So what do you think?" Acan sounded like a kid who'd just brought home a finger painting to show to mom.

"Uhhh…" The front of the bar had paintings of white fluffy clouds that turned colors as they reflected the lights from the dance floor. Behind the bar sat five blenders, hundreds of different liquor bottles in a neat line, a punch machine, and a really big fire extinguisher.

"It's, uhh, it's festive?" she replied. "Yes. That's the word I was looking for."

"Agreed. Festive is the perfect word." He smiled down at her, his turquoise eyes shimmering with the strobe lights. His long hair fell in gentle waves around his superbly sculpted cheekbones, and his lips were slightly puckered. She just wanted to brush her fingertips over his rich brown scruff and then plant a kiss on him.

He must've noticed her staring at his mouth because he leaned down and pressed his lips to hers. An instant warmth, sensual and intoxicating, washed over her.

More. I want more. She opened her mouth to him, and he took the cue.

His large hands slid down to her hips and pulled

her into his tall frame. His warm tongue mingled sensually with hers. *Ohgod. He feels so good. So sexy. So...hot! Ouch!*

She pulled away. "What was that?"

"Oops, sorry. My energy is spiking. It always happens when I'm around so many humans in a party mood. Kind of gets the old god juices flowing. Speaking of god juices, are you sure you don't want to go to my place and sample my cu—"

She held out her hand. "Nope. Thank you, but there will be no sampling. Not tonight. But you know what I would like?"

"What?"

"I'd like to know why you're so happy. I mean, you're smiling, you love being here with all of these people, and you look like you're having a good time, yet you haven't had one cocktail."

He frowned, confused. "I'm not sure. But you're right; I am having fun." A slow smile crept over his lips. "I think it's you, Margarita."

"Me? What did I do?"

He placed his hand on her cheek, softly rubbing her chin, his eyes drinking her in. She had to admit, he made her feel adored and special.

I could get used to this.

"I think," he said, "that you are like a song, one that simply puts me in a good mood. I can't ever explain why the notes have the effect. I don't even care why. I simply feel elevated. That's you, Margarita. You are my 'Bohemian Rhapsody' or my 'Pour

Some Sugar on Me.'"

Speechless, Margarita simply stared at him. No man had ever said anything so sweet, so romantic, and so beautiful to her. Not ever.

She suddenly felt herself beginning to fall toward the L-word. It was strange how all it took was one moment and a few simple words to change a person's heart. But he had. Just like that. She supposed when one stepped back and really thought about it, all of life's big moments were simply that. A moment when everything changed. You make a decision to follow your heart and move to LA. You take a run on the beach and just know that you want to open a gym. You have one moment of weakness and you're given a daughter.

Or you step into an elevator with a god.

She smiled at him. "I better warn you: If you keep talking like that, you just might win me over tonight."

"In that case, I will need to tread carefully and ensure I say many more honest and heartfelt things to you." He winked. "Now, let us get on with the next bit of fun for the evening: my work!" He gestured for her to follow him to the side of the bar. Once behind it, she watched him do a quick inventory check in the refrigerators below the counter.

Honestly, she felt kind of excited. She never imagined she'd enjoy being with him so much.

"All right." He slapped his hands together.

"Let's party." He whipped off his shirt, displaying his insanely ripped abs. If it weren't impossible, she could swear he looked even more stacked than she remembered.

Gods, I really, really want to rub baby oil on him. Followed by rubbing her naked body on him, too.

"First drink is on the house tonight!" Acan bellowed.

The crowd within earshot roared and hollered.

Acan absolutely beamed with joy as a hundred or so people queued up. The first customer was a brunette in her mid-twenties wearing white, short-short overalls and pigtails.

"Hey, Belch. You're looking fine tonight!" she yelled over the loud music. "Where you been, baby?"

"Waiting for you, beautiful." He flashed a cocky little smile.

Margarita growled. So this was his awesome plan? To have her watch him flirt with women twenty years younger than herself?

Before the young lady could say another word, Acan placed a tall glass on the counter, filled it halfway with soda—cola or root beer—and a shot of rum. He then reached under the counter and produced a tub of vanilla ice cream. He placed a scoop inside the glass and drizzled the entire thing with caramel.

Wow. That actually looked kind of good. She would tell him so, except she was kind of annoyed watching him be flirty.

The brunette's eyes went wide and began to water. "Thanks, Belch. You always know how to put me in a good mood."

"My pleasure, beautiful. Oh, there's a very handsome gentleman over in the corner, eyeing you. You should ask him to dance."

"I will!" She sauntered off, and Acan turned toward Margarita. "She was dumped at the altar a month ago. She needed a root beer bomb with a side of ego boost."

"How do you know that?"

He shrugged. "It's a gift, and I am here to serve. Would you like to try your perfect drink?"

"No, thanks. Better not."

"All right. You just say the word if you're ever ready. I know how to prepare a drink so delicious that it evokes spontaneous orgasms."

She laughed. "Why? Do your put your awesome god juice in it?"

"I've never prepared it that way, but I suppose I could."

"Eww…I was joking."

He flashed a sinful little smile. "So was I. Because if any of my cum is going into that pretty little mouth of yours, there's only one way it's getting there."

A mental image of that skated through her head, and she couldn't lie. It kind of turned her on. Not that she would admit it.

"Don't be gross." She leaned against the back counter. "Looks like your next customer is waiting."

Acan chuckled and turned to the next person in line, a tall blond guy wearing a rainbow unicorn shirt that said, "I fart cupcakes." Despite the dim lighting, Margarita noticed the man's bloodshot eyes.

Acan filled a glass with clear liquid from the dispenser and shoved it toward him. "Next!"

The guy began walking away, mid-sip. "Hey, this is water."

"Sure the fuck is," said Acan. "Come back in twenty minutes, and I'll give you a refill."

The guy walked away, looking confused.

"What was that all about?" Margarita asked.

"He's high. If I give him any liquor, he might keel over."

For some strange reason, it shocked her that Acan had rules and limits. "That's actually really sweet."

"What?" he asked.

"You looking after him."

"I'm not. I merely do not like people dying in my club. Bad for business."

Her mouth dropped open, and he cracked a smile.

"Oh, you. Very funny." She socked him right in his bulging bicep. *So, so bulgy.*

Acan went on to serve another fifty or so people, and it was nothing shy of amazing. They would walk up, and he would look them in the eyes and serve up a drink. Each person would laugh or smile, their minds completely blown that he'd given them their perfect drink. Then they'd walk away positively glowing. As Margarita watched, she realized that this had nothing to do with the drinks, really. He made them feel special, cared for, or listened to. Before long, the entire club buzzed with a contagious happiness. Even she felt it.

He's incredible, she thought. *Just incredible.*

The next person, a voluptuous black woman with pink braids and a unicorn headband, queued up.

"Why don't you give it a try?" Acan asked Margarita.

"What?" she said.

"Figure out what sort of drink she needs."

"How do I do that?" Margarita asked.

"Look into her eyes, open your mind, and see what pops into your head."

"I don't know."

"Just try it. For humanity's sake and all."

What he really meant was that tonight was about walking in each other's shoes to test their compatibility.

"Okay. Why not?" She slid over and smiled at the young woman. "Hi there. My name is Margarita."

"Like the drink?" the woman asked.

"Yeah. Like the drink. What can I get you?"

Acan stepped in. "Uh-uh-uh... That's cheating. *You* have to figure out the perfect beverage for her."

Margarita nodded. "Okay. I got this." She turned to the young woman and stared into her eyes. "Honestly, the image of a margarita keeps popping up." She shrugged. "Guess I'm not so good at this."

Seemingly out of thin air, Acan handed the young woman a margarita on the rocks. "You will require three of these tonight. One per hour, but no more. Got it?" he said to the woman.

"Thanks!" She trotted away, happy as a clam.

Margarita turned to him. "So her drink was a margarita?"

He smiled slyly.

"You already knew! Didn't you? That was a total setup," she said.

"Maybe."

"So why only three and why only one drink per hour?" It was almost like he was handing out prescriptions.

"She's a lightweight and her body can only metabolize one point five ounces of tequila per hour. She also loves to dance, so if she drinks more than that, dehydration will set in and ruin her awesome buzz."

I just love this guy, she thought, shocking herself. But did she mean it? Or did she mean that she loved how he kept surprising her or that she loved how he cared so much about people?

I don't know, but as Jess would say, I'm crushing hard on him.

"Kiss me," she demanded, batting her eyelashes and feeling eager to touch him again.

He grinned and slowly bent his head, but then stopped just inches from her lips. "I think I might hurt you if I do. I'm feeling incredibly energized in your presence. And a bit aroused. All right, very aroused. But your well-being is obviously more important."

Her heart made a little pitter-patter. *That does it, Acan, you are so getting lucky tonight.* "You know you're sort of amazing, right?"

"I am, aren't I?" He smiled playfully and brushed his thumb across her lower lip, beaming down at her. "I'm beginning to think you're pretty amazing, too."

She felt all warm and squishy inside like a teenager with a wild, irrational crush on the hot guy who was way out of her league. Only he wasn't.

He's just out of your species. Nevertheless, she was beginning to appreciate what he did for people. It wasn't just about getting them hammered. He made them feel good. He cared about what happened to them.

I can't believe I'm saying this. But I really like him. More than any man she'd ever met. A) He was hot. Seven feet of ripped muscles, perfectly tanned skin, a face that was so gorgeous it almost hurt to look at him, and eyes that penetrated the deepest layers of her soul. B) He was awkward and backwards in his way of thinking, but it kind of made him adorable. Naïve, but adorable. C) He wasn't as oblivious to others' feelings as she'd thought. He performed his duties with a sense of honor and responsibility. D) Despite being an actual god, he didn't try to make her feel small or insignificant. Quite the opposite. He made her feel special.

The only downside to him was, well, Belch. She could live with the beer belly, but she couldn't stomach his crude behavior. Swearing, drunkenness, slurring, and no pants. Degrading, X-rated talk without any filters. *But it looks like he's seen the light. He's so happy tonight.* He'd told her that she was responsible for that, and now he knew he didn't need cocktails to have fun.

Acan took a breath as they stood there beaming at each other. "I am very pleased by how well our date has gone, Margarita. It's unexpected, but has truly made me happy."

"Me too." It felt weird to admit it, but being together felt good. It felt right. Almost like they'd known each other forever. Or maybe it felt more like her feelings had always been there, locked away her entire life, waiting for Acan to show up with the key.

"Well, then," he said, "let us get the rest of these people served so you and I can perhaps go somewhere private and speak about our next steps."

His words sent warm butterflies to her stomach.

"I'd like that."

He was about to turn toward the bar when she grabbed his hand. "I'm really proud of you, Acan. I mean that. Making this kind of change in your life for me—for everyone—it just shows how big your heart is."

His smile melted away. "What change do you speak of?"

"This." She waved her hand over his fit-looking body. "Choosing a healthy life, no more drinking, acting more mat—"

"I am sorry, Margarita, if you've misunderstood." His expression soured into something grim. "But I have no plans to be anyone other than who I am."

Margarita's hopes dashed out the window. "So you have no plans to stop partying?"

"Margarita, please understand that my lifestyle," he threw out his hands, gesturing toward the dance floor and his club, "is part of the package. I am the party god, and that will never change."

Deflated, disappointed, sad, frustrated, irritated—none of those words came close to conveying how she felt. Moments ago, everything felt like perfection. They'd clicked in some crazy, soul-mate, destiny-bullcrap kind of way. None of which she'd ever believed truly existed up until tonight. Now, she didn't know what to think.

"So you plan to go back to being Belch, the drunk guy." She dropped his hand.

He stared down at his feet for a moment. "I don't honestly know, Margarita. But I can tell you this: if we are meant to be, then the rest will work out. *That* I know for certain. Relationships, just like people, must evolve as they're meant to be. Change cannot and should not be forced. Otherwise, resentment is inevitable. I have watched it happen a million times to millions of couples over my existence." He took her hand. "I must accept you as you are and you must accept me."

Easy to say, but she couldn't ignore her priorities or the facts. She had a child to look after and couldn't subject her to a life with some crazy god who was drunk all the time. As for herself, she didn't want a life like that either. *We can't work. As much as I want him, we just…can't.*

"I think I need a bio-break." She pulled her hand away and pointed to the right of the dance floor. "Bathrooms are that way?"

"Margarita," he pleaded, "let us finish the date. Perhaps spending a few more hours together will make you feel differently about things."

"I don't know. I just need," she ran her hands over the top of her head, "I need to take a moment and think."

Disappointment reflected in his eyes. "Of course." He stepped aside, allowing her to pass.

She pasted on a polite smile and slid past him, ignoring how good he felt when their bodies touched.

"Wait." He grabbed her arm.

"Yes?" she asked.

"You are coming back, right?" He stared deeply into her eyes. Was he reading her?

I don't know. I really, really don't.

"Sure." She offered a weak smile, silently pleading with him to let her be. *I need to think.*

He nodded solemnly, and she slipped away into the crowd, feeling his eyes on her the entire time. She sensed that he already knew what she'd just been thinking.

God, this is awful. Everything was happening so fast, and much was on the line. But how could she give her heart to someone who had this other side?

Dammit. Her heart hurt. Her brain ached. For the first time in her life she felt like everything was perfect, but at the same time, it was all wrong.

"You must be her," said a female voice as Margarita got in line for the bathroom.

Margarita turned to find a statuesque blonde with long legs, creamy skin, and iridescent turquoise eyes, wearing a pink minidress.

"Oh crap." Margarita covered her mouth. "Yo-won-o-dem!"

The blonde raised a brow. "I speak one hundred and seventy-seven languages, but sadly mumble is not one of them."

Margarita dropped her hand. "Sorry. It's just…" She leaned in. "You're one of them, aren't you?" The eyes were exactly like Acan's.

"Very astute. I am the Goddess of Forgetfulness, Belch's sister."

"There's a god of forgetting things?" That actually explained a lot. She forgot her shopping list, where she left her keys, to check her email daily, and to give herself breaks every four hours. Right now, she'd forgotten where she'd left her sanity.

"Goddess. Not god," the lady corrected.

"Wait. I recognize you. You were in the DJ booth."

"Right again. Aren't you a smart one? Which makes me wonder why Cimil insisted that in exactly five minutes, I will have to wipe your memory if you haven't gone all in with my brother."

"Who's Cimil?"

"She is our sister—completely bat-shit crazy, so we never quite know when she's telling the truth. But given the situation, I'm inclined to listen to her."

"Meaning?"

"Meaning millions of people will lose their heads if our brother doesn't find his mate very soon."

Margarita pulled the goddess to the side, out of earshot from anyone. "That's the thing. I'm his mate."

"So I heard. How's that workin' out for ya?"

"I don't think it's going well."

"Oh, and why not?"

"He's two different people. One is horrible and

dirty and has a giant gutter mouth. The other is very attractive and seems to want to make this world a better place."

"So…he's exactly like you?"

"Me? No. God no."

"You sure about that, honey? Because I've been alive for seventy M and that means I know people. They all have their ugly sides. It's just that they hide it on the inside, unlike my brother. Whatcha see is whatcha get."

"I can't argue with that, but when I'm at my worst, I still remember to wear pants. And I don't call women bad names."

"I see your point." She bobbed her head. "And I'm not going to lie: my brother can be a complete pig. He's reckless, rude, and insensitive at times. But that's only because he's so young."

"How young?"

"Seventy thousand years old, give or take a century or ten, but the point is, he never had boundaries, and until ten thousand years ago, he didn't have a purpose. So in our world, he's still got a lot of manning up to do."

"So he's basically an immature a-hole, like most men," Margarita assumed.

Acan's sister pointed her index finger and pulled the invisible trigger. "Yup."

"And he'll improve with age?"

"Yup again. Add a mate to the mix, and he'll probably start acting like an honest to gods man."

She shrugged. "Mates seem to have a way of balancing each other out. It's a Universe slash yin-yang thing, which is why he won't turn evil if you two hit it off."

All right. This was good news. It was almost like the time she'd hit rock bottom with nowhere to go but up. Acan had nowhere to go but more mature.

"I might be able to work with that as long as he's committed." Margarita felt elated. This was what she wanted: for them to work out.

Acan's sister toggled her head. "Well, then you've got exactly two minutes to find that out."

"Why two?"

"One minute, fifty seconds, actually. In which time, I'm going to make you forget you ever met him. Sorry, but Cimil might be insane, but she's rarely wrong."

Margarita gasped. "You're serious, aren't you?"

"As a heart attack."

Fuck. Margarita turned and sprinted back toward Acan's bar, finding it completely vacant save the line of patient customers on the other side.

Oh no. Oh no. Where is he? Margarita swiveled on her heel, her eyes searching frantically.

Nothing.

Just as she was about to make her way to the basement, she spotted him. *No. No. But why?* Her heart sank into her black boots.

On the platform in the middle of the dance floor, Acan was sandwiched between two women.

He had one bent over and was dry humping her from behind, her miniskirt hiked so high that everyone could see her unicorn panties. The other woman had her arms wrapped around him from behind with her hands shoved down the front of his pants. The crowd encircling the platform cheered and pumped their fists while the three put on their dirty show.

Ohmygod. Margarita was speechless. And hurt. This was absolutely not the sort of man she could be with. "I'm done. I'm done with you."

As if Acan heard her voice over the loud beat of the music and screaming patrons, their eyes met. Did he notice the pain in her eyes? Because his smile melted away and he looked down at himself holding the bent-over woman by the hips.

"Asshole," Margarita mouthed.

Just as she turned to leave, Acan screamed something at her and jerked the other woman's hands from his pants, but Margarita had zero to say to him. She made her way toward the front door, weaving through the wall-to-wall packed club. Just a few feet from the exit a solid wall of go-go pink stopped her.

"Sorry, babe," said Acan's sister, "but your five minutes are up." She placed her hands on Margarita's shoulders.

"Wait!" Acan's booming voice echoed over the loud music. "That wasn't me! I wasn't in control."

Everything around Margarita slowed to a glacial

crawl, and her shoulders heated up. The scene around her melted away, leaving only herself and this woman's hypnotic eyes. She then felt a strange energy burrowing deep inside her mind, searching for something.

In the background, Acan's voice thundered, "Forgetty, no! Get the fuck away from her!"

Margarita fell to the floor, the loud noise of the club, the lights, and voices of the crowd flooding her eyes and ears. She looked up and saw Acan holding his sister's wrists, the two facing each other. She looked terrified. He looked frozen in time.

"You stupid fuck! Why did you do that!" His sister released herself from Acan's grasp and grabbed him by the shoulders. "Why the fuck would you do that? Why! Godsdammit!" She shook him hard.

Acan stared blankly at his sister. "Do what? And who the hell are you?" His eyes moved around the room. "What is this place?"

Oh no.

CHAPTER TWENTY-TWO

Pacing the length of the small office on the second floor of the Randy Unicorn, the statuesque blonde mumbled profanities while Margarita sat on the edge of the stainless steel desk, thinking her hardest.

"Is there anything we can do or someone we can go to for help? Some God of Remembering or of Erasing Bad Mistakes or something?" Margarita asked. "What's your name again?"

The blonde rolled her turquoise eyes. "Call me Forgetty. Just like I told you the last five times."

"Sorry. I keep forgetting."

"Shocker. And no. There's no way to undo the damage. At the very moment he pushed you out of the way, I had my power focused on erasing him from your mind. I erased him from his mind instead. His memories—at least the important ones—are gone. For good."

"Where did they go?" Acan asked, sitting on the red sofa pushed against the wall, opposite the desk.

Margarita could hardly look at him. His vacant gaze seemed somewhere between awake and asleep and lost.

"Your sister took them away by accident," she said. "Now shush. We're trying to figure this out."

"This is bad. Very, very bad," Forgetty mumbled. "New Year's Eve is only a few weeks away. Dammit! Why did I listen to Cimil?"

"So what does this mean? What happens on New Year's Eve if he doesn't know who he is?" Margarita asked.

Forgetty pushed her fingertips through her hair and blew out a breath. "Just because he can't remember who he is doesn't mean he's powerless or any less of a danger."

"I need a martini. I'm not sure what that is, but I know I need one," Acan muttered.

Margarita cocked a brow. "Well, I guess some things can't be forgotten."

"You should go. I have no idea what he's capable of," said Forgetty.

"You're wrong. I know exactly what he's capable of."

"Really?" She crossed her very toned arms across her chest. "Did he tell you that he recently discovered he can decapitate anyone merely by snapping his fingers?"

Margarita covered her mouth with both hands. He had mentioned it, but she thought he'd been joking.

"I see you're catching on," said Forgetty.

"So what do we do?"

"You don't want him, right?"

Part of her had wanted him very much. Now, she just wanted to strangle him. Why did he have to ruin everything by acting like such a sleaze ball?

"No," Margarita replied. "Not after I saw him humping that woman on the dance floor. I can't sign up for that."

"Point taken."

"Humping is fun. I think I like humping," said Acan.

They both locked at him and barked, "Shut up!"

He frowned.

"Okay," Forgetty said, "let's assume that if you were not going to accept him, he would've gone forward with the mate mixer tomorrow night."

Margarita felt like she'd taken a blow to the stomach. "That's right. He had a mixer planned. He didn't ever believe we'd work out."

"Did you?"

"No. Not really. But it still kind of hurts."

"Get the hell over it. You said you don't want him, and that means he'll have to pick another."

The idea rubbed her wrong, but what could she do? "And?"

"And we're just going to have to help him."

"How?" Margarita asked.

"We will sort through the riffraff and pick a few women. With what we know about him, maybe we'll get lucky and find someone he likes."

"I can't play Cupid. I barely know him." The words felt like a strange lie. She felt like she'd known him her entire life, and thinking of him with someone else felt…well, it felt bad.

"Do you want him to find a mate or not?"

"Yes. Of course I do," Margarita replied. "I don't want people to die."

"I like mating. Mating rocks," Acan mumbled.

"So how are we supposed to convince any woman to want him—the real him. Or, at least, the him he will become once he sort of…"

"Gels back into his true drunken form?" asked Forgetty. "We're going to have to sell him. Convince them of how much fun he is. The king of the night and prince of the party."

Margarita swallowed hard. Forgetty was basically saying she'd have to pimp him out. "This is lame, and it makes no sense. Women have eyes and they'll see how un-fun he is."

"It will be fine. He's a god. All women want him. The trick will be convincing him to love one of them."

Margarita looked down at her feet. "You want us to trick him into falling in love?"

"You can't trick the heart. But you can persuade it. What other option do we have since you don't want him?"

Margarita shrugged. This all felt awful. She wanted to vomit. "I need to get home."

"Ah, yes. I almost forgot that you are but a weak

mortal who requires sleep."

Snotty much? "I have a daughter waiting for me, and I have a gym to run, which requires me to be there at five a.m."

"Fine." Blondie rolled her eyes. Or was her name Wanda? Margarita couldn't remember. "Can you drop him off at home?"

"I guess, but we came in his car," Margarita said.

"Take it and return it later—trust me, he won't miss it."

"What's a car?" he asked.

Diana—or was it Muffy? The woman walked over to Acan and squeezed his cheeks. "Don't you worry your pretty little head about this. You just get some rest."

The woman's cell phone beeped on the desk. She walked over and picked it up. "Fuck. Fuck. Fuck. Fuck!"

"What?" Margarita asked.

"I'm being summoned."

"By whom?"

"My brethren."

"And that's a bad thing because?" Margarita asked.

"Because it probably means they know I wiped Acan's memory and they think it's game over for finding him a mate—"

"What will they do?"

"They will want to imprison him or remove his

head."

"Jesus." Margarita winced.

"I do not like the sound of that," Acan said.

"Why would they do that?" Margarita couldn't understand these people.

"They can't let him flip and end up hurting people. Of course, they don't know him like I do, so they have not figured out that either plan won't work. Once he flips, we're all toast."

This did not sound good. Not at all.

"You need to take him, Margarita. Take him and run while I try to talk some sense into my brethren and sort this mate business out."

"What? No! I already told you that I have a daughter and a business to run."

"I will send someone to watch over your daughter, and I can have the Uchben take care of your gym."

"What's an Uchben? Wait. Never mind. Doesn't matter. I am not having strangers step in and take care of the two most important things in my life. Have your friends take care of Acan."

"I can't. Everyone I know will turn him in. They won't understand."

"But they'll be fine watching over my daughter and business?"

"Sure. I'll tell them it's a favor for a friend. They'll forget why they're doing it anyway. But they won't forget Acan or the fact that every immortal on the planet is looking for him."

"I can't. I just can't."

"Please, Margarita. This is important. Not just for him but for everyone. All I'm asking for is one day. Keep him hidden for one day while I try to fix this mess."

"And then what?"

"Come back here to the club tomorrow at midnight. I will have his perfect woman waiting and then he will be cured."

"This is crazy."

"Welcome to my world."

"I'll do it," said Margarita. "But on one condition. You don't ever touch me or my kid. No memory voodoo or whatever it is that you do."

The woman took a moment to think it over. "Deal. But you know that if you ever disclose our existence to anyone, you will be executed."

"Lovely." Margarita handed her house keys to…to…that lady. "My daughter's name is Jessica. We live at 1706 Colby Avenue, apartment D. Here's the address for my gym." Margarita handed the lady a business card from her little satchel purse. She turned to Acan. "Come on, big man, let's get going."

"Use the back door and don't let anyone see him," said Acan's sister.

"I'm sure no one will notice a seven-foot, shirtless man who looks like the mascot for the Thunder From Down Under."

"I do not know what flatulence has to do with

any of this, but I trust you'll figure out how to disguise my brother."

"Errr…okay." She took Acan's hand. "Let's go." She would call Jessica on the way to the car and let her know that a friend was coming to keep an eye on her. "Wait." She stopped halfway out the door. "Who's going to look after my daughter?"

"I will send Máax."

"Max?"

"No. Ma-ahx. You put the stress on the first *a*."

There was absolutely zero difference in the way she'd said it. "Okay. Whatever. And what does he do?"

"He's the God of Time Travel. He's married to Ashli, the Goddess of Love. They just had a baby, so he's great with kids."

Okeydokey. God of Time Travel. And Goddess of Love. "See you tomorrow night, then."

"Yup."

"What if this doesn't work?" Margarita asked. "What if you don't find him someone else?"

Something peculiar flickered in her eyes. "I'll think of something."

That didn't sit well with Margarita for some reason. This situation seemed too important to simply wing it. "See you tomorrow."

She took Acan's hand and led him down the back stairs that let them out into the alleyway behind the club. "You wait right here. Okay? I'm going around front to get your car. I'll only be a minute."

He blinked. "Okay. Wait here."

"That's right. Good god. Stay." She ran down the alley and around the corner to the main street in front of the club. She told the valet that Acan sent her for the car, and after a quick call to Acan's sister to confirm, he brought the vehicle.

But by the time Margarita got to the alley, Acan was gone.

"Oh crap." *I lost the God of Wine.*

This night just kept getting worse. First, there was learning about Acan's "flipping," then there was his shockingly disgusting behavior at the club, and then she was nearly assaulted by Whatsherface before Acan had his memory flushed down a dark hole. Now Margarita was supposed to be on the run to keep Acan from being imprisoned or killed by the most powerful—and psychotic—beings on the planet, only now she'd freaking lost him. In Los Angeles! The god could literally be anywhere. After asking the doorman at the club if he'd seen Acan again, which he hadn't, she'd hit every bar, sleazy strip club, and liquor store in a ten-block radius.

With the sun now coming up, Margarita pulled over in a small parking lot and rested her head on the steering wheel. "Oh God. What am I going to do?"

If she told Acan's sister she'd lost him, who knew what would happen? For sure, the woman wouldn't be happy and then she would probably wipe her memory. That couldn't be safe. Look what had happened to Acan.

There was a knock on the window. A tall policeman stood there, instructing her to roll down the window.

Dangit. Just what I needed.

She lowered the window. "Good morning, officer."

"Have you've been drinking, ma'am?"

"Drinking? No. I don't drink. I'm, uhh…I'm looking for my brother. He's not well and wandered off last night. You haven't seen him, by any chance? He's shirtless, seven feet tall, in really, really, really good shape?"

"No, ma'am. But if you think he's a threat to himself or others—"

"Heavens, no. No threat." *Unless you count the annihilation of millions of people.*

"Then I suggest you file a missing persons report after twenty-four hours have passed. In the meantime, this is private property. You'll have to go elsewhere to take a nap."

"Thank you, officer. I'll move my car." She started the engine and waved as they pulled out of the lot. *Okay, think, think, think.*

She took a deep breath. *I am the God of Wine. I have lost my memory. Where would I go? Where would*

I go? Her brain began to tingle and images started popping into her head. Waves. Sand. The surfers and wind.

Her eyes flew open. "He's at the beach!"

CHAPTER TWENTY-THREE

Acan stared at the waves, feeling lost. He wasn't certain why he was here—as in, on this planet—or why his memory had been taken from him. The only thing he knew for certain was that everything felt wrong. The streets weren't familiar. The people behaved strangely—rude, unfriendly, unwilling to help a tall shirtless man wandering around in the middle of the night. Whatever happened to hospitality? And what happened to his shirt?

He also knew what he'd heard from those two women back at that noisy gathering place. He was a threat. Dangerous. And he needed to find a new woman for some reason because the one he was supposed to be with—that Margarita woman—didn't want him.

Staring out at the ocean, he watched two men paddling through the waves on boards. *Strange. Everything feels so familiar, but at the same time it's not.*

"Acan! Acan!" a woman yelled, running toward him. It was the Margarita woman from earlier. The one who did not want him.

He sighed. He was in no mood for her or her insults.

She stopped right in front of him. "Where the hell have you been? Why did you just take off like that? Do you have any idea how worried I was?"

Still sitting, he looked up at her. "You're blocking my view."

"Your view?" she seethed. "Your freaking view?"

"Yes. My view. Now move."

"I've been driving around for hours looking for you. I went into the most disgusting, herpes-infested dive bars known to man. I had my ass grabbed at least ten times and had a twenty shoved down the front of my sweater. I stepped in five urine puddles, running from one liquor store to the next. And if it weren't for the fact that I'm in such great shape and can run fast, I would've been mugged! Twice!"

"You risked your life to find me?"

"Yes!"

"Why? Were you not trying to get rid of me?"

"What are you talking about?" she asked, still winded from running.

"You said you did not want me. That I had betrayed you with another woman."

Margarita exhaled. "This has got to be the weirdest date ever." She turned and sat next to him in the sand. "You didn't betray me. Not exactly."

"Then why are you attempting to find another mate for me?"

"It's complicated."

"I have the feeling that I am familiar with complicated."

"Okay. Well, when I first met you—in a hotel elevator—you weren't wearing any pants, and you were three sheets to the wind. You then proceeded to tell me I had a nice ass and tits."

He had? "Why would I walk around without pants? Or treat you in such an unchivalrous manner?"

She shrugged. "You got me. But it only gets worse. You called me old, and then I challenged you to a little fitness competition, so the next day you showed up at my gym, naked. With a giant boner."

"I do not believe you. I am a god. I would never behave with such indecency."

"From what I've seen, you've been doing it for a long time."

"So I'm basically a disgusting, drunk slob who demeans women."

"Well, you do have your good side. I mean, you seem to enjoy making people feel good and let loose. But yeah, you're kind of a pig."

"So this is why you want nothing to do with me."

"You and I made a deal last night. I would show you how it would be to live my life and you would show me yours. If at the end of the night we determined we weren't compatible, then we'd go our separate ways. And after seeing you jam your…"

She glanced toward his groin. "Your aroused penis against some woman's ass in front of six hundred people while we were on a date, I think I can safely say that I am not the woman for you."

He could not blame her. He sounded like a complete buffoon. "I am sorry, Margarita, for causing you any distress. I cannot claim to understand it. Especially when I can feel how strong the connection is between us."

"It is sad because I feel it, too. It led me right here."

The sunlight shining behind them illuminated her golden hair. And now, with more light, he could see the flecks of gold in her green eyes. "You are lovely, Margarita."

Her cheeks turned pink. "Thanks. You're not so bad yourself."

He wanted to kiss her. He wanted to hold her. Why had he fucked things up with her?

"Perhaps this is fate intervening."

"Meaning?" she asked.

"If the man I used to be wasn't good enough for you, perhaps this new man will be."

She stared at him for a very long moment. He could feel the conflict wafting from her soul. "Won't you just go back to your old ways eventually?"

He gave it some thought. "For you, I would make a vow to never return to my old ways."

She laughed, but stopped once she noticed the

stern look on his face.

"You're serious," she said. "No more partying? No more nightclubs and mayhem?"

"I may have lost my memory, but I believe in fate, Margarita. And right now, feeling how strong our link is, I wonder if this isn't a second chance. Immortals wait their entire existence to find the one person in the world who is destined for them." He leaned forward and placed a gentle kiss on her soft lips, but she didn't reciprocate.

"Sorry. I just need to think about it." She brushed a few loose strands of golden hair from her eyes.

"Yes, I imagine you must be tired after searching all night for me. My apologies."

"Let's just find a place to hide out for the day—a hotel or something."

He gave her a look, unable to block the images in his head.

"I need to sleep."

"Ah, yes. Then we will find somewhere safe."

Margarita immediately felt like something wasn't right, and she wasn't talking about the fact that Acan had lost his memory or was acting like a different person—errr…god. *Even though he is a different god.* Still the same incredibly stunning man with that stunning body and those hypnotic, jewel-colored eyes, but when he kissed her, it felt like kissing a cold fish. The spark was gone. Completely. No tingles in her toes, no twirly-birds in her stomach, no sinful aches in her core. Nothing.

I must be tired, she thought, driving them up the coast to a little motel she'd stayed at once when Jessica was five. Back then there was no such thing as vacation money, so a short one-night getaway at a beachside dive motel was the best vacation she could afford.

Margarita smiled, thinking about how tough things were back then, but those were happy times. It was the moment in Margarita's life where her faith became her constant companion. She knew that as long as she had her freedom and health, the future was wide open. For both of them. Of course, giving up was never an option. Not when you had a child to care for and you'd sacrificed everything— your family, community, and home—for the hope of a better, more fulfilling life.

She glanced at Acan, who seemed transfixed by the scenery.

"Does any of this seem familiar?" she asked, her eyes fixed on the curvy road.

"Yes. Strangely, all of it. I simply do not have any memories attached to anything."

"I can't imagine how hard this must be."

"I'm quite fine. I assure you," he said. "My only concern at the moment is you."

"Why me?"

"I don't exactly know."

"That sounds ominous."

"Nothing ominous about it. I want you to be happy. I want you to be cared for and never to worry. I want you to live in complete comfort and to only spend your time on that which gives you pleasure or happiness."

Damn. Where have you been all my life? "You don't even know me, but you feel all that?"

"Yes. I suppose it's our bond, but I do."

She didn't know how to respond. It was strange dealing with this third version of Acan.

"You know, it's funny. If you'd asked me a few days ago to describe my perfect man, I probably would've described you."

"So you are pleased by how fate has handed you what you've always wanted. That is, if you decide to take me."

It all felt too easy. Like a dream or like something she didn't deserve. "I think I'm used to working incredibly hard for anything I have."

"Ah. So you feel sacrifice is always required in order to gain something."

"Yeah. I guess so."

"And just why is that?"

She glanced at him only briefly. The two-lane road, skirting along jagged cliffs overlooking the ocean, was notorious for its sharp turns and falling rocks. "I've never actually told anyone this—not ever. Not even Jessica knows."

"Go on."

"I was raised Amish. My real name is Margaret Miller."

"Amish?" He chuckled.

"Hey, you're a god. You can't laugh at stuff like that."

"I assure you that I laugh only because you are so modern. Independent, strong minded, and very sexy, I might add. Not that Amish women cannot be any of those things, but their way of life is communal. You are a free spirit if I've ever seen one."

"God, it's so strange how well you understand me."

"Yet it is not enough."

So he knew. *Of course he does.* If she could sense where he was physically, he could surely tap into her emotional frequency. *This is all so strange.*

"I don't know how to explain it," she said. "When you were horribly drunk, you made me mad. I just wanted to strangle you. And then, when you weren't, I found you…kind of interesting. And also irresistibly sexy."

"You fucked me, didn't you?"

How embarrassing. It felt like she was telling a stranger. "Yes and no. I mean, we started but didn't finish. You needed that jade stuff."

"I remember what that is."

"Well, you weren't drunk both times—at least, you didn't seem like it—but you didn't look like you do now—perfect from head to toe—yet I didn't seem to care."

"So there was something about me that attracted you beyond my physical appearance."

"Yes, and now you're calm and acting mature and you look like…" Her eyes quickly flashed over his body. "Like a god. But it's not you."

"I see."

She hated to hurt his feelings, but honesty seemed like the only option. "I just wonder what would've happened if you'd just made a different choice last night. Because there was this moment, right before your sister zapped you and before I saw you giving an anal massage to that woman, where I believed we were going to work out. I saw a future—or really, I felt it. In my heart. And then, just like that, it all went away."

"It is a shame I would make such a foolish mistake. It makes me wonder what I was thinking."

"I don't know, because you weren't drinking. If you had been, all that—" she waved her right hand over his perfect body "—would've gone away."

"Maybe I hit my head."

"Maybe you were possessed by a rotten, womanizing asshole with an anal fetish. Wait." Something sparked in her mind. "Ohmygod. That's it. It has to be."

"What?"

"You told me that this…this thing that's happening to you causes you to become evil."

"I will have to take your word for it. I do not remember, nor do I feel evil."

"You were screaming at me in the club the moment your sister grabbed me. You said you weren't in control or something like that! You said you weren't you. You were trying to tell me and…" Margarita's eyes filled with tears. It all made so much sense now. He hadn't been trying to hurt her. He'd "flipped," as they called it.

"This is all my fault." She wiped the moisture from under her eyes. "If I'd just stopped for a second or told you sooner that I wanted to try to make us work, none of this would've happened." Why had she been so blind? "Dammit," she whispered. "Mike is still in my head, making me think that men are only going to hurt me."

"Mike? Who is Mike?"

"My ex. Never mind. He's not important." She looked at Acan, her eyes so watery she could barely see. "I fucked it up, Acan. I should've known there was something wrong with you. I'm so sorry. I fucked it—"

Acan's gaze darted to the road. "Watch out!" He reached for the steering wheel, but the moment she turned her head, all she saw were headlights and the grill of a very large truck.

∾ ᭥

Acan blacked out for several moments from the

impact of the car hitting the jagged rocks below after the car had veered off the cliff. How much time passed before his human shell regained consciousness, he didn't know, but the frigid ocean water on his face woke him from one nightmare into the horrific moment. Real.

"Margarita," he coughed out her name along with the salt water in his nose and lungs. His eyes, covered in a veil of blood, tried to focus but couldn't. Somewhere, in the back of his mind, he heard voices. Humans trying to extract them from the damaged vehicle.

"You can't move them. They might have broken necks or backs," said one man.

"They'll drown or freeze if we leave them inside."

A set of violent waves crashed into Acan's face through the shattered windshield. He gasped for air, trying to break free, but something held him in place. The two men coughed and grunted and that was when Acan realized the car was partially submerged in the water. "Margarita," he mumbled. "Get her out."

The water drained from the car with the retreat of the violent wave. Margarita lay with her head to one side, blood pouring from multiple cuts in her face. Her door flew open, and one of the men—a man in a wetsuit—dragged her out. Someone on Acan's side pulled him away from the vehicle.

Slowly, his faculties returned, and he got to his

feet with the aid of the surfer who'd come to rescue him. "Margarita. Where is she?"

"Keep going, man. We need to get you away from the waves." They stumbled through rocks and rough water, up onto a narrow strip of sand. On the cliff above, people gathered to watch.

"Just hang on, man. The paramedics are coming," said the man who held him up.

Acan's eyes focused ahead, and there, lying on the beach, was the other man, straddling Margarita. He held his palms over her heart, pumping her chest.

"No. No. No." Acan stumbled toward her, ignoring every broken bone in his body. "Margarita!" When he got to her, all he saw was her pale face and blue lips. He dropped to his knees and took her cold hand. "Margarita? Please don't go. Come back. Come back."

As if in a nightmare of his own making, Acan watched the man attempting to put life back into her body. But it was no use. She was gone.

CHAPTER TWENTY-FOUR

Acan wasn't sure how he'd gotten there, but he found himself standing inside the large empty building where he'd been with Margarita last night. For a man with so few memories to know that, for as long as he lived, there would be no day worse than this said a lot.

He looked down at his clothes covered in blood and damp with seawater. The only thing he could think about was scrubbing every inch of his soul clean from the pain inhabiting his body.

"Belch! What the hell are you doing here?" His sister stomped toward him. "And what the hell happened to your—"

"She's dead," he muttered, trying with everything he had not to cry. It didn't work. "She's fucking dead. Why the fuck is she dead?"

"Who? Who's dead?" His sister grabbed his hands.

"The car went over the cliff, and Margarita just…" He sobbed, covering his face. "We hit the rocks."

"Oh fuck. Please tell me you're joking."

"No." He placed his hands over his chest. "I can't breathe." He couldn't think or make sense of his existence.

"Ohmygods." His sister wrapped her arms around him. "I'm so, so sorry."

He pushed her away.

"Make me forget again," he yelled, pointing his finger in her face. "Erase her from my mind."

"Acan," she whispered, "I can't. It's not right. You need to stop and mourn and try to make sense of this. Otherwise it will only haunt—"

"Fuck you! This is all your fault. I should remove your head for this, you fucking fool."

Acan felt the bitter darkness crawling inside him, spreading like a virus. He'd already felt indifferent to everything, but for a few short hours, he'd had her. Margarita. Now there was no reason left to fight the wickedness threatening to consume him.

"Stop right there, brother." Forgetty drew a breath. "You don't mean that, and you vowed never to hurt me again. So while I can forgive you once for taking my head, a second time would seal your fate. Your love for me, your sister, should be sufficient to overcome anything this cruel world can throw at you. If it's not, then I can only question your loyalty."

Acan felt the darkness retreating but only temporarily. He looked down at his feet. "I'm going to have to leave. I'm not safe to be around."

"Where will you go, Acan?" she hissed. "New Year's Eve is only a few weeks away and there isn't a corner on this planet or in our world safe from you."

He blinked. "Then you will have to kill me."

"With what purpose? You'll only come right back, evil, destructive. And may I remind you that in your human form, you're less harmful. If you die, you'll be able to return to our realm and your powers will only be stronger."

Godsdammit, she was right. But he simply didn't care. Let the world sink into abyss. All he wanted was Margarita, and she was dead.

"What purpose is there of being a god if I cannot pick and choose who lives or dies, or if I cannot save my mate? Why the fuck does any of this matter?" He could not stop the tears flowing just like he could not stop his anger.

"I don't know, Acan. I really don't. But it is not our place to ask why. We are here simply to live and help them." She pointed to her side, to no one and everyone all at the same time. "And if we are lucky, someone out there will see something great in us and love us and help us not go insane while we live for eternity."

"I found her. And now she is gone." The connection he'd felt didn't lie. She had been the one.

"You might find another if you give it time. But you will never know if you allow this horrible tragedy to consume you. Please, if you give up,

Acan, the path will lead to a very dark place for everyone."

Acan stared at his sister, struggling to be the man, the god she needed him to be. In a time like this, with so little left to cling to, he found it impossible. He just wanted Margarita back. It was strange to feel so much for someone he had so few memories of. But he did. And now he just wanted his pain to end.

"I'm sorry, sister. But if I help this world continue, it only means I will have to endure an eternity of suffering. I prefer to flip and let it all end."

"No. You can't do that."

"This god is all out of compassion."

The Goddess of Forgetfulness slid her cell from her pocket, ready to call the emergency mailbox that would summon her brethren. They had to be told. But in the back of her mind, she also knew it would do little good. If Acan flipped, there was no way to stop him from hurting millions of people. Not prison. Not taking away his mortal shell. They might minimize some damage if he were incapacitated, but the spike in his powers on New Year's wasn't something he controlled. That was the issue.

Godsdammit. Why did I listen to Cimil? Had Forgetty kept her hands to herself and not tried to wipe Margarita's mind, none of this would've happened. Had Cimil known the outcome?

Of course she did. She always knew. But why would she want this to happen? This of all things?

Why? Why? She replayed the moment where it all went so terribly wrong. She'd spoken to Margarita near the bathroom and convinced her to give Acan the chance he deserved. Margarita ran out to the dance floor, looking for Acan, and found him dirty dancing with some woman. From there, it all went south.

Forgetty toggled through her contacts and dialed the only number she could ever call in a case like this. "Hi, it's me. There's been an accident— Acan's mate is dead. I'm going to need you to break the law and deliver a letter."

She listened.

"Yes, *that* law. Yes, I know what's at risk, but you owe me, and you know I will cover your tracks."

She listened again.

"Thank you." She ended the call and went up to the office on the second floor, getting a piece of paper and a pen from the drawer.

She sat down at the desk and thought very carefully about what she would say.

Dear Margarita...

CHAPTER TWENTY-FIVE

Margarita lined up for the bathroom, wondering what the hell she was doing at this stupid unicorn club on a date with a god. This wasn't going to work out. It couldn't. She and Acan were two different people—or beings or whatever—and their worlds didn't mesh.

"You must be her," said a female voice from behind her.

Margarita turned to find a statuesque blonde wearing a pink minidress, with long legs, creamy skin, and iridescent turquoise eyes.

"Oh shit." Margarita covered her mouth. "Yo-won-o-dem!"

The blonde raised a brow. "I speak one hundred and seventy-seven languages, but sadly mumble is not one of them."

Margarita dropped her hand. "Sorry. It's just…" She leaned in. "You're one of them, aren't you?" The eyes were exactly like Acan's.

"Very astute. I am the Goddess of Forgetfulness, Belch's sister."

Acan's sister and she continued talking about how her brother behaved like two different men, but that he still had a lot of maturing to do. It seriously gave Margarita second thoughts about their future. Perhaps all that was required to make them work was a little patience and an open mind.

Then the goddess told her she had two minutes to make a choice or face getting a memory whammy.

Margarita gasped. "You're serious, aren't you?"

"As a heart attack," said Acan's sister.

Shit. Margarita turned and sprinted back toward Acan's bar, finding it completely empty save the line of patient customers on the other side. *Oh no. Oh no. Where is he?* Margarita swiveled on her heel, her eyes searching frantically. Nothing.

"Hi there." A tall, well-built man, with long honey brown hair and the same brilliant turquoise eyes as Acan, stepped out of the crowd and stood in front of her. He had a fierceness in his gaze that immediately set off alarm bells.

She took a step back. "Who are you?"

"My name is Máax, and I want you to listen very carefully, Margarita. You are to read this letter quickly, turn around, and head straight for the front door." He shoved a folded-up piece of paper at her.

"I don't understa—"

"Hurry, woman. Time is running out. Take it."

She grabbed the thing from his hand.

"Don't think. Just do. Jessica needs you," he

said.

Her heart sank to her shaking knees. What was happening? She unfolded the letter and quickly scanned the handwritten note, the flashing lights of the club making it difficult to read, but not impossible.

What the hell? She looked up and the man was gone. She spun on her heel, but there was no sign of him. She stood there for a moment, feeling her stomach knot into a ball of terror. She then turned and sprinted for the front door, pushing people out of her way.

Just a few feet from the exit a solid wall of go-go pink stopped her.

"Sorry, babe," said Acan's sister, "but your five minutes are up.' She reached for Margarita's shoulders, but Margarita stepped away.

"Back the fuck off." She shoved the note at her. "And get the *hell* out of my way."

The woman's eyes darted from Margarita's face to the note and back again. "What is that?"

"A warning. From you." Margarita dropped the note at the woman's feet, stepped around her, and left the club.

∾ ∾

The next morning, Acan came to on the floor of his new living room, with a train wreck inside his pounding skull.

"Gods fuck me." He sat up, pressing his palms to the sides of his head, and noticed two warm bodies next to him. A brunette and a blonde. Naked. All three of them.

"What the...?" He jostled the brunette's shoulder. "Who are you? What are you doing in my house? Where the fuck is Margarita?"

The woman rolled the other way, giving him her back—or butt cheeks. "Who's Margarita?" she mumbled.

"She is my...mate." He whispered that last word, feeling an ache in his heart as he recalled Margarita standing behind the bar with him last night. She'd just served a drink to a woman with pink braids, and there was this moment when he looked at Margarita, thinking, *This could work between us. This could really work.* But then he'd explained to her that he could not stop being the party god, and the hope and joy vanished from her eyes. How could she have not understood that? Why couldn't she simply accept him as he was and let their relationship take its natural course? Either way, he knew she was going to end the night walking away. From him. From them. She then made an excuse to go to the bathroom. From there, it was all a blank.

He glanced over at the two sleeping women and then down at his stomach. Flat. Perfect. *So I did not drink, but I cannot remember anything? Oh hell.* He must've flipped last night. Losing Margarita had set him off. *This can't be good.*

Panicked, he shook the brunette. "Hey. What happened last night? Did we fuck?"

No response.

He tweaked her bare butt cheek.

"Ow!" She opened her brown eyes.

"What did we do last night?"

The woman scrubbed her face with her hands. "You made us drinks and we watched *Love Boat* reruns. You said it was some special kind of sleepover."

"So we didn't have sex?" he asked.

"No."

He felt instant relief, though he wasn't exactly sure why. That being said, "Then why are we naked?"

The woman pointed to the other side of the room, where a Twister mat lay spread across the floor.

So I turned evil, made them watch Love Boat *reruns, and we played naked Twister.* "Jesus, I'm becoming Cimil." *Gods, I hope that is the worst of last evening.*

Fear struck him hard. The last time he'd blacked out, he'd succumbed to the evil inside him and then decapitated his brothers and sisters.

He quickly dialed Forgetty, but it went to voicemail. *Fuck. What happened last night?*

He grabbed his car keys and drove straight for the club. One hour later he arrived and parked in the back alley. He ran inside to find Forgetty behind his bar, cleaning up.

"Oh, thank gods." He let out a sigh. "Why the fuck weren't you answering your phone?"

She looked at him only for a moment. "Sorry. Must've left it on vibrate."

"No. It's fine. I just thought I'd maybe hurt you again or something." He rubbed his brow. "I blacked out again last night."

"Yeah. I know."

"But I didn't remove anyone's heads or anything, correct?"

"Nope. You were just a rude bastard, which is why I kicked you out," she said, her voice indifferent.

"And Margarita?"

"She, uhhh…left." Forgetty began drying off the clean glasses and putting them under the counter.

"But she's all right?"

"Alive and kicking," Forgetty said.

"So it's over, then. She has rejected me."

"I honestly don't know, Acan." She didn't sound happy. Was she worried that he would give up?

"Sister, do not concern yourself. I am going through with the party tonight. I will find a woman. I am sure of it."

Forgetty smiled at him, but her usual spark of light was missing from her eyes. "I hope you do, brother."

"Is something the matter?"

"I have to take a break for a while. I'm leaving town in a few hours."

"You are going on vacation?"

"Yes. A vacation."

"Now? Why now? I understood you were to assist me this evening at the mixer."

"You'll be fine without me. We have five bartenders lined up, and I pulled the DJ from our other club in San Diego."

Her odd behavior did not sit well with him. "Are you certain that nothing has happened?"

"Yup. Hunky dory. I just need a few days off to decompress. I might go visit a few old friends."

Something was definitely bothering her, because she would never leave at such a difficult time. Especially when New Year's was so close. That said, if she did not want to discuss it, he would not push. She had her reasons to keep to herself.

"Very well, enjoy your rest. I will see you when you come back?"

She shrugged. "Sure."

He sensed she was lying, but he had to let it go. He had to focus on tonight, on clearing his heart and mind of Margarita. It wasn't what he wanted, but she'd rejected him last night, and his duty was to his brethren and to the people who would be harmed if he didn't halt his transformation. He had no choice but to move on. It was the right thing to do. The only thing to do.

"See you later, sister." He turned to head back out to his car.

"Brother?"

"Yes?"

"Don't forget to wear pants tonight."

He glanced down. *Dammit. Again?*

He smiled awkwardly. "I will not forget. But the shirt is staying off. Can't let these abs go to waste. The fate of the world lies in the balance."

Forgetty bobbed her head. "Guess it can't hurt. Break a leg."

"Thank you." He got to his car, feeling like things were off. Very, very off. But why?

It is something I will have to figure out later. Because tonight, he and his rock-hard abs needed to attract the perfect woman. *Yes, we will save the world.* He patted his stomach.

CHAPTER TWENTY-SIX

Since returning from the club last night, Margarita had not been able to stop crying and checking on Jessica, who slept in her room. There was no doubt in Margarita's mind that the letter had been real and, for some reason, she'd been given another chance by that god.

Why? It didn't matter. She'd cheated death. *Death.* And it terrified her. It wasn't the way life worked. We were supposed to live the lives given to us, no matter how long or short. Still, she couldn't help but feel grateful to get this second chance to watch her daughter grow up. And as of today, she would make every moment count.

Finally, around seven in the morning, Margarita decided it was time to make a few changes in her life, starting by turning over a new leaf with her daughter.

She went into Jessica's bedroom, hugging a box of tissues. "Jess? Honey? Wake up. We need to talk."

Jessica opened her groggy green eyes. "What's

wrong?"

"Everything. Everything and nothing."

"I don't understand."

"Neither do I, but I'm going to tell you a story…"

An hour later, Jessica sat with her back up against her headboard, her sweet little face pale and her eyes filled with confusion. "So you're Amish. And you left my father because he hit you, not because you didn't love each other enough."

"I only lied to protect you, Jessica. I wanted you to have an easier life, but now I realize I robbed you of the chance to really know me and why I am the way I am."

"I always wondered why you never dated."

"Part of me feels like, and will always feel like, the people I love will just turn their backs on me. But that's what you need to know about me, Jessica. I will never turn my back on you. I will always be there to cheer for you no matter what you choose to do in life. And even when you push back and act like an insensitive teenager, I will never make you feel unloved. I am here for you, and going forward, I will make more time for us. Less time at the gym, less worrying, less work."

"What about your plans to franchise and make more money?"

Margarita didn't want to tell Jessica that she was supposed to have died, and by some miracle, a deity came out of nowhere and delivered a letter that changed her fate. That was the sort of story that could shake a child's world.

I myself still don't understand what happened. She only knew that she was alive.

Margarita smiled. "Some things are more important than money."

Jessica smiled back. "So does this mean you're finally going to start dating again?"

"God, no. I think I'd like to focus on us a little more. There'll be time for dating once you're off to college."

"What about that guy from last night? He seemed nice. So tall...and wow. So tall."

Margarita frowned. She didn't like her daughter appreciating Acan's, errr...tallness or anything else.

"He is nice. In a way. But I don't think we're meant to be. His, umm...work takes up a lot of his time. And he loves what he does, so I couldn't and wouldn't expect him to change just for me."

"That's too bad. Because...wow. He was so," Jessica sighed and shook her head appreciatively, "tall."

"Yep. Tall. Among many, many other things." *Such as he's hung like a stallion and kisses like the God of Panty Melting.* Even right now, just thinking about it made her all toasty down there. *And changing subjects...* "Hey, want to go for a jog? We can stop for pancakes at the place around the corner on the way back."

"Sure." Jessica clapped. "Let me get dressed.

Oh, and before I forget, my friend Kara is having a birthday movie thing at her house tonight. Her parents will be there. Can I go?"

"Just be home by nine. It's a school night. Now, go get dressed. It's a beautiful day outside."

Margarita and Jessica had a fantastic day. Probably more fantastic for Margarita simply because she now knew how much she had to be grateful for. Being alive. Being there to watch her daughter grow and find love and maybe have her own children someday.

All it had cost her was Acan. But there was little choice but to put him out of her head and move on. She'd escaped with her life and that was what mattered. *That and my daughter obeying my damned rules.*

Five past ten, Jessica still hadn't come home. "Dammit, Jess." Margarita had sent several texts that Jess decided to ignore. *You would think that after this morning, Jessica would change her damned ways.*

But what could Margarita expect? Things were not going to change overnight, and her daughter was still a teenager.

Margarita called Kara, and when she didn't answer, there was no choice but to get in the damned car and retrieve her daughter. Why did Jessica insist on making things so much harder than they had to be?

Wearing black yoga pants and a T-shirt, Margarita slipped on her running shoes, grabbed her purse and keys, and headed for Kara's house only to arrive ten minutes later and find Kara's mother at a complete loss for words. "I'm so sorry, but Jessica isn't here. The party ended at nine."

"What? Where did she go?" The rage pumped in Margarita's veins.

"Come in. We'll ask Kara." Kara's mother, a full-figured woman with short dark hair, disappeared down the hallway of their small ranch-style home. After a few minutes, she returned to their living room with Kara in tow.

"Tell her! Tell her right now, Kara, or so help me you will be grounded for six months!" said her mother.

"Mom, I don't know." Kara's dark hair fell over her eyes as she looked at the ground.

She was lying.

"Kara, honey," said Margarita. "I don't know how to explain this to you in a way you'll fully understand, but I am going through a rough time right now. And maybe Jessica is fine, and maybe she doesn't need me, but I need her. I need to know she's okay. Can you understand that?"

Kara grumbled under her breath. "She Ubered to some club with Ophelia."

"A club? What's the name?" Margarita asked.

"I don't remember. It's some big party for this billionaire guy who's looking for a date."

Oh hell no. "Is it called the Randy Unicorn?"

"Yeah. That's the place."

Shit. Shit. Shit. Why would Jessica go there?

"Thanks." Margarita sprinted for her car.

CHAPTER TWENTY-SEVEN

Acan could not believe how many men had shown up for this evening's event. *Dammit, Jill!* There were perhaps five percent women and ninety-five percent men. Gay men. Very nice, but very gay.

"I'm sorry," Jill had said right before they'd opened the doors. "How was I supposed to know I shouldn't put rainbows and an animal with a big phallic symbol on its head all over the ads?"

"Did you at least say the word *wife* in these ads?"

"I said *partner* because I didn't want to frighten off any women who might not be ready for marriage but might be okay with a committed relationship." Jill had begun to cry, which resulted in his feeling sorry for her and offering another raise.

With that, Jill picked herself up and continued the task of coordinating the evening—organizing the staff, greeting guests, and discreetly handing out VIP passes to the second floor, where Acan would get a chance to serve the selected women a cocktail. He would use his special gift to determine if a potential mate was here tonight. He knew that any woman worth her salt would order her perfect cocktail for the occasion. So few actually did. They ordered something safe, something familiar, or they ordered "their drink," which was code for "I don't know how to color outside the lines. Ever." Any potential mate of his would order her ideal beverage for this very particular occasion, demonstrating a respect for the sacred, time-honored tradition of getting intoxicated. *That will be my sign.*

As the staff below got the evening going, and Jill handed out passes to women who might fit his criteria—love to party, hot, hot, love to party—the women began filing upstairs one by one, each female a bigger disappointment than the last.

"I'll have a light beer," said a perky blonde. "Oh. Nice abs. Work out a lot?"

"No. Here's your 'beer.' Now you may leave." He waved the woman—an unnaturally skinny thing, who looked like she survived exclusively on kale chips—to the exit.

She huffed and marched toward the stairway leading back down to the main floor.

Light beer, he scoffed. *It is an insult to beer. They should call it that which is left over when beer takes a hot piss on an effervescent snowman and crawls into a can to die.*

"Next!" he yelled.

The following women weren't much better. Miss Vodka Tonic ordered a wine spritzer. *Wrong!*

Wine Spritzer lady ordered a dirty martini. *Wrong!* Kalua and Cream gal asked for champagne. *Sacrilege! What the hell is the matter with you, woman!* It made him sick, seeing all of this incorrect drink pairing.

After the thirty-fifth woman, Acan felt completely discouraged. *Margarita was right. This isn't going to work. It can't.* The Universe wasn't going to help him out and have the perfect woman magically walk into his club. She'd already given him a mate. But sadly, Margarita didn't want to give her heart to him and nothing in this world could force her. Just like he couldn't force himself to look at any of these women no matter how beautiful. *What the hell am I going to do? I'm screwed.*

Suddenly, his chest began to tighten and his legs turned ice-cold. He felt like someone had pulled the stopper from his awesome bathtub filled with awesome Acan light.

Fuck. Not now. No, no, no. He was flipping again. But this time he felt the powerful change coming on, sweeping through him like fire ants devouring everything in their path. He wouldn't come back after this. He would stay evil.

Fuck! Dammit. No! He planted his hands on the bar, bowing his back. A frigid fire raged through his head, and his heart collapsed in on itself. He didn't want this. He didn't want to change. More importantly he didn't want to hurt anyone.

He reached to his side, under the counter, for

the large chef's knife he kept for slicing limes. He had to take himself out. A temporary solution, but what if he hurt the people here tonight? His happy unicorn-loving gays, the handful of women looking for love—or free drinks—same thing—and his staff.

He gripped the knife's handle, trying to think. If he killed himself, he might return to this realm, but what if he did not? What if he stayed in the realm of the gods, where his reach into this world wasn't limited by his human shell?

Acan gritted his teeth, the icy malevolent energy burrowing through him. He couldn't win. Either way, he would hurt millions. *Fuck you, Universe*, he grunted in his head. *I never wanted to be a god. I never asked for this role. But I've tried my best, and this is the thanks I get? You can just bite me.*

"Hi," said a perky little voice. "Can I have a Sugar Free Red Bull with Cherry Sprite and a twist of lime?"

Acan looked up at the young blonde wearing too much makeup. He opened his mouth to tell her to run, but when his eyes met hers—*Green. So, so green*—he noticed something amazing.

"That's…that's…your perfect drink." He couldn't believe it.

"Really?" She shrugged. "I've never tried it before. Just sounded good, yanno?"

He gazed in wonderment at her full lips, oval face, golden hair, and emerald green eyes, feeling an instant connection. Her energy washed over him from across the counter like a brilliant light filling a dark room, sending the creatures of the night scurrying for cover. The ice in his veins began to melt. His heart swelled. His light began pulsing, pushing back the evil.

He blinked at the young woman. "Do-do I know you?" he said in a scratchy voice.

"Jessica!" a woman bellowed across the room from the direction of the bouncer at the doorway.

Acan's eyes focused on the tomato red face of…"Margarita?"

"You!" She pointed at him, pushing past the bouncer. "You get away from my daughter."

Her daughter? He looked at the face underneath the five pounds of makeup. She was indeed Jessica, Margarita's sixteen-year-old daughter.

He stepped back from the bar, thoroughly confused.

"Mom, what are you doing here?" Jessica barked.

"What am *I* doing here? What am *I* doing here? If you were smaller, I would spank the crap out of you. Okay, I'd also have to believe in spanking, but if I did and you were twenty pounds lighter, I would give you a paddle to remember."

Acan couldn't help but smile. He was so happy to see Margarita.

"You think this is funny, Mr. God of Wine? I will send your nut sack flying into the next galaxy if you ever—and I mean ever!—look at my daughter like that again."

"Mom! You're totally embarrassing me," Jessica whined.

"You ain't seen nothing yet. Where the hell is Ophelia?" Margarita demanded.

Jessica shrugged. "I dunno. Dancing downstairs somewhere."

"You go find her and meet me at the front door while I have words with Mr. Party Pants here."

Jessica scurried off, and Margarita turned the full force of her rage toward him. "How could you?"

He held up his hands. "I couldn't. I didn't." Nevertheless, he couldn't deny that seeing Jessica had saved him.

"I saw the way you were looking at her, Acan. Don't fucking fuck with me."

Wow, such language. Very hot. "I was only looking at her like that because I felt something powerful between us."

Margarita's green eyes flared. "She's sixteen!"

"No. It's not like that. I-I feel like she's special. I feel drawn to her."

"Wow. Just wow. You are the biggest prick I've ever—"

"I mean." He shut his eyes. "I mean, I believe that whatever connection I have with you connects to her, too. In a purely platonic sense. But, Margarita, *you* are the one. There can't be another. I see that now."

"No. No! You stay away from us. I will not have

our lives taken by some evil, murdering monster."

"Monster?" Had she seen him flip last night?

"Yes, a monst—never mind!" She turned and headed for the stairs

He ran around the bar and stopped her before she got there. "Wait. Why did you run out last night?"

"It doesn't matter. Because I'm done. Enjoy your party."

"Margarita, this is important," he growled. "Because there will not be another for me, not ever, and everything is on the line."

"I told you I'm done. Now let me leave," she growled.

"I know you feel it too, Margarita. I know you feel the strong connection, and it's only becoming stronger. Seeing Jessica just now made me realize that."

"I can't…do this. Not with you." Her eyes filled with tears.

"Why?"

"I got a warning last night, Acan. And I don't know if it was God looking out for me or fate or just dumb luck, but I know that I didn't leave behind my entire Amish family, fight every day for a better life for my daughter, and bust my butt to make this world a healthier place only to have my life snuffed out in an instant by you."

"By me? I would never—wait. You're Amish?" And why did he feel like they'd already spoken about this?

She shot him a look.

"Sorry, it is simply that you are so modern—entrepreneur, single mom, and that body? So hot."

She continued glaring.

"Not the time?" he said sheepishly. "All right. Tell me about the warning."

"Some guy stopped me on the way back from the bathroom last night and handed me a note."

"What guy?"

"I can't remember his name—he was tall like you. Same color eyes. He handed me a note signed by your sister that said I died—or would die—or something like that if I didn't stay away from you. It told me to run like hell and not to question or let your weird sister touch me. I didn't understand."

Forgetty had been trying to wipe Margarita's memory? Without his approval?

Acan's mind did several loop-ti-loops. "The man who gave you the note, his name wouldn't happen to be Máax, would it?"

"Yes. That was the guy."

"Where's the note?" he asked.

"I shoved it at your sister—the DJ."

This had to be why Forgetty was so upset this morning. Perhaps she'd read the note and felt leaving town would avoid a repeat of whatever happened? Sadly, there wasn't enough information to know for sure.

"I believe," he said, "that something went wrong

last night. Very, very wrong."

"I don't understand."

"Máax is my brother, the God of Time Travel, which he's technically not permitted to do without a majority vote by the gods and only for matters of extreme apocalyptic-scale emergencies, which means he risked everything to come find you."

Margarita's face contorted. "I'm sorry, but did you say time travel?"

"Well, he cannot travel through time on his own. He must have the aid of a black jade tablet created by the Maaskab, an ancient sect of very violent bloodthirsty Mayan priests. But yes, time travel."

"Mayan-priest-jade-tablet-whats?"

"Never mind. It's complicated." His mind raced. He'd flipped last night. Perhaps he had hurt Margarita during that episode and Forgetty had tried, but failed, to intervene? *Yes, that is the only explanation. The only one.* Otherwise, why would his brother risk severe punishment to help avoid Margarita's death? Acan would call his brother and ask, but Máax would not know anything because whatever events sparked his journey last evening had been avoided—*Gods, I hope!* In any case, the version of Máax who would know the details no longer existed. It had all been erased at great risk to his brother.

All this led Acan to one conclusion: "That's it, woman. We're done playing games." He grabbed

Margarita's hand and started dragging her toward the bar.

"Hey, what are you doing?" she protested.

"I'm ending this," he growled.

"Ending what?"

"I refuse to put your life in danger simply because you *think* we won't work out."

She jerked her hand back. "You're dangerous."

"Not if you accept me."

"You're a bad example for my daughter and a complete pig when you're in party mode." She took back her hand, stopping in her tracks.

He grabbed her by the shoulders, refusing to let her leave. "These past few days I've proven that I can have just as much fun hosting the party as being the party. That said, yes, we will need to get wild with drink from time to time, but I am certain I will behave much better with you at my side. We can also agree in advance which holidays will be our wild days."

"I can't do this. It's too crazy." She stepped back, freeing herself.

He stepped toward her. He had to make her listen. He had to make her see the truth. "What's crazy, my dear woman, is the pathetic life I've been living. I want a life that isn't simply about waking up naked in a taco truck with a pile of hungover women on top of me, or a life of inspiring humans with my ability to consume five kegs of beer in one night." He took her hand. "I want a life that is not lived at the bottom of a bottle. I want to wear pants so you are the only one who sees my enormous shaft—because it really is enormous. And you, Margarita, are the only cocktail I need."

She blinked at him, confused. She still wasn't convinced. But that was because she didn't fully understand he was out of time and that everything happened for a reason.

"Let me make you a drink, Margarita. One drink."

"You think giving me alcohol will make me change my mind? That's ridiculous."

He raised a brow. "I am the God of Wine and Intoxication. If there is one thing I've learned, it's that sometimes we need to let our guard down in order to see the truth. Or to dance naked on a tabletop, but that is neither here nor there. Let me make you a damned drink, woman!"

She huffed. "Okay. Fine. Make me the stupid special drink."

Finally. With a room full of women watching them both, he walked around to the other side of the bar and stood in front of her. He stared into her beautiful green eyes and focused his mind, searching for what would be the ideal beverage at this exact moment in her life. Because in this moment, she needed to be convinced that they were meant to be.

"Got it!"

✑ ✒

Margarita watched Acan go to work behind the bar, grabbing different bottles, pouring them into little glasses, measuring every drop going into his concoction. He looked like a mad scientist.

Meanwhile, she couldn't deny that his words had reached through to her. They definitely had. But last night had terrified her. Would he ever understand how it felt to be a mother and want nothing more than to love and protect your child? Especially when you were all she had?

His world seemed dangerous, unpredictable, and very unhealthy. And how could he, this deity, be a good father or husband?

On the other hand, if she accepted him, he wouldn't be a danger to anyone and that included Jessica and herself. So if last night was a disaster avoided, was tonight their second chance?

As Margarita tried to wrap her mind around all of the pieces, she watched Acan carefully pour the ingredients into an extra-tall glass, creating layer upon layer of different colors—reds, greens, purples, oranges and yellows. The crowd around them of mostly women oohed and ahed with each additional layer as if watching someone build a towering house of cards that could crumble at any moment.

"I hope you're not expecting me to drink all that," Margarita said. There had to be a half gallon of alcohol in that thing.

Acan grinned but kept his eyes and steady hands focused on his work.

"Mom? We were waiting downstairs, but some weird redheaded woman wearing a clown suit with a strap-on said we should come back up here." Jessica and her friend stood there looking at her.

"Oh, sorry. I just…" Margarita's words faded as Acan struck a match.

"Mom?" Jessica gasped.

"Christ." Margarita stepped back, pushing Jess behind her. "You're going to blow us all up!"

Holding the lit match, Acan stared into her eyes. "Not tonight." He dropped the match into the glass and a giant ball of rainbow-colored flames burst from the top.

"Ooooh. Aaaahh," said the crowd.

The flames began taking shape.

"Is that…a unicorn?" Margarita asked.

"Yes," Acan said triumphantly.

"And that's my special drink?"

"Be patient. The best part is coming." He held out his hands to silence the crowd.

The unicorn figure died with a puff. Leaving behind an empty glass.

How strange. My perfect cocktail drinks itself?

Acan scooted the glass toward her. "Look inside."

She stepped forward and carefully leaned over the bar to look inside. Charred to the bottom of the glass were the words "I love you."

She looked up at him, trying to process.

"Margarita, I woke up this morning, having no

memory of last night past the point of you leaving. Yet despite my enormous disappointment, I realized that the only thing I could think of today was finding a mate so that I would not turn into a horrible, decapitating monster and end up hurting you. But now I know that you are the one I want, you are the one I was meant to love. And there isn't anything I wouldn't do for you, including spending my eternity with another woman who wouldn't make me happy. Which I now realize is ridiculous because if she didn't make me happy, then I would still turn into a horrible evil god. So yeah, that makes no sense. But I think we do, Margarita. I look at you and your child and I know it is time to move on with my life and be a man. Who wears pants."

Tears trickled from Margarita's eyes. If she said yes to him, it would mean taking a huge leap of faith. Not only for her, but for her daughter, too.

"Mom?"

Margarita looked at Jessica, then at Acan and then back at Jessica.

"One second," she said to Acan and pulled her daughter aside. "Jessica, see that really tall man right there?"

"Yeah?"

"He wants to be a part of our lives. Permanently. How do you feel about that?"

"I just want to see you happy, Mom. That's why I came here tonight."

Margarita crinkled her brows in question.

"The ad on Facebook said some successful businessman who liked to party was looking for someone special to share his life with. I recognized him from our apartment last night and thought I should tell him to pick you. You need a guy you can have fun with, Mom. All you do is work and worry. And the last thing you need is another person to take care of. He has his own money, so that wouldn't be a problem."

"So you think I should be with him?" It surprised Margarita that Jessica wanted this to happen and wasn't concerned about sharing attention.

"I mean, yeah, he's way younger than you, but he's pretty cute and seems really into you."

"Wait. You think he's younger than me?" Margarita asked.

"He's like twenty-five or something, right?"

Margarita had to tell Jessica everything. No more secrets. "Try seventy thousand. That's the thing, Jessica. He's a god. An actual, real live deity, and he's kind of crazy. But I think he could be good for us, and I think he needs us, too."

Jessica blinked. "Sorry, but did you just say god?"

"Of wine and decapitation."

"Are you being serious right now?" Jessica asked.

"Completely."

"Ohmygod. That's so cool," Jessica squealed.

"You will absolutely change your mind about

that when you see him in party mode. It's pretty horrible."

Jessica lifted a brow.

"He forgets to wear pants, swears like a sailor, and drinks obscene amounts of alcohol," Margarita explained. "But I think we should give him a chance. Honestly, I don't see another choice at this point."

"So you love him?" Jessica asked.

Margarita had to give that question some thought. She became a reckless, horny mess in his presence. He infuriated her with his cockiness, but his devotion to others fascinated her. She especially loved how people became instantly happy when he walked into a room. And last night, before that scary crap happened with Máax, had been one of the funnest nights she'd had in a long time. However, and more importantly, she'd never met a man that made her feel like this. Adored, special, and the most important thing in his life. Her heart thrummed with happiness in his presence and told her one thing: *We are meant to be together.* This was fate, and she couldn't turn her back on it any more than she could stop wanting him.

Margarita rubbed her brow. "I'm not sure the word love could ever come close to describing how I feel about him. There just aren't any words."

"I'll take that," said Acan from behind her.

She turned and looked up at him. "You were listening?"

"I may be a deity, but I'm still a man. We don't like being held in suspense for very long. Especially after one has prepared the legendary Randy Unicorn flagship drink and has proposed."

"You proposed?" Margarita asked.

"Yes. Right now," he said.

"When?" she asked.

"Now. I'm doing it now." He looked at Jessica. "As long as your daughter will accept me."

Jessica kind of nodded, but appeared to be too awestruck to speak.

Acan grinned at Jessica. "Good. Because in that case, you're grounded, young lady. You should never sneak into bars and you should always tell your mother where you're going. This city is not safe for children to be running around at night."

Jessica's jaw dropped. "I think I just changed my mind."

"And I think I just made up mine. Yes!" Margarita popped up on her tiptoes, threw her arms around his neck, and kissed him on the lips.

Acan beamed. "I'm going to assign a few of our security guards to her," he whispered. "She's a sneaky one. I can see it in her eyes."

"And I can see we are going to be very happy together," said Margarita, instantly feeling her heart blossom with a profound sense of joy. Okay, and a lot of passion. She seriously ached for him right now.

"I am already happy, which is why you must

go," he said.

She gave him a quizzical look.

"It's not appropriate for your child to see so much joy." He winked and glanced down toward his pants.

"Oh. That kind of happy." She looked into his hypnotic turquoise eyes. She'd never done something as crazy as this, agreeing to be with a man—god—she hardly knew, but her faith had always carried her through. "I really want you right now."

"Yep." He pulled her arms off his neck and twirled her around. "Time for you to go." He gave her a little smack on the ass. "I'll see you tomorrow so we can discuss the terms of our living arrangement and the sharing of powers."

"Sharing of powers?"

"I will explain tomorrow." Wincing, he waved her off, angling the front of his body away from Jessica. His "joy" had to be uncomfortable and she wanted nothing more than to help him with it; however, now was not the time.

Her body shaking with hormones and adrenaline, but in a good way, Margarita took one final look at her beautiful man and left the club.

"Mom? Are you really going to let that man ground me?" Jessica asked as they slid into the car.

"Nope. *I'm* going to ground you." She looked at her daughter. "And I love you, Jessica. More than anything and that will never change."

"I love you, too."

Margarita started the car, eager to get Ophelia and themselves home. "Man, I so need a glass of wine." Her eyes went wide. Oh no. She totally had the urge to party. "This is going to be interesting."

CHAPTER TWENTY-EIGHT

After a restless night of very erotic dreams about Acan, Margarita was woken by the doorbell at five a.m. *Ugh. Monday. And I'm already late for work.*

She opened the door to find a dozen red roses in a glass vase. *Wow.* She picked them up and inhaled deeply. She couldn't remember the last time someone gave her flowers. They put an instant smile on her face.

She took them inside, placed them on the kitchen counter, and read the card:

> *Good morning, my sexy Margarita. I will be running a few minutes late this morning, but Brutus will be there shortly to take your daughter to school and will accompany her home.*
>
> *Many Sweet Nothings,*
> *Acan*

Margarita reread the note. She didn't remember having a date with Acan this morning. There was another knock at the door. Hopeful it might be

Acan, she opened it and looked up, up, up at a huge man with elephant-sized biceps, a crew cut, and fierce turquoise eyes. He wore black cargo pants and a black T-shirt that emphasized a powerful chest.

"I am Brutus, ma'am. Here to escort your daughter until I decide who to assign to her permanently."

Margarita rubbed her face. "Can you hold on a second?" She closed the door and went for her cell to call Acan, who answered immediately.

"Hello, my delicious lime- and tequila-flavored beverage. Did you sleep well? Because I've been hard as a rock, thinking about—"

"Yes, yes. I'm completely horny for you, but there's a man at my door."

"Yes. That is Brutus. He is one of our toughest immortal soldiers. He kills things—little things, big things, evil things. He is extremely dangerous."

What the hell? "Ummm…and you want him to take Jessica to school why?"

"Margarita, I cannot send a complete wimp to watch over your most prized possession. What sort of mate would I be?"

"She's a person, not a possession. And she's only going to school, so I really don't understand what's going—"

"Are you aware that roughly one hundred and fifty thousand humans perish each and every day? And that there is currently a plague of evil turning those who've been charged to protect humans, including our army of good vampires, into blood-thirsty monsters, and we expect that number to triple before this epidemic has run its course?"

Holy shit. "I'm sorry, did you say vampires?"

"Yes."

"Okay. Brutus sounds awesome. Acan, when can we see each other?" Not only did she have a million nervous questions, but she felt incredibly anxious to see him. It was as if her body was going through Acan withdrawals and her woman parts would not stand down. "Acan, I have some serious," she lowered her voice so Jessica wouldn't accidentally overhear, though Jessica remained in bed, "I have serious *needs*. I think I might actually be combusting." Was this normal when one decided to "mate" with a god?

"I like the sound of that," he said. "And you can see me very soon."

Her doorbell rang. It was probably that Brutus guy. "Hold on," she said and went to answer the door. "Sorry, please come in…" Acan stood there wearing a very nice suit, light blue dress shirt and black tie. His hair was brushed to a silky shine that made her want to run her fingers through it. His short beard had been trimmed down to a neat stubble.

"You're here," she said, thoroughly surprised.

"Yes. Did you get the flowers?"

"I did, thank you. But…wow. You look…" She gulped. "Hot."

He grinned. "Yes, well. Today is the start of a new chapter in my life, and I thought I might try dressing like a grown-up. By the way, Brutus is down in his car—a black SUV—ready to go when your daughter is."

Margarita stood there, completely speechless. All she wanted was to climb the big hunk of sexy man standing in her doorway and ride him like the stallion that he was. "Thanks. And the-the new look wa-wa-works." She shuddered with arousal, unable to peel her eyes away from the substantial bulge hanging down his tailored pant leg.

"I'm glad you approve," he leaned in to whisper. "But if it makes you feel any better, I'm still commando."

"I ca-can see tha-that." The image of his naked cock scorched its way through her head.

"So are you ready?" he asked.

"For what?"

"There is much to be done—including showing you the home I've acquired for you and Jessica and, of course, taking care of those *needs* you mentioned." He leaned in close, giving her a whiff of his intoxicating smell. "I too couldn't wait to see you, which is why I came before you left for work. I am kidnapping you for the day."

"Can you back up to that part about the home?"

"Margarita, before you say anything strong and womanly—such as I should always consult you on all decisions—you should know it has already been purchased. And it would be such a shame to let such a nice house with a view of the ocean, chef's kitchen, private gym, swimming pool, movie theater, bowling alley, and fun room all go to waste. Of course, if you hate it and insist on living here, we could do that, but I do not see a sprinkler system, and that is a problem."

Margarita's head spun in sinful circles. Being near Acan was turning her "need" into torture.

"Gah, gah...but I—and there's work. School. Jessica. God, it's hot in here." She pulled at the neck of her pink pajama top.

Acan held out his hand. "I think your *needs* are getting in the way of speaking, but I believe you're concerned about moving and the impact to Jessica or your gym. Fear not, the home is only a thirty-minute drive north from your business and nearly the same for Jessica's school. I've also arranged for a few of our top Uchben trainers to oversee your gym for the next few days while you settle in. Of course, there will be a honeymoon, too, and—"

"Stop. No more talking. I need *that*." Her eyes flashed down to his groin. "I need it now," she growled. Her c-spot was throbbing with erotic pulses, and her entire body felt like a sexy sinful rubber band about to snap.

"I think now that you've accepted me, the bond between us is only increasing."

She didn't care why. She just needed him to fuck her, and she needed it now. "Grrr..."

He smiled. "Now *this* is going to be fun."

Margarita brushed her teeth, quickly changed into jeans and a white T-shirt with her gym's logo, and woke up Jessica for school. One look at Brutus, and Jess was giddy. "I get my own badass bodyguard? Saaweet!"

"Remember, Jessica," said Acan, "you are not permitted to tell anyone our secret. If you do, you will find a very upset, bloodthirsty unicorn on your doorstep, who will take you to a very bad place." Acan had winked at Margarita, but she hadn't been one hundred percent convinced he'd been joking.

"Unicorns are real? Freaking awesome!" Jessica had yelled, sparking a look of frustration on Acan's face.

Welcome to parenthood, Margarita had thought.

With Jess taken care of, she and Acan headed out. All Margarita could think of was sating the gnawing lust churning inside her body. He, on the other hand, seemed calm and collected.

"How did I become the mindless, horny teenager, and you're the mature one?" she asked.

He smiled slyly. "Well, I am an ancient deity, and you're just a baby in my world."

"Well, this baby is about to die of a heart attack if she doesn't get her way."

The smile on his beautiful lips fell off a sharp

cliff.

"Did I say something wrong?" she asked.

He loosened his tie, leaving one hand on the steering wheel. "Turning over a new leaf today wasn't the only reason for the suit. Nor was Brutus at your home simply because I am in love with you."

She sighed. Hearing him say those words melted her heart. She was beginning to see how closed off she'd been to love, to him, and to life in some respects. Jessica had been right; Margarita had been all about worrying and work. In an instant, Acan had changed all that and she wondered if he wasn't what she'd been waiting for her entire life. Because she had to admit, they were special.

"So why the suit? Why Brutus?" she asked.

"I had to attend an emergency meeting with my brethren this morning. It seems that yesterday, my brother Zac flipped and has gone on a violent killing spree. He has vowed to continue until he finds Tula, a woman he is involved with. Or not involved with. It's complicated."

Margaret covered her mouth. "Jesus."

"Not to worry. We will catch him, and unlike me, he does not have the power to influence the masses. Still, it is concerning to have him roaming free, so I felt Brutus was a necessary precaution given yesterday's nonevent."

"You mean how I almost died."

He glanced at her with a stern expression. "One

can never be too careful, Margarita. Which is why I also petitioned to take you to Mexico."

Mexico? "I'm not following."

Acan turned and hit Highway 1, heading north up the coast. She suddenly felt a strange déjà vu washing over her.

"The thing is, Margarita, that your life is fragile, and while it is impossible to make you into a god, we can give you our light. The portal to my world is in Mexico."

She still wasn't quite understanding. "What light? What's in the portal?"

"If I take you through it to the other side, to my real home, you will become immortal—a demigoddess. Not indestructible, but much more resilient. You will never grow old and you will live forever— as long as your body remains intact."

Acan moved in the opposite lane and passed a slow-moving truck edging up a steep grade.

"Careful," she said, feeling incredibly nervous. He wasn't driving fast, but the narrow two-lane road was dangerous with all of its blind turns and falling rocks from the cliffs above in some areas.

Acan glanced over at her. "I cannot lose you, Margarita."

"Acan, I can't. I don't want to live forever."

He flashed a glance her way, hurt reflecting in his eyes. "So you're saying no?"

"Yes, I'm saying no."

Acan looked back at her again just as she saw

the grill of a large truck coming around the blind turn, heading straight for them.

"Watch out!" she screamed.

CHAPTER TWENTY-NINE

For the rest of the drive, Margarita and Acan went back and forth, screaming at each other.

"You almost got us killed!" she yelled.

"Yes. Because it isn't every day a god finds the perfect woman and she refuses to accept the gift of immortality."

"But I want to live my life."

"Just not with me!" he yelled.

"Yes. With you! But I'm a mother. I don't want to watch my daughter grow old and die. It's not supposed to be that way."

"So then I have to watch you grow old and die? Watch your body wither into nothing and then be left all alone for eternity? I've only just found you and fifty years—or however long you've got—won't be enough. It's a blink of an eye for me."

With that Margarita took a steadying breath. Her adrenaline was high and her nerves shaken badly after almost slamming into that truck. Thank God she'd been watching the road. Another split second and Acan wouldn't have been able to swerve in time.

I'd be dead right now. For the second time in two days. Which was why she couldn't blame him for how he felt. Hell, she might feel the same way if in his shoes. But she believed, now more than ever, that life was precious, every moment a gift. Living forever took that away.

"Do you love me, Margarita?" he asked.

God, it had been years since she'd said those words to a man. She'd locked them away in a safe place so she'd never use them again, but the time had come to let them out.

"Well?" He waited.

She closed her eyes and drew a slow breath. "Yes. I love you."

"Good," he said. "Then that means I can fight to change your mind." He took a sharp left and headed down a long driveway cutting through a thick stand of breathtakingly tall pine trees.

"And I can respect a man who won't stop fighting for what he wants. But I don't want you to have false hope. It wouldn't be right."

"I'm a god. We don't hope. We do. And I *will* win this battle."

She supposed he could, though in her heart, the last thing she could ever want would be to bury her daughter. She liked the idea of getting old and being able to experience her life as it was meant to be lived. And after she was gone, she realized, Acan would always be there to look after Jess and her grandchildren and great-grandchildren. He would never be alone. He would always be loved.

The thought warmed Margarita's heart, sparking a big smile.

Still in a huff, Acan grumbled, "Why are you so happy?"

She shrugged. "That was our first real fight."

A moment passed and then he chuckled. "Indeed it was, and I have a feeling it won't be our last. We still have a lot of getting to know each other." He pulled up to a large iron gate and stopped the car, turning his body to look at her. "I cannot tell you how much I am looking forward to it, Margarita." He leaned over to kiss her, and her body went straight into sexual overdrive. Adrenaline rush, erotic aches deep inside her core, painfully erect nipples.

The heat from his lips suddenly grew intolerable.

"Ouch!" she pulled back.

He flashed a mischievous smile. "That's what you get for making me upset."

She slapped his leg. "You brat! Now open that gate. And there better be a big bed in there or me and my needs will go elsewhere."

He frowned. "You and your needs are about to get your planet rocked." He lowered his window, punched a code into a small keypad, and the gates slid open.

Margarita's blood pressure soared. *This is it.*

We're finally going to have sex. But now she felt nervous. It was different before when they were just two people. Now she knew the truth. He was a god, and frankly, it still blew her mind. "Bring it o-on?"

He flashed a devilish grin. "Oh, I'm bringing it."

Acan wanted to project confidence for Margarita's sake, but for the first time ever, he felt nervous about having sex. He wanted it to be special and perfect. Yet at the same time, he also wanted to pound her into next Tuesday and make her scream his name. Was that so wrong?

The car skirted along the curvy driveway between skyscraper pine trees and thick bushes. "Here we are."

"It seems to have a lot of privac..." Margarita's voiced faded as they came up over the small hill and the scenery opened up. Manicured lawns stretched across the horizon and just beyond that was a never-ending stretch of blue ocean.

Her face lit up. "Wow."

"So you approve?" He felt relieved. He'd never bought a home before. Houses, yes. An amphitheater, warehouse, and taco trucks, too. But a home where one made memories and filled it with love? Never.

"How can anyone not approve of that view?"

she asked.

"My sister Akna, the Goddess of Fertility, hates the ocean. She says it gives her hives."

"All right, so one person on the planet wouldn't approve."

"There's also Ah-Celiz, the God of Eclipses. He detests anything mildly inspiring," he said.

"I really can't wait to meet your family. They sound so cheerful."

"You have no idea." He turned the bend and the full house came into view—huge marble pillars sat beside the twenty-foot-high front door made of stained glass. Two large rectangular fountains stretched from the side of the home all the way out to the ocean, giving it a romantic, dramatic feel.

"This is amazing," she said.

"And it is fit for my queen—six acres, twelve bedrooms including the guesthouse, a lap pool, sauna, yoga room, full gym, and three-thousand-bottle wine cellar."

"Ah. So that's why you bought it. The wine cellar."

"Actually it was the master suite that sealed the deal. Care to see it first?"

She nodded. "I'm not sure I'll make it that far." She slid her hand over his groin, sending a jarring arousal through his dick.

"I will carry you!" He didn't want their first time as a real couple to be on the hood of a car. *That can be later tonight.*

He shut off the engine and quickly made his way around the car, scooping Margarita into his arms.

He charged through the front door, up the grand staircase, and headed straight for the master suite. Margarita's laughter filled the air as she bounced in his arms.

"Here we are!" He stepped through the doorway and lowered her to her feet, watching the expression on her beautiful face.

Margarita's eyes scanned the enormous bedroom, where a balcony overlooked the Pacific Ocean and brought in plenty of light. If they wanted to sleep in, one press of the button would close the blackout curtains. The extra-long king-sized bed had been made with white satin sheets—per his instructions to Jill—but the couches, TV, and other furniture remained to be unpacked.

"It will all be put together soon," he said, "but allow me to show you the closet." He guided her past the palatial bathroom—time for that later—to the walk-in closet with enough racks for her to buy a new pair of shoes every day for three years and not run out of space.

"This is really—wow."

"And look at this." He pulled out the drawer to their side. "Many, many toys to please you with."

"Uh. Is that a rubber fist?" She looked mortified.

Dammit, Jill. Very funny. He slammed the

drawer shut.

"We don't have to use any of those things for our first time. But if you change your mind later, I have handcuffs, feathers, vibrators, ass tickl—"

"Nope. I'm all good."

The two stood there, a thick fog of awkwardness lurking between them. He had to do something fast or the moment would be ruined.

"I bought you a gift," he said.

"You really didn't have to—"

"You will definitely want this." He walked over to the wall on the right and pulled back some of the shelving to reveal a walk-in safe. "It's in here." He punched in the code "TastyMargarita," and it sprang open.

"Jeez. Are you opening a bank in our closet?" she asked with a smile.

"Come take a look." They entered the little room containing walls of shelving and drawers. In the middle was a granite table and a small box sitting on top. "That is for you. Go ahead. Open it."

"What is it?" she asked.

"Take a look."

She walked over to the table and slowly took the thing. From her hesitation, he sensed she already knew what was inside. She opened it and stared, but her expression remained unreadable.

"Do you like it?" he asked.

"It's a ring. Shaped like a tiny bottle of wine."

"It's an engagement ring, but it opens."

She popped the miniature clasp that revealed a small compartment inside. "Ohmygod. Are those tiny diamond-incrusted running shoes?"

"Yes, and the stones around the edge of the bottle are very special." He smiled. "Black jade."

She smiled. "I love it. It's crazy. But I love it."

He stepped toward her. "It's an engagement ring. I had it made last night. Pulled the guy out of bed at two in the morning to get it done."

Her wide eyes were filled with a strange expression. "You don't need to do all of this for me," she whispered.

"I want to see you happy. I want you to feel like your life is a never-ending celebration. Which is why you're going to take time off work and we are going to travel. You'll get massages every day, have a personal chef, you'll get to jog on any beach—"

"Acan." She took his hand and squeezed. "Stop. I don't want all that."

She pushed herself up on her tiptoes and reached for his neck to pull his mouth down to hers. She kissed him softly. "I'm nervous too," she whispered, "but this is all I need." She then shoved her soft little hand down the front of his pants, giving him a jolt. "And that. That is really, really good."

He made a deep grumble. "That does feel nice." She began playing with the tip, rubbing it between her thumb and forefinger.

She slid her hand out and looked up at him. "So

are you going to put this thing on me?" She held up the tiny box.

He quickly grabbed it, plucked it out, and slid it on her ring finger. "Perfect fit." He took her hand and pulled her back into the bedroom.

"Wait." She stopped a few feet from the bed.

"What?"

"Can I get pregnant if I'm wearing this ring?"

"Yes. But all you have to do is remove it immediately afterwards."

"What if I want to get pregnant?"

His body felt cold all of a sudden. "Right now?"

She shrugged. "I'm almost fifty, but I'm in great shape."

He swallowed hard. "Uh…uh…"

She smiled. "I'm just kidding. Jessica was my one and only. I'd like to keep it that way."

"Oh. That's a relief. Babies frighten me. Especially all of their miniature body parts. It's just weird—wait. You're almost fifty?"

She grinned. "Well, forty-five, really."

He threaded his fingers in her hair. "Well, you are really hot." He kissed her hard.

"You're pretty hot, too, for a seventy-thousand-year-old man." She smiled and returned to kissing him.

❧ ❧

Margarita couldn't wait a moment longer. This was

the one thing she'd been fantasizing over and dreaming about since she'd met him and they'd had those wildly sexy encounters. She unbuttoned his pants and slid them down to his ankles, allowing him to step out while he shed his coat, tie, and dress shirt.

She stepped back and took in the full view. Strong, lean, muscled body. Soft brown hair cascading down wide shoulders. Abs that rippled like powerful waves frozen in time, and a huge, huge penis.

"Wow. It looks so much different in a private setting."

He smiled and pulled her in close, pressing his hard shaft against her. "How does it look now?"

The heat of his cock warmed her stomach, but made her insides sizzle.

"It looks really lonely." She slid her hand between them and wrapped her fingers around his cock, enjoying the thickness of him in her hand.

A deep grumble of approval erupted from his muscled chest and he bent his head to kiss her. His tongue, warm and sweet, slid across the crease in her lips, coaxing her to open for him. She did. He kissed her slow at first, allowing her to taste him, allowing her to savor the sensual rhythm of his tongue.

Oh, God. What a kiss. Slow and demanding. Sexual and heated.

She began moving her hand, stroking the length of his long dick with equally sensual movements. He groaned, which only made her want to pleasure him more. Maybe with her mouth. She felt absolutely ravenous for him.

Wanting to go to her knees, she broke their kiss and found a feral, hungry look in his eyes. It stopped her in her tracks and flooded her core with a hard rush of throbbing warmth.

He suddenly pushed her back onto the bed and peeled down her jeans. Eager to get him inside her, she removed her shirt, exposing her painfully erect nipples.

"Your breasts are amazing. And those legs." He drew a breath, standing there looking at her naked body, his thick cock engorged and straining, looking like he was about to explode.

What was he waiting for? She was hot, wet, and so ready.

"Open your legs," he commanded in a low voice. "I want to see you."

Another erotic rush spiked through her. She liked this commanding, dominating side of him.

Doing as he asked, she slowly parted her thighs and watched the intensely carnal look in his eyes. He was pleased by what he saw.

"Mmm…that's right." He took his thick cock in his large hand and began slowly stroking himself. "Now," he said in a sinfully low voice that sent goose bumps down her spine, "touch yourself. Show me how you like it."

She'd never done anything like this with a man,

but watching him stroke his rock-solid cock, sliding that big hand at a leisurely pace over the velvety skin, made her ready to come instantly. She'd never been so turned on and in need of a release.

His animalistic gaze stuck to her most intimate spot, she slid her hand down to her swollen bud and gently stroked it. "I'm going to come," she said.

With a devilish smile, he said, "Show me."

By the time he said the words, it was too late. She felt the sexual tension snap like the cable on a bridge. She couldn't stop.

"That's right," he said, watching her as she whimpered through her orgasm. It passed quickly, lacking the proper friction and pressure of a hard shaft to turn it into anything more. She didn't know what to make of this. Why let her get so worked up only to have her pleasure herself?

She blew out a long breath and looked at him. He'd dropped his hands and was no longer pleasuring himself.

"Is that what you wanted?" she asked, her voice breathy.

"That was so you have something to compare to." He climbed onto the bed and slid between her legs, placing the tip of his shaft at her heated slick entrance. "And so you remember why you don't ever want to stop living a life with me." His gaze locked with hers, he thrust into her with one smooth stroke, burying himself to the hilt.

She gasped, her body unaccustomed to his size,

her inner walls clenching in response.

This time he didn't tell her to relax, but pulled out and slammed into her again with a demanding thrust, as if taking what was his. And it hurt so good.

She moaned in response and dug her fingers into his back.

He pulled out and thrust again, watching her face as he took her hard.

He suddenly bent his head and whispered into her ear, "Are you ready, Margarita?"

"Ready for what?" she panted, her mind a messy fog of sexual need and lust.

Whatever he did sent her straight into a mind-bending orgasm. Her entire body bucked with punishing, sinful waves of hard spasms. "Ohgods. Ohgods." She groaned, explosions rocking the deepest part of her core and radiating out through every limb. As she came, he continued pumping his thick cock into her, filling her, stretching her, pressing into her g-spot.

"Holy crap," she whimpered. There were no thoughts, no sense of time, no limit to the space her body occupied. Everything around her became one giant ball of pulses and carnal explosions. She felt him inside her and all around her. Nothing was separate.

As he gave her one final thrust, she held her breath and curled her toes, wondering if she might never come back down to Earth.

As she clung to him, a few moments passed and he pulled out.

Her body began instantly relaxing.

"How do you feel?" he asked, brushing her hair away from her sweaty forehead.

"What was that?" She looked into his turquoise eyes brimming with male ego.

"Foreplay."

"Foreplay?"

"Yes. Foreplay." He flipped her over onto all fours and gripped her hips.

"Wait. I think I need a brea—"

He slammed inside her from behind, stealing her breath.

"Ohgods," she moaned, forgetting what she had been about to say. There was only him inside her.

"Don't move," he commanded. He moved his hand to her hips and leaned into her, driving as deep as he could go, bottoming out at the entrance to her womb. She instantly felt his hot cum jetting inside her, and her body ignited with another round of explosive orgasms.

"Oh, God. How. Do. You. Do. That?" she panted, grabbing fistfuls of sheets. She bowed her back while he drove into her again from behind, pounding out her release in wave after wave of euphoric shudders. This time, her mind and body separated, going in two different directions. One floated on a cloud; the other savored the feel of his long slick shaft hammering into her.

Every time she felt her orgasm flagging, he would come more, sparking another insane release. She never imagined sex could be so incredible.

Just when she thought she couldn't possibly take any more, he pulled out and flipped her over onto her back, covering her with his large body. His mouth was on her, his tongue inside her, on her neck and earlobes and the sides of her mouth.

"You're amazing." She placed her hands on the sides of his face, enjoying the roughness of his short whiskers.

"I'm glad you approve."

"You have no idea." She pushed her mouth to his and kissed him hard. She breathed him in, allowing his sweet, intoxicating scent to fill her lungs and mix with her mind. She'd never felt so connected to another person—at least not in this way, where every molecule of their bodies touched.

"I can't believe I almost walked away," she said in between kisses.

He pulled back and gazed into her eyes. "I can't believe I almost let you."

But as they lay there, covered in each other's sweat, their warm, naked bodies pressed tightly together, she had the strangest feeling that none of this was an accident. They had landed exactly where they were meant to land.

"I love you," she said.

"And I love you, too." He began slowly moving inside her, his hard strong body gliding over her while his hands took hold of hers. He moved them above her head.

Gently pumping his hips, he continued staring into her eyes. "Are you ready?"

"For what?" She hoped he wasn't planning to go get the sex toys. She wasn't ready for that. *And so unnecessary.*

"Like I said, that was just foreplay. Now I'm going to make love to you."

What? How much more of this could she take?

She blinked. "Uh. Okay. I just need to be home for dinner. And able to walk straight."

"I can make sure you get home on time." He bent his head and whispered in her ear, "You're already home, Margarita. You are with me."

She turned her head and gazed into his hypnotic, blue-green eyes. "Yes. I *am* home."

EPILOGUE

"Well, that was a beautiful beach wedding. I especially liked all of the little lights in the shape of wine bottles over the archway." Cimil sighed, sitting next to Roberto inside their custom-made stretch Volvo, waiting for the car ahead to clear Acan's driveway so they could unload. The children—gods bless their spunky evil little souls! So delightful—played "put out the cigarette" toward the back of the car, while their "guest" whimpered in agony.

"You know, my love," said Roberto, straightening his bowtie, looking extra delicious with his milk-chocolaty skin and dark eyes, "I think it's okay to let the children have their fun, but perhaps we can leave your victims at home on family fun night."

Cimil shrugged and gave the front of her strapless green dress a tug. "Sure, baby. Whatever makes you happy. I just thought we needed to keep the kids occupied while we bring in the New Year."

Roberto sighed with contentment. "Another year."

"Yep. One more year." Cimil turned her head

and gazed out the window, hoping Roberto would not see the truth in her eyes. Somehow, he always knew. But this was one secret he could never learn. Not ever. Because nothing was as it seemed. Then again, when was it ever?

"Any news about Zac?" he asked.

Cimil shook her head. She'd had lots of news, mostly from all of the pissed-off dead people Zac had created, but she'd come up empty-handed in the premonition department. "Nothing that will help us capture him, which truly fucks with the old piñata." She pointed to her head. "It's like he's ten steps ahead of me, which is impossible. I'm the master of the ten-steps-ahead program. Yanno? What if he outsteps me and finds her?"

Roberto patted her leg. "Do not worry, my love. Zac will never find Tula."

Cimil hoped that was the case because Tula was special. She didn't know exactly how or why yet, but the dead never lied. Unless they were the bad dead, in which case they lied about everything, so all one needed to do was take the opposite of what they said. Still, very black and white.

"Let's not think about it tonight," she said. "Acan's powers are about to hit max velocity and I want to get a front-row seat. It's a total rush."

"Agreed. I will take out your brother Votan. He always wants to hog Belch on New Year's."

Their stretch Volvo pulled up to the front of the palatial home, and the valet opened the door.

"Good evening. Welcome. If you're part of the wedding reception, please take the walkway to the right for photos. If you are here for the New Year's celebration, please go straight inside and deposit any matches or lighters in the bowl. Acan and Margarita are requesting there be no fires of any sort this evening."

"What? No matches?" Cimil barked. "What kind of party is this?"

"Do not worry," said Roberto, patting his groin. "I have all of the fire you will need tonight."

"Oh gods, you so float my Love Boat." Cimil jumped on top of him and began kissing him wildly.

"Uh, ma'am?" said the valet. "Everyone's waiting, and there are children present."

Not breaking from ravishing her hubby, Cimil waved him off. "Kids, out of the car! And take your toy with you."

∂∾ ∾∾

"Two minutes to midnight on the East Coast." Acan took Margarita's hand as they stood in the middle of their large living room decorated with silver streamers and balloons, filled with his closest friends and his family. Margarita's daughter, her purple panty friends, and quite a few celebrities from her gym had come, too. Mostly men. *Grrr…*He hadn't known that Margarita had such a fan club, but it wasn't a surprise. She was really hot.

As for Forgetty, she still hadn't returned, but he knew she would when she felt ready. They were like peas and carrots.

Only now I have butter, too. He beamed down at Margarita. It was strange to have someone in your life and learn that they were the missing ingredient all along. Now that he had her, he felt content, and while he still loved doing his job, he enjoyed being alert and conscious while he did it.

He'd even passed on making tonight one of their official party nights. It was their wedding night, after all, and he didn't want to miss a thing.

Acan bent down and gave Margarita a kiss on her soft lips. She looked stunning with her golden hair in soft waves falling down her back and her little white reception dress that showed off her athletic body and awesome tits. He patted himself on the back. *I snagged a hotty.* The hottest MILF on the planet. And if he had his way, he was going to have her around forever. There was always hope that she'd warm up to the immortal idea.

"So tell me again why your powers spike at midnight East Coast time?" Margarita asked.

"I'm not exactly sure."

"Well, I've been feeling your energy rising all day." She gave him a wink.

He had fucked her about five times this morning. Then he made love to her, nice and slow, three more times. Still, it hadn't been enough according to her. She said it felt like her entire body just wanted to party, and since she didn't drink, that meant she wanted her favorite vice: him.

"Are you ready?" He smiled, feeling his body thrumming with energy while their guests increased in rowdiness, laughing and cheering.

"Oh, I love it when you say that. Something good always happens right after," she replied.

The guests began the countdown and so did Acan. "Ten, nine, eight, seven, six, five, four, three…"

Boom. Party time!

Margarita turned to him, her green eyes wide. "Holy crap. That's awesome!" She ran for the bar in the corner, plucked a bottle of champagne from one of the buckets, and poured it over her head. The guests roared with "Woohoos!"

With a giant grin, Acan simply stood there staring as Margarita bathed herself in bubbly, howling, "Party! Party! Party!"

"Well, well, well." He folded his arms over his chest. "I think I found my party queen after all."

Zac hated the fucking ocean. He hated the salty air, he hated the movement and those stupid birds that kept following behind them, looking for a handout, and he especially hated fucking boats.

"Can't this piece of shit move any faster?" he

growled at the captain and chucked his bottle of whisky over the side from the top deck where they sat.

"Sorry, sir. This is as fast as she goes."

"Fucking hunk of junk."

"Ye-yes, sir. It is a hunk of ju-junk. Would you care for another bottle? There are plenty in the bar."

The bar? Where all of those dead bodies lay in a heap, just where he'd left them? "You go. I hate the sight of blood. Makes me queasy."

The captain and owner of this luxury vessel, an older gentleman with a long gray beard, looked like he might wet himself. "I would be delighted to get you a beverage. Are you able to steer?"

"No. But if we crash, who gives a shit? You're the only one who will die."

"Uh-huh, very good, sir." The man scurried off, and Zac walked around to the railing. "Like we're going to hit anything in the middle of the gods-damned fucking ocea…" His eyes caught a glimmer of light reflecting in the darkness, high above what appeared to be open water. He looked again, hoping his eyes weren't playing tricks. Another shimmer of light from the front of the boat bounced off something ahead.

"Ha. There you are, you motherfucking island." He smiled sadistically and yelled over his shoulder, "Hey! Captain, get your ass back up here!" Zac looked back out across the dark ocean. "Think you can hide Tula from me, Cimil?" he whispered.

"Think fucking again."

There was no corner of this Earth safe from him. Not even El Corazón Island.

Zac pulled out a long machete from his waistband and thumbed the blade to check the sharpness. "Gods, I fucking hate mermen. This is going to be so fun."

TO BE CONTINUED (Muahaha...)

AUTHOR'S NOTE

Hi, all! I'll make my note short and sweet this time (no story breakdown needed for this one. LOL). First, I hope you all enjoyed GOD OF WINE. I'm tellin' ya, after the last few months (elections…ugh) and just plain old stressy life, I so needed to let my silly loose. I'm guessing many of you did as well. Anyway, I have three more books planned in this series, and I hope to publish two of them next year (2017): The Goddess of Forgetfulness, Brutus, and Colel (Goddess of Bees). Seriously, I keep going back and forth as to which I'll do next, so if any of you are DYING for one or the other, let me know. Maybe you'll help get me off the fence!

Also, some have asked about Zac and Tula getting their own book. I have not ruled it out, but had originally planned to have their story play out over the next few novels. I'll keep folks posted (via my newsletter) as the Goddess of Inspiration guides me! Or you can check in here for updates on new Immortal Matchmaker titles: www.mimijean.net/immortal_matchmakers.html

As always, I have SIGNED BOOKMARKS (first-come basis) for those who love to collect my personally crafted swag. Be sure to mention if you took the time to show some BOOK LOVE with an awesome REVIEW (very much appreciated!) so I can include extra "thank you" swag from either this book or one of my upcoming releases (Ten Club!! Woohoo!).

Since NEW YEAR'S EVE is coming, don't miss the list of my readers' all-time favorite party anthems in the back! Belch would be so proud. So many rockin' songs, you guys!!

Enjoy your New Year's, everyone, and don't forget to say a silent prayer of thanks to Belch if you find yourself filled with an insatiable need to get wild and crazy on his special night.

Happy Reading,
Mimi
#Madeitdirty   #Lovemyreaders   #UnicornsAreEvil
#PantsManParts

Mimi's PLAYLIST

"Wings" by Birdy

"Neptune" by Sleeping At Last

"Big Jet Plane" by Angus & Julia Stone

"On the Road" by Houndmouth

"So What" by Pink

"Blow Me (One Last Kiss)" by Pink

"Can't Feel My Face" by The Weeknd

"Tubthumping" by Chumbawamba

"Roxanne" by The Police

"Paper Aeroplane" by Angus & Julia Stone

"Young And Beautiful" by Lana Del Rey

"Prayer In C" by Robin Schulz

"Take You Higher (Club Mix)" by The Goodwill

"Black Crow" by Angus & Julia Stone

"Rawnald Gregory Erickson the Second" by
      STRFKR

"Sweet Disposition" by The Temper Trap

"Midnight City" by M83

"Sweater Weather" by The Neighbourhood

"Fade Into You" by Mazzy Star

"Naïve" by The Kooks

"When Did Your Heart Go Missing?" by Rooney

"The Funeral" by Band of Horses

"Something Good Can Work" by Two Door
      Cinema Club

"Animal" by Miike Snow

"Fantasy" by Galimatias

What's YOUR Biggest Party Anthem of All Time?
I asked my readers and here were their responses!

Ailsa Cousins: "Oops Upside Your Head" by The Gap Band

Alicia Fleming: "Save A Horse (Ride A Cowboy)" by Big and Rich

Alison Herman Schooley: "More Than A Feeling" by Boston

Allene Hogan: "Born In The USA" by Bruce Springsteen

Amanda Jacqueline: "Lola's Theme" by The Shapeshifters

Amanda LeJeune: "Welch Bottoms Up" by Brantley Gilbert

Amy Laura Russell: "Up All Night" by Alex Clare

Amy Lazarus: "Rocket Scientist" by The Teddybears

Anita Nalla: "Tubthumping" by Chumbawamba

Ann Victor: "Everybody Knows Your Name" (Theme song to Cheers) by Gary Portnoy

Anna Brooks: "Who Let The Dogs Out" by Baha Men

Anna Johnson: "Love Man" by Otis Redding

Ashley Behrens: "Thunderstruck" by AC/DC

Becky Covert: "Radar Love" by Golden Earring

Bethany Klein: "M. O. V. E." by Luke Bryan

Brandy Miller: "S.O.B." by Nathaniel Rateliff and the Night Sweats

Carmela Hazzard-Viera: "Celebration" by Kool and the Gang

Carolyn Maciejko: "Closer" by Nine Inch Nails

Carrie Hamilton: "Just Dance" by Lady Gaga

Carrie Wear: "Staying Alive" by Bee Gees

Casey Nicholson: "Can't Stop The Feeling" by Justin Timberlake

Casey Seiple-Faumuina: "O.M.G" by Kanye West

Cathy Atchison: "Party All The Time" by Eddie Murphy

Chelsea Dudley and Michele Emery Hayes: "You Shook Me All Night Long" by AC/DC

Chinelo Chukwuka: "Back in Black" by AC/DC

Christen Marie Salles: "I'm Gonna Be (500 Miles)" by The Proclaimers

Christine Poss Sturgill: "Shots ft. Lil Jon" by LMFAO

Danielle Kostetsky: "Instant Replay" by Dan Hartman

Deanna Young and Harriett Murray Beck: "Push It" by Salt-N-Pepa

Deby Hadfield: "Sexy And I Know It" by LMFAO

Deidre Leus: "Pump It" by Black Eyed Peas

Denise Gallagher McCaul: "ChaChaChaa"

Diane Powe: "Let's Groove" by Earth Wind and Fire

Dina Reyna: "Give Me Everything" by Pitbull

Erika Simek "Piano Man"

Faye Bass: "Yeah" by Usher

Gurt Brown: "Dancing In The Street" by David Bowie & Mick Jagger

Hannah Roberson: "Hey Ya" by OutKast

Helen Doogan: "Run Runaway" by Slade

Helen Glue: "Relight My Fire" by Lulu

Jamie McGonigle Biggs, Rebecca Mclaughlin, and Michelle Rogers: "Get The Party Started" by Pink

Jane Kagarise: "Beast Of Burden" by Bette Midler

Janiel Kramer and Myria Noble: "I'm Too Sexy" by

Right Said Fred

Jenny Davis Bell: "She Drives Me Crazy" by The Fine Young Cannibals

Jill Swicegood: "Dude Looks Like a Lady" by Aerosmith

Jozanne Wihongi: "Party" by Beyoncé

Julia De Brito: "Bulletproof" by La Roux

Julia Stevens: "Hot Stuff" by Donna Summer

Kaleena Kaderabek: "If I Had You" by Adam Lambert

Kat Ann and Denise Gould: "Bohemian Rhapsody" by Queen

Kathryn Kirsten O'Toole: "Paradise By The Dashboard Light" by Meat Loaf

Katie Morgan: "Carry on my Wayward Son" by Kansas

Kelsey Dwyer Mogavero: "Party Hard" by Andrew W. K.

Krystal Rancourt: "Sweet Home Alabama" by Lynyrd Skynyrd

Kyla McNamara and Diane Dykes: "Uptown Funk" by Bruno Mars

Laura Clark: "Dancing With Myself" by Billy Idol

Laura Sabatino: "Kickstart My Heart" by Motley Crue

Leah Browne: "Closer" by The Chainsmokers

Leigha Price and Amanda Johnson: "Living On A Prayer" by Bon Jovi

Linda Brandt: "Bad To The Bone" by George Thorogood

Linda Davies and Carol Heisz: "Pony" by Ginuwine

Linda Greenlees: "Primal Scream" by Rocks

Lindsay K Lo Kolodziej: "If You Could Read My Mind" by Starz on 54

Lisa Lockwood: "Pump Up The Volume" by M.A.R.R.S.

Lisa Wootton: "Came here to forget" by Blake Shelton

Lizzie Donaldson: "Victim Of Love" by Erasure

Louise Sparrow: "Gigi D'Agostino bla bla bla" by zyxdance

Mandy Moran, Kristi Reynolds Hammond, Kathryn Synoracki Dillard, Dawn Trampe, Jessica Ramos, and Beth Webb: "Pour Some Sugar On Me" by Def Leppard

Manika Pathak: "This Is What You Came For" Calvin Harris ft Rihanna

Martha Foman: "Sexy Back" by Justin Timberlake

Mary Schanz: "Hot Stuff" by Donna Summer

Melba Solis Zuniga: "Enter The Sandman" by Metallica

Micelle Daly: Anita Leigh Breau: "Raise Your Glass" by Pink

Michelle Sarra: "Walk This Way" by Aerosmith

Monica Woodmansee: "Just Dance" by Cotton Eyed Joe

Monique Daoust: "Dancing Queen" by Abba

Nadine Crago: "The Boys Are Back in Town" by Thin Lizzy

Nadine Nicholson: "Old Time Rock And Roll" by Bob Seger

Nancy Huber: "She's A Brick House"

Natalie Person: "This Is How We Do It" by Montell Jordan

Niamh Mc Shane: "Rock The Boat" by Hues Corporation

Nic Smith: "Keep On Moving" by Five

Nicola Heatley-Willis: "Better The Devil You Know" by Kylie Minogue

Patrice Williams: "The Near Future" by Irving Berlin

Paula Ryan: "Kiss Me Deadly" by Lita Ford

Peggy Walther: "Up Around The Bend" by Creedence Clearwater Revival

Rachel Goakes: "Barracuda" by Heart

Rebecca Stoltzfus: "Formation" by Beyoncé

Regina R Olivares: "Nobody But Me" by Michael Buble

Rita Richards: "Animal"

Robyn Rison: "Your Entertainment" by Adam Lambert

Samantha Gelman: "Baby Got Back" by Sir Mix A Lot

Samantha Johnson: "Stuck in your head" by I Prevail

Sandra Rambin Neeley: "Drink in my hand" by Eric Church

Sandy Hammond Ambrose: "Burn It To The Ground" by Nickelback

Sarah Cash: "Jump Around" by House of Pain

Sherae Ballanger Brown: "I'll Sleep When I'm Dead" by Bon Jovi

Shurlea Koger: "Taking Care Of Business" by Bachman–Turner Overdrive

Simone Abraham: "My Songs Know What You Did In The Dark" by Fall Out Boy

Sophie Phipps: "Work It" by Missy Elliott

Teri Berry: "I Wanna Rock N Roll All Night" by KISS

Terri Casolaro Seminuk: "Celebration" by Kool and the Gang

Terry Austin: "One Wild Night" by Bon Jovi

Terry Plumart: "Party Rock Anthem" by LMFAO

Tina Lynn: "We're Not Gonna Take It" by Twisted Sister

Tobias Chintz: "Purity Ring" by Fineshrine

Toni Galligan: "Party Up" by DMX

Tonya Vertrees Jacobs: "Rockin Into The Night" by 38 special

Tracie Tough: "Ride On Time" by Black Box

Tracy Breed: "Let The Music Play" by Shannon

Trenna Harris: "Rock N Roll All Night" by KISS

Wendy Renwall: "Sanchez Sugar" by Maroon 5

Yvette Grimes: "Yeah!" by Usher ft. Lil Jon, Ludacris

Yvonne Nickson: "Love Shack" by The B52s

ACKNOWLEDGEMENTS

I can never give enough thanks to the awesome people in my life who help get these books done, but I'll try anyway! Kylie Gilmore, Dali, Ally, Latoya, Pauline, and Paul…THANK YOU!

A big thank you to my Street Team, the pimp-masters and raging lunatics who keep me inspired with hotties.

And a giant hug to my men—Javi, Seb, and Stef. Thank you for folding clothes and making sure I'm fed occasionally.

With Love,
Mimi

UPCOMING RELEASES

Get ready! Coming January 31, 2017
The Finale of the King Series

For BUY LINKS, EXCERPTS, AND MORE:
www.mimijean.net/king_trilogy_books.html

DON'T MISS OUT ON NEW IMMORTAL RELEASES!

Sign up for Mimi's Newsletter – Free Swag, Special Book Giveaways, and Random Useless Crap!

SIGN UP HERE: https://goo.gl/9NZiqR

Character Definitions
The Gods

Although every culture around the world has their own names and beliefs related to beings of worship, there are actually only fourteen gods. And since the gods are able to access the human world only through the portals called cenotes, located in the Yucatán, the Mayans were big fans.

Another fun fact: The gods often refer to each other as brother and sister, but the truth is they are just another species of the Creator and completely unrelated.

Acan—God of Wine and Intoxication: Also known as Belch, Acan has been drunk for many millennia. He generally wears only tightie whities, but since he's the life of the party, he's been known to mix it up and go naked, too. Whatever works.

Ah-Ciliz—God of Solar Eclipses: Called A.C. by his brethren, Ah-Ciliz is generally thought of as a giant buzz kill because of his dark attitude.

Akna—Goddess of Fertility: She is so powerful, it is said she can make inanimate objects fornicate and that anyone who gets in the same room as her ends up pregnant. She is often seen hanging out with her brother Acan at parties.

Backlum Chaam—God of Male Virility: He's responsible for discovering black jade and figuring out how to procreate with humans.

Camaxtli—Goddess of the Hunt: Also once known as Fate until she was discovered to be a fake and had her powers stripped away by the Universe. She's now referred to as "Fake."

Colel Cab—Mistress of Bees: Though she has many, many powers, "Bees" is most known for the live beehive hat on her head. She has never had a boyfriend or lover because her bees get too jealous.

Goddess of Forgetfulness—She has no official name that is known of and has the power to make anyone forget anything. She spends her evenings DJing because she finds the anonymity of dance clubs to be comforting. Her partner in crime is Acan, the God of Wine.

Ixtab—Goddess of Happiness (ex-Goddess of Suicide): Ixtab's once morbid frock used to make children scream. But since finding her soul mate, she's now the epitome of all things happy.

K'ak (Pronounced "cock")—The history books remember him as K'ak Tiliw Chan Yopaat, ruler of Copán in the 700s AD. King K'ak is one of Cimil's favorite brothers. We're not really sure what he does, but he can throw bolts of lightning, wears a giant silver and jade headdress with intertwining serpents, and has long black and silver hair.

Kinich Ahau—ex-God of the Sun: Known by many other names, depending on the culture, Kinich likes to go by Nick these days. He's also now a vampire—something he's actually not so bummed about. He is mated to the love of his life, Penelope, the Ruler of the House of Gods.

Máax—Once known as the God of Truth, Máax was banished for repeatedly violating the ban on time travel. However, since helping to save the world from the big "over," he is now known as the God of Time Travel. Also turns out he was the God of Love, but no one figured that out until his mate, Ashli, inherited his power. Ashli is now the fourteenth deity, taking the place of Camaxtli, the Fake.

Votan—God of Death and War: Also known as Odin, Wotan, Wodan, God of Drums (he has no idea how the hell he got that title; he hates drums), and Lord of Multiplication (okay, he is pretty darn good at math so that one makes sense). These days, Votan goes by Guy Santiago (it's a long story—read ACCIDENTALLY IN LOVE WITH…A GOD?), but despite his deadly tendencies, he's all heart.

Yum Cimil—Goddess of the Underworld: Also

known as Ah-Puch by the Mayans, Mictlantecuhtli (try saying that one ten times) by the Aztec, Grim Reaper by the Europeans, Hades by the Greeks…you get the picture! Despite what people say, Cimil is actually a female, adores a good bargain (especially garage sales) and the color pink, and she hates clowns. She's also bat-shit crazy, has an invisible pet unicorn named Minky, and is married to Roberto, the king of all vampires.

Zac Cimi—Once thought to be the God of Love, we now know differently. Zac is the God of Temptation, and his tempting ways have landed him in very hot water. Because no matter how temptingly hot your brother's mate might be, trying to steal her is wrong. He is currently serving time for his crime in Los Angeles with Cimil, running the Immortal Matchmakers agency.

Not the Gods

Andrus: Ex-Demilord (vampire who's been given the gods' light), now just a demigod after his maker, the vampire queen, died. He is now happily mated to Sadie, a half-succubus who spends her days feeding off of her delicious new hubby and going to casting calls in LA.

Ashli: Ashli actually belongs over in the GODS section, but since she was born human, we'll keep her here. Ashli is mate to Máax, God of Time Travel. Unbeknownst to him, he was also the God of Love. Ashli inherited his power after they started falling in love. Maybe the Universe thought a woman should have this power?

Brutus: One of the gods' elite Uchben warriors. He doesn't speak much, but that's because he and his team are telepathic. They are also immortal (a gift from the gods) and next in line to be Uchben chiefs.

Charlotte: Sadie's golf-loving half sister and the intended mate to Andrus Grey. Only, Andrus, being the rebel that he is, decided he could pick his own damned woman, Sadie. Charlotte is now happily mated to Tommaso, Andrus's BBF. They're one big happy family! Oh, and her daddy is an incubus.

Helena Strauss: Once human, Helena is now a

vampire and married to Niccolo DiConti. She has a half-vampire daughter, Matty, who is destined to marry Andrus's son, according to Cimil.

Margarita Seville: Once a member of the Amish community, Margarita now lives in LA, following her calling to make the world a healthier place. She owns a successful gym and has a teenage daughter, Jessica, who's hell-bent on making her life miserable.

Matty: The infant daughter of Helena and Niccolo, destined to marry Andrus's son.

Niccolo DiConti: General of the Vampire Army. Now that the vampire queen is dead, the army remains loyal to him. He shares power with his wife, Helena Strauss, and has a half-vampire daughter, Matty.

Reyna: The dead vampire queen.

Roberto (Narmer): Originally an Egyptian pharaoh, Narmer was one of the six Ancient Ones—the very first vampires. He eventually changed his name to Roberto and moved to Spain—something to do with one of Cimil's little schemes. He now spends his days lovingly undoing Cimil's treachery, being a stay-at-home dad, and taking her unicorn Minky for a ride.

Sadie: Charlotte's half sister and mated to Andrus Grey, Sadie is an aspiring actress who discovered she's also half incubus.

Tommaso: Once an Uchben, Tommaso's mind was poisoned with black jade. He tried to kill Emma, Votan's mate, but redeemed himself by turning into a spy for the gods. He is now mated to Charlotte.

Tula: The incorruptible administrative assistant at Immortal Matchmakers, Inc.

About the Author

MIMI JEAN PAMFILOFF is a *USA Today* and *New York Times* bestselling romance author. Although she obtained her MBA and worked for more than fifteen years in the corporate world, she believes that it s never too late to come out of the romance closet and follow your dream. Mimi lives with her Latin lover hubby, two pirates-in-training (their boys), and the rat terrier duo, Snowflake and Mini Me, in Arizona. She hopes to make you laugh when you need it most and continues to pray daily that leather pants will make a big comeback for men.

Sign up for Mimi's mailing list for giveaways and new release news!

STALK MIMI:
www.mimijean.net
twitter.com/MimiJeanRomance
pinterest.com/mimijeanromance
instagram.com/mimijeanpamfiloff
facebook.com/MimiJeanPamfiloff

17806384R00195

Printed in Poland
by Amazon Fulfillment
Poland Sp. z o.o., Wrocław